序 言

　　「全民英語能力分級檢定測驗」依不同英語程度，分為初級、中級、中高級、高級和優級五級。一般高中生通過「中級英語檢定測驗」之後，在申請大學或推甄時，就比別人多了一項能力的認證，自然容易脫穎而出。

　　本公司所出版的「中級英語聽力檢定①～④」，由於內容完全仿照全民英檢格式，深具演練價值，而獲得廣大讀者的肯定。有鑒於此，本公司再接再勵，推出了最新版的「中級英語聽力檢定⑤」，繼續服務所有考生。

　　本書秉持內容充實的原則，並特別注意因應時事出題，讓考題永遠能跟得上時代，命中率當然倍增。有志一次通過全民英檢中級檢定的考生，一定要善加利用本書，考前至少要有兩個月的準備時間，一個星期要做完一回測驗，然後再花時間把公佈字彙背熟，那麼中檢證書就勢在必得了。

　　全書共八回，每一回 45 題，分為看圖辨義、問答，以及簡短對話三種題型。讀者在做本書的測驗時，最好訓練自己在二十五分鐘內作答完畢，因為實際考試時間為三十分鐘，讓自己習慣在較短的時間內寫完，考試時會更得心應手。

　　本書在編審及校對的每一階段，均力求完善，但恐有疏漏之處，誠盼各界先進不吝批評指正。

編者 謹識

English Listening Comprehension Test
Test Book No. 1

This listening comprehension test will test your ability to understand spoken English. In this test, each conversation, statement and question will be spoken JUST ONE TIME. They will not be written out for you. There are three parts to this test. Special instructions will be given to you at the beginning of each part.

Part A

In Part A, you will see several pictures in your test book. For each picture, you will be asked 1 to 3 questions. For each question, you will hear four possible answers. Choose the best answer according to what you see in the picture.

Example:

You will see:

You will hear: What is this?
     A. This is a table.
     B. This is a chair.
     C. This is a watch.
     D. This is a doll.

The best answer to the question "What is this?" is B: "This is a chair." Therefore, you should choose answer B.

A. <u>Questions 1-2</u>

B. <u>Questions 3-4</u>

C. <u>Questions 5-7</u>

D. <u>Questions 8-9</u>

E. <u>Questions 10-12</u>

F. <u>Questions 13-14</u>

G. <u>Question 15</u>

Part B

In Part B, you will hear 15 questions. After you hear a question, read the four possible answers in your test book and decide which one is the best answer to the question you have heard.

Example:

You will hear: What does your father do?

You will read: A. He's 50 years old.
B. He's a teacher.
C. He's hungry.
D. He's in Los Angeles.

The best answer to the question "What does your father do?" is B: "He's a teacher." Therefore, you should choose answer B.

Please go to the next page. ⇨

16. A. I know exactly what a giraffe looks like.
    B. For sure, I can help.
    C. Neither can I.
    D. You have no imagination!

17. A. No, I'm taking it.
    B. Yes, there is an aisle seat.
    C. That's what I told you.
    D. No. It's free.

18. A. No problem. I'll tell you some other time.
    B. That's OK. Take your time.
    C. Sorry, do you have the time?
    D. It's not worth the wait.

19. A. I know the perfect way.
    B. I've been there before twice.
    C. Yes, just follow this road.
    D. The museum is open today.

20. A. Yes, I'm making it now.
    B. A roast.
    C. I'm on a diet.
    D. Dinner is at eight.

21. A. No need to worry.
    B. I missed my bus.
    C. Do you need help?
    D. I'll see you then.

22. A. I saw it last week.
    B. Very silently.
    C. It was really boring.
    D. I had the best score.

23. A. How is it used?
    B. I've never used a
       cell phone.
    C. No thanks. I'd like
       to see new ones only.
    D. Most people use cell
       phones.

24. A. Yes, it has been put
       on the bus.
    B. I already took the bus.
    C. Why don't you call
       the bus station?
    D. I have his backpack
       here.

25. A. He made a grocery
       list.
    B. She left school early
       to go shopping.
    C. Yes, he picked her
       up this afternoon.
    D. No, she had to work
       late.

26. A. Yes, he took it out
       before.
    B. Not again! I just
       took him to the vet.
    C. I told him not to go
       out.
    D. Well, take her for a
       walk then.

27. A. And you?
    B. That was fun.
    C. Me neither.
    D. What a relief!

28. A. That's $57.64.
    B. Of course we have your size.
    C. Only if you take two.
    D. I bought the last one yesterday.

29. A. That's for sure.
    B. I'll come back.
    C. I'm not off till 3:30.
    D. There's no time.

30. A. I didn't have any coffee today.
    B. I'd love to.
    C. I never liked it.
    D. Coffee's ready!

Part C

In Part C, you will hear 15 conversations between a man and a woman. After each conversation, you will hear a question about the conversation. After you hear the question, read the four possible answers in your test book and choose the best answer to the question you have heard.

Example:

<u>You will hear</u>: (Man)   How do you go to school every day?

              (Woman) Usually by bus. Sometimes by taxi.

              (Tone)

              Question: How does the woman go to school?

<u>You will read</u>: A. She always goes to school on foot.
                B. She usually rides a bike.
                C. She takes either a bus or a taxi.
                D. She usually goes to school by bus, never by taxi.

The best answer to the question "How does the woman go to school?" is C: "She takes either a bus or a taxi." Therefore, you should choose answer C.

Please go to the next page. ⇨

31. A. She thinks Frank is
dating Sally.
   B. She thinks James and
Sally are fighting.
   C. She thinks James and
Sally are romantically
involved.
   D. She thinks Frank likes
Sally.

32. A. It has a color screen.
   B. She saw it on TV.
   C. It can play movies
and music.
   D. It's small.

33. A. At their office.
   B. At an Italian restaurant.
   C. It is not stated.
   D. At the cafeteria.

34. A. He is seldom late.
   B. He's running to
work.
   C. He must have had
an accident.
   D. He is usually late.

35. A. She wants to save
power by turning
out the lights.
   B. She thinks her
father is right.
   C. She does care about
turning out the
lights.
   D. She thinks it's
unimportant to turn
out the lights.

36. A. It will be fun.
    B. He is unenthusiastic about it.
    C. He is happy to go on vacation.
    D. He is interested in doing it.

37. A. At the train station.
    B. At the bakery.
    C. At the dentist's.
    D. At the eye doctor's.

38. A. He is going to attend Stanford next year.
    B. He is talking to a woman from Stanford.
    C. He hopes to be accepted at Harvard.
    D. He is going to make an application to Harvard.

39. A. At a convenience store.
    B. At an ice cream shop.
    C. At a movie theater.
    D. At the woman's school.

40. A. She has no problem.
    B. She can't quit smoking.
    C. She can't sleep at night.
    D. She is suffering from stress.

41. A. The man.
    B. The woman.
    C. Nobody.
    D. We cannot tell.

42. A. Tomatoes.
    B. Mushrooms.
    C. Spaghetti.
    D. Milk.

43. A. The woman lives with
       the man.
    B. Susan lives near the
       man.
    C. The man and woman
       are classmates.
    D. The woman usually
       drives herself.

44. A. He is a doctor.
    B. He is an auto
       mechanic.
    C. He is a film maker.
    D. He is a TV
       repairman.

45. A. A new computer.
    B. Outer space.
    C. A computer
       software program.
    D. Satellites that take
       photos from space.

Listening Test 1 詳解

Part A

For questions number 1 and 2, please look at picture A.

1. (**D**) Question number 1: What is the boy on the right doing?

    A. He is cold.

    B. He's building a snowman.

    C. He's admiring the snowman.

    D. He is throwing a snowball.

    * build〔bɪld〕v. 建造；製作
    snowman〔'snoˏmæn〕n. 雪人
    admire〔əd'maɪr〕v. 讚賞；欽佩　　throw〔θro〕v. 丟
    snowball〔'snoˏbɔl〕n. 雪球

2. (**C**) Question number 2: What are the girls wearing?

    A. Snowball.

    B. Scarves.

    C. Earmuffs.

    D. Hats.

    * wear〔wɛr〕v. 穿；戴
    scarves〔skɑrvz〕n. pl. 圍巾（單數爲 scarf〔skɑrf〕）
    earmuff〔'ɪrˏmʌf〕n. 禦寒耳罩

For questions number 3 and 4, please look at picture B.

3. (**B**) Question number 3: Why is the girl on the left crying?

    A. She doesn't like fishing.

    B. Her fishing net broke.

    C. The boy won't let her fish.

    D. Her fish died.

    * fishing〔'fɪʃɪŋ〕*n.* 釣魚　*adj.* 釣魚的；捕魚的
       net〔nɛt〕*n.* 網子　　break〔brek〕*v.* 破裂
       fish〔fɪʃ〕*v.* 釣魚　*n.* 魚　　die〔daɪ〕*v.* 死掉

4. (**B**) Question number 4: How many children are fishing now?

    A. One.

    B. Two.

    C. Three.

    D. Four.

For questions number 5 to 7, please look at picture C.

5. (**C**) Question number 5: Why is the man unhappy?

    A. He does not like the food.

    B. He has a knife and fork.

    C. He cannot use chopsticks.

    D. He has a mild fever.

    * knife〔naɪf〕*n.* 刀子　　fork〔fɔrk〕*n.* 叉子
      chopsticks〔'tʃɑp,stɪks〕*n. pl.* 筷子
      mild〔maɪld〕*adj.*（病情）輕的
      fever〔'fivɚ〕*n.* 發燒

6. (**A**) Question number 6: Please look at picture C again.
What is the waitress carrying?

    A. Dumplings.   B. Fish.

    C. Rice.   D. Soup.

    * waitress〔'wetrɪs〕 *n.* 女服務生
      carry〔'kærɪ〕 *v.* 攜帶；拿   dumpling〔'dʌmplɪŋ〕 *n.* 水餃
      rice〔raɪs〕 *n.* 米飯   soup〔sup〕 *n.* 湯

7. (**B**) Question number 7: Please look at picture C again.
What can we tell from the picture?

    A. The customer is not Chinese.

    B. The man doesn't know how to use chopsticks.

    C. The waitress is tired.

    D. The man is waiting for his friends.

    * tell〔tɛl〕 *v.* 知道；看出   customer〔'kʌstəmɚ〕 *n.* 顧客
      chopsticks〔'tʃɑp,stɪks〕 *n. pl.* 筷子
      tired〔taɪrd〕 *adj.* 疲倦的   ***wait for*** 等待

For questions number 8 and 9, please look at picture D.

8. (**D**) Question number 8: What is happening in this picture?

    A. A pretty lady is dreaming of Picasso.

    B. An artist is making a statue.

    C. The artist is falling in love with his model.

    D. A lady is having her portrait painted.

    * happen〔'hæpən〕 *v.* 發生   pretty〔'prɪtɪ〕 *adj.* 漂亮的
      dream〔drim〕 *v.* 夢見   Picasso〔pɪ'kɑso〕 *n.* 畢卡索
      artist〔'ɑrtɪst〕 *n.* 藝術家；畫家   statue〔'stætʃu〕 *n.* 雕像
      fall in love with 愛上   model〔'mɑdl̩〕 *n.* 模特兒
      portrait〔'portret〕 *n.* 肖像；畫像   paint〔pent〕 *v.* 畫

9. (**B**) Question number 9: Please look at picture D again.
What style is the artist's painting?

A. Beautiful.　　　　B. Abstract.
C. Realistic.　　　　D. Romantic.

* style〔staɪl〕 *n.* 風格　　abstract〔æb'strækt〕 *adj.* 抽象的
realistic〔͵riə'lɪstɪk〕 *adj.* 寫實派的
romantic〔ro'mæntɪk〕 *adj.* 浪漫派的

For questions number 10 to 12, please look at picture E.

10. (**C**) Question number 10: Where is the boy?

A. He is in the swimming pool.
B. He is dreaming.
C. In the sea.
D. Visiting an aquarium.

* *swimming pool* 游泳池　　visit〔'vɪzɪt〕 *v.* 參觀
aquarium〔ə'kwɛrɪəm〕 *n.* 水族館

11. (**C**) Question number 11: Please look at picture E again.
What does the boy hope to see?

A. A colorful fish.
B. A dolphin.
C. A mermaid.
D. A lady.

* colorful〔'kʌləfəl〕 *adj.* 五顏六色的
dolphin〔'dɑlfɪn〕 *n.* 海豚
mermaid〔'mɝ͵med〕 *n.* 美人魚

12. (**A**) Question number 12: Please look at picture E again. Which animal is NOT in the picture?

    A. A whale.   B. A crab.

    C. A fish.   D. An octopus.

   * whale〔hwel〕*n.* 鯨魚   crab〔kræb〕*n.* 螃蟹
    octopus〔'ɑktəpəs〕*n.* 章魚

For questions number 13 and 14, please look at picture F.

13. (**C**) Question number 13: What is going on outside the boy's home?

    A. The weather is very cold.

    B. There are clouds in the sky.

    C. There is a strong storm.

    D. There is a serious earthquake.

   * ***go on*** 發生   weather〔'wɛðɚ〕*n.* 天氣
    cloud〔klaud〕*n.* 雲   sky〔skaɪ〕*n.* 天空
    storm〔stɔrm〕*n.* 暴風雨   serious〔'sɪrɪəs〕*adj.* 嚴重的
    earthquake〔'ɝθ͵kwek〕*n.* 地震

14. (**D**) Question number 14: Please look at picture F again. Why is there water inside the boy's home?

    A. The boy forgot to turn off the tap.

    B. The boy wanted to go swimming.

    C. The water came through the window.

    D. The boy's house was flooded.

   * ***turn off*** 關掉（瓦斯、自來水等）
    tap〔tæp〕*n.* 水龍頭   flood〔flʌd〕*v.* 淹水

For question number 15, please look at picture G.

15. (**D**) Question number 15: What are they doing?

    A. The two girls are carrying the boy.

    B. They are racing against each other.

    C. The boy is pushing the two girls.

    D. They are racing as a team.

    * carry 〔'kærɪ 〕 v. 抱；背

      race 〔 res 〕 v. 與…賽跑 < against >

      push 〔 puʃ 〕 v. 推   team 〔 tim 〕 n. 隊伍

Part B

16. (**C**) I can't imagine being a giraffe.

    A. I know exactly what a giraffe looks like.

    B. For sure, I can help.

    C. Neither can I.

    D. You have no imagination!

    * imagine 〔 ɪ'mædʒɪn 〕 v. 想像

      giraffe 〔 dʒə'ræf 〕 n. 長頸鹿

      exactly 〔 ɪg'zæktlɪ 〕 adv. 精確地

      look like 看起來像   *for sure* 一定；當然

      neither 〔'niðə 〕 adv. 也不

      imagination 〔 ɪˌmædʒə'neʃən 〕 n. 想像力

17. (**D**) Excuse me, is this seat taken?

    A. No, I'm taking it.

    B. Yes, there is an aisle seat.

    C. That's what I told you.

    D. No. It's free.

    * ***Excuse me***. 抱歉；對不起。　　seat〔sit〕*n.* 座位
       take〔tek〕*v.* 佔（位子）；就（座）　　aisle〔aɪl〕*n.* 走道
       aisle seat 靠走道的座位
       free〔fri〕*adj.* 空著的；沒有使用的

18. (**B**) Sorry to keep you waiting.

    A. No problem. I'll tell you some other time.

    B. That's OK. Take your time.

    C. Sorry, do you have the time?

    D. It's not worth the wait.

    * keep〔kip〕*v.* 使　　wait〔wet〕*v. n.* 等待
       some other time 改天　　***Take your time***. 慢慢來。
       Do you have the time? 你知道現在幾點嗎？
       worth〔wɝθ〕*adj.* 值得…的

19. (**C**) Is this the right way to the museum?

    A. I know the perfect way.

    B. I've been there before twice.

    C. Yes, just follow this road.

    D. The museum is open today.

    * way〔we〕*n.* 路　　museum〔mju'ziəm〕*n.* 博物館
       perfect〔'pɝfɪkt〕*adj.* 正確的　　twice〔twaɪs〕*adv.* 兩次
       follow〔'falo〕*v.* 順著（道路等）前進
       open〔'opən〕*adj.* 開著的；營業中的

20. (**B**) What are we having for dinner tonight?

    A. Yes, I'm making it now.

    B. A roast.   C. I'm on a diet.

    D. Dinner is at eight.

    * have〔hæv〕v. 吃；喝　　roast〔rost〕n. 烤肉
    be on a diet 節食

21. (**A**) I totally forgot about our meeting!

    A. No need to worry.   B. I missed my bus.

    C. Do you need help?   D. I'll see you then.

    * totally〔'totḷɪ〕adv. 完全地　　meeting〔'mitɪŋ〕n. 會議
    need〔nid〕n. v. 必需；需要
    miss〔mɪs〕v. 錯過　　then〔ðɛn〕adv. 到那時候

22. (**C**) How did you like the new Batman movie?

    A. I saw it last week.   B. Very silently.

    C. It was really boring.   D. I had the best score.

    * batman〔'bætmən〕n. 蝙蝠俠
    silently〔'saɪləntlɪ〕adv. 安靜地
    boring〔'borɪŋ〕adj. 無聊的　　score〔skor〕n. 成績；分數

23. (**C**) Could I interest you in a used cell phone?

    A. How is it used?

    B. I've never used a cell phone.

    C. No thanks.　I'd like to see new ones only.

    D. Most people use cell phones.

    * interest〔'ɪntrɪst〕v. 使感興趣　　used〔juzd〕adj. 二手的
    cell phone 手機　　use〔juz〕v. 使用

24. (**C**)　Oh, no. I left my backpack on the bus!

　　A. Yes, it has been put on the bus.

　　B. I already took the bus.

　　C. Why don't you call the bus station?

　　D. I have his backpack here.

　　* leave〔liv〕*v.* 遺留

　　　backpack〔'bæk,pæk〕*n.* 背包

　　　station〔'steʃən〕*n.* 車站

25. (**D**)　Didn't she pick up the groceries?

　　A. He made a grocery list.

　　B. She left school early to go shopping.

　　C. Yes, he picked her up this afternoon.

　　D. No, she had to work late.

　　* ***pick up*** 買；開車載（某人）

　　　grocery〔'grosəɪ〕*n.* 食品雜貨

　　　list〔lɪst〕*n.* 清單　***make a list*** 列一張清單

　　　late〔let〕*adv.* 到很晚

26. (**D**)　The dog wants to go out again.

　　A. Yes, he took it out before.

　　B. Not again! I just took him to the vet.

　　C. I told him not to go out.

　　D. Well, take her for a walk then.

　　* vet〔vɛt〕*n.* 獸醫　　walk〔wɔk〕*n.* 散步
　　　then〔ðɛn〕*adv.* 那麼

27. (**C**) I couldn't understand a word of what he said.

    A. And you?   B. That was fun.

    C. Me neither.   D. What a relief!

    * understand〔ˌʌndɚˈstænd〕v. 了解　　***And you?*** 那你呢？

      fun〔fʌn〕adj. 有趣的　　neither〔ˈniðɚ〕adv. 也不

      relief〔rɪˈlif〕n. 放心；鬆一口氣

      What a relief! 真是令人鬆一口氣！

28. (**C**) Could you give me a discount on this?

    A. That's $57.64.

    B. Of course we have your size.

    C. Only if you take two.

    D. I bought the last one yesterday.

    * discount〔ˈdɪskaʊnt〕n. 折扣

      size〔saɪz〕n. 尺寸；大小　　take〔tek〕v. 買

29. (**C**) How does 3:00 sound?

    A. That's for sure.   B. I'll come back.

    C. I'm not off till 3:30.   D. There's no time.

    * sound〔saʊnd〕v. 聽起來　　***That's for sure.*** 那當然。

      not⋯till~ 直到~才⋯　　off〔ɔf〕adv. 休假地；不工作地

30. (**B**) Would you like to get some coffee?

    A. I didn't have any coffee today.

    B. I'd love to.

    C. I never liked it.

    D. Coffee's ready!

    * have〔hæv〕v. 喝　　ready〔ˈrɛdɪ〕adj. 準備好的

Part C

31. (**C**) W: Did you see the way James looked at Sally?

M: Yeah. I wonder if something's going on.

W: Well, Frank told me he saw them leave work together yesterday. Maybe they're dating.

(TONE)

Q: What does the woman think?

A. She thinks Frank is dating Sally.

B. She thinks James and Sally are fighting.

C. She thinks James and Sally are romantically involved.

D. She thinks Frank likes Sally.

* way〔we〕*n.* 樣子   yeah〔jɛ〕*adv.* 是的（＝ *yes* ）
wonder〔'wʌndɚ〕*v.* 想知道   ***go on*** 發生
leave work 下班   date〔det〕*v.* 約會；和…約會
fight〔faɪt〕*v.* 打架
romantically〔ro'mæntɪk!ɪ〕*adv.* 浪漫地
involved〔ɪn'vɑlvd〕*adj.* （與異性）有很深關係的

32. (**D**) W: Have you seen this new mp3 player?

M: Yeah, it's really cool. It has a color screen and it can play movies as well as music.

W: And what's best, it fits in the palm of your hand.

(TONE)

Q: What impressed the woman most about the mp3 player?

A. It has a color screen.   B. She saw it on TV.

C. It can play movies and music.

D. It's small.

* **mp3** 音樂格式檔   player〔'pleɚ〕n. 播放器

cool〔kul〕adj. 酷的；很棒的

color〔'kʌlɚ〕adj. 彩色的

screen〔skrin〕n. 螢幕   play〔ple〕v. 播放

as well as 以及   **what's best** 最棒的是

fit in 適合；正好塞得進   palm〔pɑm〕n. 手掌

impress〔ɪm'prɛs〕v. 使印象深刻

33.(**C**) W: I'm so sick of this cafeteria food. It's always the
         same.

     M: I know what you mean. Maybe we should go out
         somewhere for lunch.

     W: How about that new Italian place?

     M: Hmm… I ate there yesterday.

     W: Well, I'll let you choose then.

     (TONE)

     Q: Where are the two planning to eat?

     A. At their office.   B. At an Italian restaurant.

     C. It is not stated.   D. At the cafeteria.

* **be sick of** 對～厭倦   cafeteria〔ˌkæfə'tɪrɪə〕n. 自助餐廳

same〔sem〕adj. 相同的   mean〔min〕v. 意思是

Italian〔ɪ'tæljən〕adj. 義大利的   place〔ples〕n. 餐館

choose〔tʃuz〕v. 選擇   then〔ðɛn〕adv. 那麼

plan〔plæn〕v. 打算   state〔stet〕v. 說明

34. (**D**) M: Where's Jacob? It's already 9:30.

W: Are you kidding? He's always running behind schedule.

(TONE)

Q: What does the woman imply about Jacob?

A. He is seldom late.

B. He's running to work.

C. He must have had an accident.

D. He is usually late.

* kid〔kɪd〕v. 開玩笑　run〔rʌn〕v. 運轉；保持在特定水平
schedule〔'skɛdʒʊl〕n. 計畫；時間表
behind schedule 落後於計畫；遲於規定的時間
imply〔ɪm'plaɪ〕v. 暗示　seldom〔'sɛldəm〕adv. 很少
late〔let〕adj. 遲到的　　**must have + p.p.** 當時一定~
accident〔'æksədənt〕n. 意外

35. (**D**) M: I've told you a thousand times: Don't forget to turn out the lights when you leave.

W: Whatever! It's no big deal, Dad.

M: Well, you can decide how important it is when you're paying the power bill, young lady.

(TONE)

Q: What is the woman's attitude?

A. She wants to save power by turning out the lights.

B. She thinks her father is right.

C. She does care about turning out the lights.

D. She thinks it's unimportant to turn out the lights.

* time〔taɪm〕n. 次數　**turn out** 關掉
light〔laɪt〕n. 燈　whatever〔hwɑt'ɛvɚ〕pron. 隨便
No big deal. 沒什麼大不了。　decide〔dɪ'saɪd〕v. 決定
pay〔pe〕v. 支付　power〔'pauɚ〕n. 電力
bill〔bɪl〕n. 帳單　attitude〔'ætə,tjud〕n. 態度
save〔sev〕v. 節省　**care about** 關心；在乎
unimportant〔,ʌnɪm'pɔrtn̩t〕adj. 不重要的

36. (**B**)　W: Could you do me a favor and water my plants while
I'm away next week?

M: Uh, I guess so. How many times should I water them?

W: Well, the ones upstairs need to be watered three
times, and the ones on the first floor should be
watered twice, but the ones in the…

M: Why don't you just leave me some instructions?

(TONE)

Q: How does the man feel about watering the plants?

A. It will be fun.

B. He is unenthusiastic about it.

C. He is happy to go on vacation.

D. He is interested in doing it.

* favor〔'fevɚ〕n. 恩惠；幫忙　**do sb. a favor** 幫某人的忙
water〔'wɔtɚ〕v. 給…澆水　away〔ə'we〕adv. 不在
guess〔gɛs〕v. 猜　**I guess so.** 我想是可以的。
upstairs〔'ʌp'stɛrz〕adv. 在樓上　floor〔flor〕n. 樓層
twice〔twaɪs〕adv. 兩次　leave〔liv〕v. 留給；留下
instructions〔ɪn'strʌkʃənz〕n. pl. 指示
unenthusiastic〔,ʌnɪn,θjuzɪ'æstɪk〕adj. 不熱心的
go on vacation 去渡假　**be interested in** 對～有興趣

37. (**C**) M: Now open wide and keep your tongue down.

W: Is this going to hurt?

M: Not at all. I just need to check the teeth at the back.
Try to relax.

(TONE)

Q: Where did this conversation happen?

A. At the train station.

B. At the bakery.

C. At the dentist's.

D. At the eye doctor's.

* wide〔waɪd〕*adv.* 張大地　　tongue〔tʌŋ〕*n.* 舌頭
hurt〔hɜt〕*v.* 疼痛　　***not at all*** 一點也不
check〔tʃɛk〕*v.* 檢查　　teeth〔tiθ〕*n. pl.* 牙齒
relax〔rɪˈlæks〕*v.* 放輕鬆
train station 火車站　　bakery〔ˈbekərɪ〕*n.* 麵包店
dentist's *n.* 牙醫診所 (= *dentist's office*)

38. (**C**) W: What does it say?

M: It says I've been accepted at Stanford next year.

W: Wow! That's great news. Aren't you excited?

M: Oh, absolutely, but I'm still waiting to hear back
from Harvard.

(TONE)

Q: What can we tell about the man?

A. He is going to attend Stanford next year.

B. He is talking to a woman from Stanford.

C. He hopes to be accepted at Harvard.

D. He is going to make an application to Harvard.

* say〔se〕v. 寫著　　accept〔əkˋsɛpt〕v. 接受
wow〔waʊ〕interj. 哇啊　　excited〔ɪkˋsaɪtɪd〕adj. 興奮的
absolutely〔ˋæbsəˌlutlɪ〕adv. 當然
hear from 得到…的消息；收到…的信
tell〔tɛl〕v. 得知　　attend〔əˋtɛnd〕v. 上（學）
application〔ˌæpləˋkeʃən〕n. 申請

39. (**B**)　M：What flavor do you want?

W：Hmm… I can't decide.　There are just too many.

M：Well, you can have a taste if you can't choose.

W：May I try mint chocolate?

(TONE)

Q：Where did this conversation take place?

A.　At a convenience store.　B.　At an ice cream shop.

C.　At a movie theater.

D.　At the woman's school.

* flavor〔ˋflevɚ〕n. 味道；口味
decide〔dɪˋsaɪd〕v. 決定　　have〔hæv〕v. 吃
taste〔test〕n. 一口；少量　　choose〔tʃuz〕v. 選擇
mint〔mɪnt〕n. 薄荷　　**take place** 發生
convenience store 便利商店　　theater〔ˋθiətɚ〕n. 電影院

40. (**C**)　M：Well, the test results are back and there's nothing
to worry about.

W：Oh, that's a relief.　Are you sure I'm okay?　I still
can't get a good night's sleep.

M：You're just fine.　I would, however, suggest that
you try to give up smoking.　That could be
contributing to your problem.

(TONE)

Q：What is the woman's problem?

A．She has no problem.

B．She can't quit smoking.

C．She can't sleep at night.

D．She is suffering from stress.

* result〔rɪˋzʌlt〕*n.* 結果

　back〔bæk〕*adv.* 返回；回來　　relief〔rɪˋlif〕*n.* 放心

　get a good night's sleep 晚上睡個好覺

　suggest〔səgˋdʒɛst〕*v.* 建議　　***give up*** 戒除

　smoking〔ˋsmokɪŋ〕*n.* 吸煙

　contribute〔kənˋtrɪbjut〕*v.* 促成

　contribute to 是⋯的部份原因；造成

　quit〔kwɪt〕*v.* 戒除

　suffer〔ˋsʌfɚ〕*v.* 遭受；因⋯而受苦＜*from*＞

　stress〔strɛs〕*n.* 壓力

41. (**B**) M：Hey! There's no soda left! Did you finish it off?

　　　W：Well, nobody else was drinking it.

(TONE)

Q：Who finished the soda?

A．The man.

B．The woman.

C．Nobody.

D．We cannot tell.

* soda〔ˋsodə〕*n.* 汽水　　left〔lɛft〕*adj.* 剩下的

　finish off 吃完；喝光　　else〔ɛls〕*adj.* 其他的

　tell〔tɛl〕*v.* 知道

42. (**C**) M：What should we make for dinner?

W：I don't know. How about spaghetti?

M：That would be okay.

W：Oh, wait! There're no tomatoes left.

M：Well, I can go pick some up. Do you need anything else?

W：Yeah, could you get some mushrooms and milk?

(TONE)

Q：What will the couple have for dinner?

A. Tomatoes.　　　　B. Mushrooms.

C. Spaghetti.　　　　D. Milk.

* spaghetti〔spə'gɛtɪ〕n. 義大利麵
tomato〔tə'meto〕n. 番茄　***pick up*** 買
get〔gɛt〕v. 買　　mushroom〔'mʌʃrum〕n. 蘑菇
couple〔'kʌpl̩〕n. 夫婦　　have〔hæv〕v. 吃

43. (**C**) W：Thank you so much for dropping me off. You really didn't have to.

M：Hey, no need to thank me. It's on my way anyhow.

W：So will you be coming to class next week?

M：Actually, I won't be. Maybe you can get a ride with Susan—she's coming for sure.

(TONE)

Q：What can we tell from the conversation?

A. The woman lives with the man.

B. Susan lives near the man.

C. The man and woman are classmates.

D. The woman usually drives herself.

* ***drop off*** 讓…下車　　***on one's way*** 在某人途中
  anyhow〔'ɛnɪ,haʊ〕*adv.* 無論如何；反正
  actually〔'æktʃʊəlɪ〕*adv.* 事實上
  ride〔raɪd〕*n.* (汽車等的) 乘坐　　***for sure*** 一定
  tell〔tɛl〕*v.* 得知　　***live with*** 與…同住；與 (異性) 同居

44. (**D**) M：I can't tell what the problem is from looking at it here. I'll have to take it back to the shop and open it up.

W：Are you serious? That means I won't be able to watch my favorite show tonight.

(TONE)

Q：What does the man do for a living?

A. He is a doctor.

B. He is an auto mechanic.

C. He is a film maker.

D. He is a TV repairman.

* tell〔tɛl〕*v.* 看出　　***take back*** 將…帶回
  open up 打開　　serious〔'sɪrɪəs〕*adj.* 認真的
  mean〔min〕*v.* 意思是　　***be able to V.*** 能夠
  favorite〔'fevərɪt〕*adj.* 最喜歡的　　show〔ʃo〕*n.* 節目
  do for a living 以…謀生　　auto〔'ɔto〕*n.* 汽車
  mechanic〔mə'kænɪk〕*n.* 技工　　film〔fɪlm〕*n.* 影片
  maker〔'mekɚ〕*n.* 製作者
  film maker 影片製作人；電影導演
  repairman〔rɪ'pɛrmən〕*n.* 修理工人

45. (**C**) M : Have you heard of Google Earth?

W : No. What's that?

M : It's a three-dimensional model of the earth made up of satellite pictures. It lets you look at photos of any place on earth taken from outer space.

W : Wow, that's amazing. Where can I get it?

M : Just download it and install it on your PC. It's free!

(TONE)

Q : What are the two people talking about?

A. A new computer.

B. Outer space.

C. A computer software program.

D. Satellites that take photos from space.

* ***hear of*** 聽說

dimensional〔dəˋmɛnʃənḷ〕*adj.* …度空間的

model〔ˋmɑdḷ〕*n.* 模型   ***be made up of*** 由…組成

satellite〔ˋsætḷˏaɪt〕*adj.* 衛星的   photo〔ˋfoto〕*n.* 照片

take〔tek〕*v.* 拍（照片）   space〔spes〕*n.* 太空

outer space 外太空

amazing〔əˋmezɪŋ〕*adj.* 令人吃驚的

download〔ˋdaʊnˏlod〕*v.* 下載

install〔ɪnˋstɔl〕*v.* 安裝

PC 個人電腦（＝*personal computer*）

free〔fri〕*adj.* 免費的   software〔ˋsɔftˏwɛr〕*n.* 軟體

program〔ˋprogræm〕*n.* 程式

English Listening Comprehension Test
Test Book No. 2

This listening comprehension test will test your ability to understand spoken English. In this test, each conversation, statement and question will be spoken JUST ONE TIME. They will not be written out for you. There are three parts to this test. Special instructions will be given to you at the beginning of each part.

Part A

In Part A, you will see several pictures in your test book. For each picture, you will be asked 1 to 3 questions. For each question, you will hear four possible answers. Choose the best answer according to what you see in the picture.

Example:

<u>You will see</u>:

<u>You will hear</u>: What is this?

      A. This is a table.
      B. This is a chair.
      C. This is a watch.
      D. This is a doll.

The best answer to the question "What is this?" is B: "This is a chair." Therefore, you should choose answer B.

A. <u>Questions 1-2</u>

B. <u>Questions 3-5</u>

C. <u>Questions 6-8</u>

D. <u>Questions 9-11</u>

E. <u>Questions 12-13</u>

F. <u>Questions 14-15</u>

Part B

In Part B, you will hear 15 questions. After you hear a question, read the four possible answers in your test book and decide which one is the best answer to the question you have heard.

Example:

<u>You will hear</u>: What does your father do?

<u>You will read</u>: A. He's 50 years old.
　　　　　　　　　B. He's a teacher.
　　　　　　　　　C. He's hungry.
　　　　　　　　　D. He's in Los Angeles.

The best answer to the question "What does your father do?" is B: "He's a teacher." Therefore, you should choose answer B.

Please go to the next page. ⇨

16. A. Not now, thanks.
    B. Why should you care?
    C. Yes, it's true.
    D. I haven't seen any.

17. A. Oh, don't go to the
       trouble.
    B. No, the door is locked.
    C. I just left.
    D. The door looks fine.

18. A. I'm sorry. You can't
       do that.
    B. I'm afraid we are sold
       out.
    C. No, I sold my stocks
       in that company.
    D. These are not
       stockings.

19. A. I heard what you were
       saying.
    B. Yeah, they're delicious.
    C. And you have a burger,
       too.
    D. Would you like fries
       with that?

20. A. A lot of time.
    B. Twice a year.
    C. Only once.
    D. Not anymore.

21. A. I'm so sorry!
    B. I meant to tell you.
    C. That's all right.
    D. How did you do it?

22. A. I wrote a letter to
       Susan.
    B. I don't know. I can't
       find it anywhere.
    C. Yes, it's my pen.
    D. I did a lot with it.

23. A. This is not fun
       anymore.
    B. I had a lot of fun
       there.
    C. Nothing at all.
    D. Have fun!

24. A. Yes, I'm on Friday.
    B. Yes, they are going on Friday.
    C. No, by Friday it will be over.
    D. No, I have too much to do.

25. A. Thanks, I could use one.
    B. I'm breaking my back.
    C. I'm going to break it.
    D. No, I haven't.

26. A. Yes, I used to.
    B. No, I'm not used to it.
    C. Yes, I'm used to it.
    D. Yes, I used it.

27. A. I don't have twenty dollars.
    B. It's worth twenty dollars.
    C. It's about two kilos.
    D. It is more than twenty dollars' worth.

28. A. I did the same thing.
    B. I told her I did the same.
    C. I would do the same thing.
    D. I am just doing what she did.

29. A. She likes them both.
    B. It is red and orange.
    C. He likes red and orange.
    D. She doesn't have any.

30. A. It uses gas.
    B. I don't know how it works.
    C. The stove is in the kitchen.
    D. Oops! I forgot to turn it off.

Part C

In Part C, you will hear 15 conversations between a man and a woman. After each conversation, you will hear a question about the conversation. After you hear the question, read the four possible answers in your test book and choose the best answer to the question you have heard.

Example:

<u>You will hear</u>: (Man)   How do you go to school every day?

(Woman) Usually by bus. Sometimes by taxi.

(Tone)

Question: How does the woman go to school?

<u>You will read</u>: A. She always goes to school on foot.
    B. She usually rides a bike.
    C. She takes either a bus or a taxi.
    D. She usually goes to school by bus, never by taxi.

The best answer to the question "How does the woman go to school?" is C: "She takes either a bus or a taxi." Therefore, you should choose answer C.

Please go to the next page. ⇨

31. A. The woman will not
       be able to see the
       dentist.
    B. The man will take
       the woman to the
       dentist's.
    C. It is past 2 p.m.
    D. The woman is at the
       dental appointment
       now.

32. A. At McDonald's.
    B. On her way to
       McDonald's.
    C. At home.
    D. On her way home.

33. A. The woman should buy
       a cell phone that plays
       mp3s.
    B. The woman's cell phone
       is quite old.
    C. The woman doesn't need
       to buy a new cell phone.
    D. The woman should sell
       her phone and buy an
       mp3 player.

34. A. He is a coward.
    B. He doesn't think the
       boat is safe.
    C. He gets dizzy when he
       rides in boats.
    D. He has a fear of the water.

35. A. Encourage the man.
    B. Find a job for the man.
    C. Tell the man how to find a job.
    D. Tell the man what jobs are available.

36. A. The woman would not sell the umbrella to the man.
    B. The man was able to buy the umbrella.
    C. The man forgot to pay the woman.
    D. The man was not able to buy the umbrella.

37. A. He studied on Sunday.
    B. He didn't know about the test.
    C. He went hiking on Saturday.
    D. He already took the test.

38. A. Once in a while.
    B. When he is hungry.
    C. Almost never.
    D. When he does not want pasta.

39. A. He wants to buy a cat with a black patch.
    B. He has lost his cat.
    C. He thinks he has found the woman's cat.
    D. He can't find the woman's cat.

40. A. Because it is not so bad.
    B. Because she can't afford healthy food.
    C. Because she really likes its taste.
    D. Because she is what she eats.

41. A. On Monday.
    B. On Thursday.
    C. On Saturday.
    D. We cannot tell.

42. A. The new teacher will
       teach the woman.
    B. The new teacher
       teaches English.
    C. The woman has a crush
       on the new teacher.
    D. The man will be in the
       new teacher's class.

43. A. Because his classmate
       is getting married.
    B. Because he cannot work
       on Friday.
    C. Because the client
       cannot show up.
    D. Because he has not
       finished the work.

44. A. At the police
       station.
    B. At the woman's
       office.
    C. At the man's home.
    D. At the woman's
       son's school.

45. A. He thinks it is
       superstitious.
    B. He thinks it attracts
       ghosts.
    C. He thinks it is
       harmless.
    D. He thinks it is
       creepy.

Listening Test 2 詳解

Part A

For questions number 1 and 2, please look at picture A.

1.(**C**) Question number 1: Where are the people?

    A. Skating.   B. Snowy.

    C. Switzerland.   D. Skiing.

    * skate〔sket〕*v.* 溜冰   snowy〔'snoɪ〕*adj.* 下雪的

    Switzerland〔'swɪtsələnd〕*n.* 瑞士   ski〔ski〕*v.* 滑雪

2.(**C**) Question number 2: Please look at picture A again.

    What happened to the boy?

    A. He is skiing.   B. The girl hit him.

    C. He fell down.   D. He lost his skates.

    * happen〔'hæpən〕*v.* 發生   hit〔hɪt〕*v.* 打

    fall down 跌倒

    lose〔luz〕*v.* 遺失（三態變化為：lose-lost-lost）

    skates〔skets〕*n. pl.* 溜冰鞋

For questions number 3 to 5, please look at picture B.

3.(**B**) Question number 3: What is the boy doing?

    A. Playing with fire.   B. Lighting a firecracker.

    C. Putting out a firecracker.

    D. Watching fireworks.

    * *play with fire* 玩火；做危險的事   light〔laɪt〕*v.* 點燃

    firecracker〔'faɪr,krækə〕*n.* 鞭炮

    put out 熄滅；撲滅   firework〔'faɪr,wɝk〕*n.* 煙火

4. (**C**)   Question number 4: Please look at picture B again.

What holiday are the children celebrating?

A. Dragon Boat Festival.

B. The Lantern Festival.

C. Chinese New Year.

D. Mid-Autumn Festival.

* celebrate〔'sɛlə,bret〕v. 慶祝

dragon〔'drægən〕n. 龍　　boat〔bot〕n. 船

festival〔'fɛstəvḷ〕n. 節慶

Dragon Boat Festival　端午節

lantern〔'læntən〕n. 燈籠　　mid-　中間的

autumn〔'ɔtəm〕n. 秋天

Mid-Autumn Festival　中秋節

5. (**D**)   Question number 5: Please look at picture B again.

What is the girl doing?

A. No, she's not doing it.

B. It's a firecracker.

C. Plugging her ears.

D. Playing with sparklers.

* plug〔plʌg〕v. 用塞子塞住

ear〔ɪr〕n. 耳朵

sparkler〔'spɑrklə〕n. (散出火花的、手持的)煙火

For questions number 6 to 8, please look at picture C.

6. (**D**) Question number 6: What can we tell about the woman?

A. No, she didn't scold the dog.

B. She does not like dogs.

C. He told her it is a bad dog.

D. She is quite wealthy.

* tell〔tɛl〕v. 知道　　scold〔skold〕v. 責罵
quite〔kwaɪt〕adv. 非常
wealthy〔'wɛlθɪ〕adj. 富有的

7. (**B**) Question number 7: Please look at picture C again.
What might the boy be saying?

A. Of course he is angry.

B. Hey lady! Your dog!

C. He will clean it up.

D. Here, doggy. Here!

* angry〔'æŋgrɪ〕adj. 生氣的　　*clean up* 清掃乾淨
doggy〔'dɔgɪ〕n. 小狗（= *doggie*）

8. (**C**) Question number 8: Please look at picture C again.
What is true about the picture?

A. The boy is going to school.

B. The boy is very happy.

C. The woman is not attentive to her dog.

D. The woman told the dog to pee on the boy.

* attentive〔ə'tɛntɪv〕adj. 注意的　　pee〔pi〕v. 小便

For questions number 9 to 11, please look at picture D.

9. (**C**) Question number 9: What is happening in the picture?

    A. A boy drowned, so his friend is calling the police.

    B. The girl threw the lifesaver.

    C. Someone is drowning.

    D. The police are rescuing a drowned boy.

    * happen〔'hæpən〕v. 發生　　drown〔draʊn〕v. 淹死；溺水

      police〔pə'lis〕n. 警察　　*the police* 警察；警方

      lifesaver〔'laɪf‚sevɚ〕n. 救生圈

      drowning〔'draʊnɪŋ〕adj. 快要淹死的

      rescue〔'rɛskju〕v. 解救

      drowned〔draʊnd〕adj. 溺水的；淹死的

10. (**B**) Question number 10: Please look at picture D again.
    What is the girl going to do?

    A. She is going to swim to her friend.

    B. She will throw the lifesaver.

    C. She is yelling help at the drowning boy.

    D. She is calling the police to rescue the boy.

    * yell〔jɛl〕v. 大叫　　help〔hɛlp〕interj. 救命

11. (**C**) Question number 11: Please look at picture D again.
    What do we know about the boy in the water?

    A. He drowned.

    B. He was rescued by the police.

    C. He cannot swim.

    D. He was rescued by the girl.

For questions number 12 and 13, please look at picture E.

12. (**B**) Question number 12: What can we tell about the picture for sure?

      A. The girl is with her parents.

      B. The girl is thirteen years old.

      C. They told her, "Happy Birthday!"

      D. It is evening.

      * *for sure* 確定地

13. (**C**) Question number 13: Please look at picture E again. What food will the people probably eat?

      A. Ice cream.   B. Soda.

      C. Cake.   D. Wine.

      * probably (ˈprɑbəblɪ) *adv.* 可能   *ice cream* 冰淇淋

      soda (ˈsodə) *n.* 汽水   wine (waɪn) *n.* 酒

For questions number 14 and 15, please look at picture F.

14. (**C**) Question number 14: What are the children doing?

      A. Because it is too windy.

      B. Flying their kites.

      C. Fighting over their kites.

      D. The boy did it.

      * windy (ˈwɪndɪ) *adj.* 多風的；風力強的

      fly (flaɪ) *v.* 放（風箏）   kite (kaɪt) *n.* 風箏

      fight (faɪt) *v.* 爭鬥   *fight over*… 爲了…而爭鬥

15. (**A**) Question number 15: Please look at picture F again.
    Why are the children unhappy?

    A. Their kites are tangled together.

    B. Yes, they are.

    C. The weather is too windy.

    D. Neither of them are happy.

    * tangle〔'tæŋgl̩〕v. 纏結　　weather〔'wɛðɚ〕n. 天氣
    neither〔'niðɚ〕pron. 兩者都不

Part B

16. (**A**) Can I get anyone some more coffee?

    A. Not now, thanks.

    B. Why should you care?

    C. Yes, it's true.

    D. I haven't seen any.

    * get〔gɛt〕v. 替~拿　　care〔kɛr〕v. 在乎

17. (**A**) May I show you to the door?

    A. Oh, don't go to the trouble.

    B. No, the door is locked.

    C. I just left.

    D. The door looks fine.

    * ***show sb. to the door*** 送某人到門口
    trouble〔'trʌbl̩〕n. 麻煩；費事
    go to the trouble 特意　　lock〔lɑk〕v. 鎖上

18. (**B**) Do you have any of these in stock?

    A. I'm sorry. You can't do that.

    B. I'm afraid we are sold out.

    C. No, I sold my stocks in that company.

    D. These are not stockings.

    * stock〔stɑk〕*n.* 存貨【不可數名詞】；股票【可數名詞】

    have…in stock 有…的存貨

    sell out 賣光   stockings〔'stɑkɪŋz〕*n. pl.* 長襪

19. (**B**) I've heard that they have really tasty burgers.

    A. I heard what you were saying.

    B. Yeah, they're delicious.

    C. And you have a burger, too.

    D. Would you like fries with that?

    * tasty〔'testɪ〕*adj.* 美味的

    burger〔'bɝgə〕*n.* 漢堡

    delicious〔dɪ'lɪʃəs〕*adj.* 美味的   have〔hæv〕*v.* 吃

    fries〔fraɪz〕*n. pl.* 薯條（= *French fries*）

20. (**C**) How many times have you been to California?

    A. A lot of time.   B. Twice a year.

    C. Only once.   D. Not anymore.

    * time〔taɪm〕*n.* 次數

    California〔ˌkælə'fɔrnjə〕*n.* 加州

    twice〔twaɪs〕*adv.* 兩次   once〔wʌns〕*adv.* 一次

    anymore〔'ɛnɪˌmɔr〕*adv.* 再也（不）；（不）再

21. (**C**) Oh, I'm sorry. I didn't mean to do that.

  A. I'm so sorry!   B. I meant to tell you.

  C. That's all right.   D. How did you do it?

  * mean〔min〕v. 有意；打算　***That's all right.*** 沒關係。

22. (**B**) Where is that pen?

  A. I wrote a letter to Susan.

  B. I don't know. I can't find it anywhere.

  C. Yes, it's my pen.

  D. I did a lot with it.

  * letter〔'lɛtɚ〕n. 信

23. (**C**) What's so funny?

  A. This is not fun anymore.

  B. I had a lot of fun there.

  C. Nothing at all.

  D. Have fun!

  * funny〔'fʌnɪ〕adj. 好笑的；有趣的

  fun〔fʌn〕adj. 有趣的　***have a lot of fun*** 玩得很愉快

  at all 一點也（不）　***Have fun!*** 玩得愉快！

24. (**D**) Can you finish this by Friday?

  A. Yes, I'm on Friday.

  B. Yes, they are going on Friday.

  C. No, by Friday it will be over.

  D. No, I have too much to do.

  * finish〔'fɪnɪʃ〕v. 完成　over〔'ovɚ〕adv. 結束；完畢

25. (**A**) You look exhausted—take a break!

    A. Thanks, I could use one.

    B. I'm breaking my back.

    C. I'm going to break it.

    D. No, I haven't.

    * exhausted〔ɪg'zɔstɪd〕*adj.* 筋疲力竭的

      break〔brek〕*n.* 休息　*v.* 折斷；扭傷…的關節；打破

      could use 想要　***I could use one.*** 在此指「我是想要休息。」

      back〔bæk〕*n.* 背部

26. (**A**) Did you play baseball?

    A. Yes, I used to.   B. No, I'm not used to it.

    C. Yes, I'm used to it.   D. Yes, I used it.

    * ***used to*** 以前常常　***be used to*** 習慣於

27. (**B**) How much is twenty dollars' worth?

    A. I don't have twenty dollars.

    B. It's worth twenty dollars.

    C. It's about two kilos.

    D. It is more than twenty dollars' worth.

    * worth〔wɜθ〕*n.* 價值　*adj.* 值…的

      kilo〔'kɪlo〕*n.* 公里（= *kilometer*）

28. (**C**) What would you do if you were her?

    A. I did the same thing.

    B. I told her I did the same.

    C. I would do the same thing.

    D. I am just doing what she did.

    * same〔sem〕*adj.* 相同的

29. (**A**) Which one does she like better? Red or orange?

   A. She likes them both.

   B. It is red and orange.

   C. He likes red and orange.

   D. She doesn't have any.

   * *like better* 比較喜歡
     orange〔'ɔrɪndʒ〕 *n.* 橘色　 *adj.* 橘色的

30. (**D**) How come the stove is on?

   A. It uses gas.

   B. I don't know how it works.

   C. The stove is in the kitchen.

   D. Oops! I forgot to turn it off.

   * *How come~?* 為什麼~？　　 stove〔stov〕 *n.* 爐子
     on〔ɑn〕 *adv.* 開著　　 gas〔gæs〕 *n.* 瓦斯
     work〔wɜk〕 *v.* 運作　　 oops〔ups〕 *interj.* 糟糕
     turn off 關掉

Part C

31. (**C**) W: Hey, when was my dental appointment again?

   M: Oh my goodness! It was today at 2 p.m.! You
   should be there now! Get going.

   (TONE)

   Q: What can we tell from the conversation?

   A. The woman will not be able to see the dentist.

   B. The man will take the woman to the dentist's.

C. It is past 2 p.m.

D. The woman is at the dental appointment now.

* dental〔'dɛntḷ〕 *adj.* 牙科的
  appointment〔ə'pɔɪntmənt〕 *n.* 預約；約會
  My goodness! 天啊！；糟糕！　　***get going*** 動身；出發
  tell〔tɛl〕 *v.* 知道　　conversation〔͵kɑnvə'seʃən〕 *n.* 對話
  be able to V. 能夠～　　dentist〔'dɛntɪst〕 *n.* 牙醫
  dentist's *n.* 牙醫診所（= *dentist's office*）
  past〔pæst〕 *prep.* 超過

32.(**B**) W: Hello.

M: Hi, could I talk to Fanny?

W: Hold on a sec. Fanny! Telephone! Fanny? Oh, I'm
　　sorry. Fanny just left. May I take a message?

M: No, that's fine. She must be on her way to meet me.

W: Well, she said she was going to McDonald's.

M: That's where I am now.

(TONE)

Q: Where is Fanny now?

A. At McDonald's.　　B. On her way to McDonald's.

C. At home.　　D. On her way home.

* ***hold on*** 不要掛斷電話；稍待
  sec.〔sɛk〕 *n.* 片刻；一會兒（= *second*）
  message〔'mɛsɪdʒ〕 *n.* 訊息；留言
  May I take a message? 你要留話嗎？
  on *one's* ***way to***～ 在某人去～的途中
  McDonald's〔mək'dɑnḷdz〕 *n.* 麥當勞

33. (**C**)　W: I should buy a new cell phone.　This one is so old.

　　　　　M: What are you talking about?　You got it last year.

　　　　　W: Yeah, but it can't even play mp3s.

　　　　　M: Well, why don't you just buy an mp3 player?　It would be a lot cheaper.

　　　　　(TONE)

　　　　　Q: What does the man think?

　　　　　A. The woman should buy a cell phone that plays mp3s.

　　　　　B. The woman's cell phone is quite old.

　　　　　C. The woman doesn't need to buy a new cell phone.

　　　　　D. The woman should sell her phone and buy an mp3 player.

　　　* ***cell phone***　手機　　　get〔gɛt〕*v.* 買

　　　　play〔ple〕*v.* 播放　　***mp3*** 音樂格式檔

　　　　player〔'pleɚ〕*n.* 播放器　　cheap〔tʃip〕*adj.* 便宜的

　　　　a lot cheaper 便宜很多　　quite〔kwaɪt〕*adv.* 非常

34. (**C**)　M: There's no way I'm getting into that boat.

　　　　　W: Don't be such a baby.　It's perfectly safe!

　　　　　M: I'm sure it is, but that's not my problem.

　　　　　W: Well, what's wrong then?

　　　　　M: I get seasick really easily.

　　　　　(TONE)

　　　　　Q: Why won't the man get in the boat?

A. He is a coward.

B. He doesn't think the boat is safe.

C. He gets dizzy when he rides in boats.

D. He has a fear of the water.

* **_There's no way~_**　　~門都沒有；我才不要~
　boat〔bot〕*n.* 船　　baby〔'bebɪ〕*n.* 孩子氣的人
　perfectly〔'pɝfɪktlɪ〕*adv.* 十分；非常
　safe〔sef〕*adj.* 安全的　　then〔ðɛn〕*adv.* 那麼
　seasick〔'si͵sɪk〕*adj.* 暈船的　　**_get in_** 上（車、船等）
　coward〔'kauɚd〕*n.* 膽小鬼　　get〔gɛt〕*v.* 成為；變得
　dizzy〔'dɪzɪ〕*adj.* 暈眩的　　ride〔raɪd〕*v.* 搭乘
　fear〔fɪr〕*n.* 恐懼；害怕

35.（ **A** ） M：I've been looking for months, but I still can't find
　　　　　　a job.

　　　　W：Well, don't let it get you down. Just keep trying
　　　　　　and I'm sure something will come up.

（TONE）

　　　　Q：What does the woman try to do?

　　　　A. Encourage the man.

　　　　B. Find a job for the man.

　　　　C. Tell the man how to find a job.

　　　　D. Tell the man what jobs are available.

* **_get sb. down_** 使某人情緒低落　　try〔traɪ〕*v.* 嘗試
　come up 發生　　encourage〔ɪn'kɝɪdʒ〕*v.* 鼓勵
　available〔ə'veləbḷ〕*adj.* 可獲得的

36. (**B**)　M：I'll take that blue umbrella.

　　　　　W：That's $160.

　　　　　M：Uh, I only have $155.　Can I give you the rest next
　　　　　　　time?

　　　　　W：Well, I guess so—but don't forget.

　　　　　(TONE)

　　　　　Q：What can we tell from this conversation?

　　　　　A.　The woman would not sell the umbrella to the man.

　　　　　B.　The man was able to buy the umbrella.

　　　　　C.　The man forgot to pay the woman.

　　　　　D.　The man was not able to buy the umbrella.

　　　*　take〔tek〕v. 買　　umbrella〔ʌm'brɛlə〕n. 雨傘
　　　　rest〔rɛst〕n. 其餘的東西　　guess〔gɛs〕v. 猜
　　　　I guess so. 我想是可以的。　　tell〔tɛl〕v. 得知
　　　　conversation〔ˌkɑnvə'seʃən〕n. 對話
　　　　pay〔pe〕v. 付錢給~

37. (**B**)　M：How was your weekend?

　　　　　W：It was okay.　How about you?

　　　　　M：Oh, it was great.　I watched movies all day Saturday
　　　　　　　and played computer games with my friends on
　　　　　　　Sunday.　How about you?

　　　　　W：Well, I went hiking on Saturday, but I studied
　　　　　　　all day Sunday for the test.

　　　　　M：What test?

　　　　　W：The test in class today.

　　　　　M：Uh-oh…

(TONE)

Q：What can we tell about the man?

A. He studied on Sunday.

B. He didn't know about the test.

C. He went hiking on Saturday.

D. He already took the test.

* weekend〔ˈwikˌɛnd〕*n.* 週末　　***all day*** 整天

hike〔haɪk〕*v.* 健行；遠足　　take〔tek〕*v.* 參加；接受

38. (**C**)　W：I hope you like pasta.

M：Actually, I don't really.

W：Well, too bad 'cause that's what we're having for dinner.

M：How come you never ask me before you start cooking?

W：Hey, if you want to pick and choose, then you can cook once in a while.

(TONE)

Q：How often does the man make dinner?

A. Once in a while.

B. When he is hungry.

C. Almost never.

D. When he does not want pasta.

* pasta〔ˈpɑstɑ〕*n.* 通心粉；義大利麵

actually〔ˈæktʃʊəlɪ〕*adv.* 事實上

'cause〔kɔz〕*conj.* 因為（ = *because* ）

pick and choose 挑三揀四　　***once in a while*** 偶爾

39. (**B**)　M：Have you seen a young cat with a black patch
　　　　　　　around his right eye?

　　　　W：I don't think so.　What color is his body?

　　　　M：He's all white, except for the black patch.

　　　　W：Sorry, I haven't seen him.

　　　　(TONE)

　　　　Q：Why is the man asking about the cat?

　　　　A.　He wants to buy a cat with a black patch.

　　　　B.　He has lost his cat.

　　　　C.　He thinks he has found the woman's cat.

　　　　D.　He can't find the woman's cat.

　　　　* patch〔pætʃ〕*n.* 眼罩　　***except for*** 除了
　　　　　lose〔luz〕*v.* 遺失

40. (**C**)　M：How can you eat fast food every day?　It's so
　　　　　　　unhealthy.

　　　　W：I know, but it tastes so good.

　　　　M：Yeah, but fast food is such junk.

　　　　W：Oh, don't worry so much.　It can't be that bad.

　　　　M：Just remember: You are what you eat.

　　　　(TONE)

　　　　Q：Why does the woman eat fast food every day?

　　　　A.　Because it is not so bad.

　　　　B.　Because she can't afford healthy food.

C. Because she really likes its taste.

D. Because she is what she eats.

* ***fast food*** 速食　　unhealthy〔ʌnˋhɛlθɪ〕*adj.* 不健康的

taste〔test〕*v.* 嚐起來　*n.* 味道

such〔sʌtʃ〕*adj.* 這樣的；如此的

junk〔dʒʌŋk〕*n.* 無價值的東西

remember〔rɪˋmɛmbɚ〕*v.* 記得

You are what you eat. 你吃什麼，就變成什麼樣。

afford〔əˋfɔrd〕*v.* 負擔得起

healthy〔ˋhɛlθɪ〕*adj.* 健康的

41. (**C**)　M：How much is a ticket to Taichung?

W：It's $330.

M：But the sign says $280.

W：That's from Monday through Thursday.　The weekend rate is higher.

(TONE)

Q：When did this conversation probably take place?

A. On Monday.　　　　B. On Thursday.

C. On Saturday.　　　　D. We cannot tell.

* ticket〔ˋtɪkɪt〕*n.* 票；車票　　sign〔saɪn〕*n.* 告示

say〔se〕*v.* 寫著　　through〔θru〕*prep.* 直到

rate〔ret〕*n.* 費用；價格

probably〔ˋprɑbəblɪ〕*adv.* 可能

take place 發生　　tell〔tɛl〕*v.* 知道

42. (**D**) M：Have you seen the new math teacher?

W：Yeah, he looks cool. He's much younger than the other teachers.

M：I have him for third period today.

W：Really? Let me know what you think of him.

(TONE)

Q：What do we learn from the conversation?

A. The new teacher will teach the woman.

B. The new teacher teaches English.

C. The woman has a crush on the new teacher.

D. The man will be in the new teacher's class.

* math〔mæθ〕*n.* 數學　　cool〔kul〕*adj.* 酷的
period〔'pɪrɪəd〕*n.* (上課的) 節；堂
learn〔lɜn〕*v.* 得知　　crush〔krʌʃ〕*n.* 迷戀
have a crush on *sb.* 迷戀某人

43. (**D**) W：Are you serious? You can't just cancel the meeting.

M：What am I supposed to do? I have nothing to show the client—the work isn't finished yet.

W：Well, it would be if you hadn't taken Friday off last week.

M：But it was my classmate's wedding. I couldn't miss it.

(TONE)

Q：Why does the man have to cancel the meeting?

A. Because his classmate is getting married.

B. Because he cannot work on Friday.

C. Because the client cannot show up.

D. Because he has not finished the work.

* serious〔'sɪrɪəs〕adj. 認眞的　cancel〔'kænsl̩〕v. 取消
  meeting〔'mitɪŋ〕n. 會議　*be supposed to V.* 應該～
  show〔ʃo〕v. 給～看　client〔'klaɪənt〕n. 顧客
  finish〔'fɪnɪʃ〕v. 完成　yet〔jɛt〕adv. 尙（未）
  take off 休息；休假　wedding〔'wɛdɪŋ〕n. 婚禮
  miss〔mɪs〕v. 錯過　*get married* 結婚
  show up 出席；出現

44.(**D**)　M：Mrs. Lin, I think your son could do a lot better—he
　　　　　　just seems a little distracted in class.

　　　　W：Do you have any idea why?

　　　　M：Actually, I caught him playing games on his cell
　　　　　　phone the other day. That could be one reason.

　　　　W：Well, I'll take it away from him for a while, and
　　　　　　see if he gets the message.

(TONE)

Q：Where did this conversation probably take place?

A. At the police station.　B. At the woman's office.

C. At the man's home.

D. At the woman's son's school.

* *do better* 表現得更好　seem〔sim〕v. 似乎
  distracted〔dɪ'stræktɪd〕adj. 分心的
  actually〔'æktʃuəlɪ〕adv. 事實上
  catch〔kætʃ〕v. 撞見（某人正在做…）　*cell phone* 手機
  the other day 前幾天　reason〔'rizn̩〕n. 理由；原因
  take away 拿走　*for a while* 暫時；一會兒
  get the message 明白對方的意思　*police station* 警察局

45. (**C**)　W：Don't whistle!　You'll attract ghosts.

　　　　　M：You don't actually believe that nonsense, do you?

　　　　　W：Not really, but it still creeps me out.　Please just stop.

　　　　　M：Okay, have it your way.　But I still think you're being too superstitious.

　　　　(TONE)

　　　　Q：What does the man think about whistling?

　　　　A. He thinks it is superstitious.

　　　　B. He thinks it attracts ghosts.

　　　　C. He thinks it is harmless.

　　　　D. He thinks it is creepy.

* whistle〔'hwɪsḷ〕v. 吹口哨

　attract〔ə'trækt〕v. 吸引；招引

　ghost〔gost〕n. 鬼

　actually〔'æktʃʊəlɪ〕adv. 真地

　nonsense〔'nɑnsɛns〕n. 無意義的話；胡說八道

　not really 事實上沒有

　creep〔krip〕v. 令～毛骨悚然

　creep sb. **out** 嚇壞某人

　have it one's **way** 隨心所欲

　superstitious〔‚supə'stɪʃəs〕adj. 迷信的

　harmless〔'hɑrmlɪs〕adj. 無害的

　creepy〔'kripɪ〕adj. 令人毛骨悚然的

English Listening Comprehension Test
Test Book No. 3

This listening comprehension test will test your ability to understand spoken English. In this test, each conversation, statement and question will be spoken JUST ONE TIME. They will not be written out for you. There are three parts to this test. Special instructions will be given to you at the beginning of each part.

Part A

In Part A, you will see several pictures in your test book. For each picture, you will be asked 1 to 3 questions. For each question, you will hear four possible answers. Choose the best answer according to what you see in the picture.

Example:

<u>You will see</u>:

<u>You will hear</u>:   What is this?
　　　　　　　　A. This is a table.
　　　　　　　　B. This is a chair.
　　　　　　　　C. This is a watch.
　　　　　　　　D. This is a doll.

The best answer to the question "What is this?" is B: "This is a chair." Therefore, you should choose answer B.

A. Questions 1-2

B. Questions 3-4

C. Questions 5-7

D. Questions 8-10

E. Questions 11-12

F. Questions 13-15

Part B

In Part B, you will hear 15 questions. After you hear a question, read the four possible answers in your test book and decide which one is the best answer to the question you have heard.

Example:

<u>You will hear</u>: What does your father do?

<u>You will read</u>: A. He's 50 years old.
B. He's a teacher.
C. He's hungry.
D. He's in Los Angeles.

The best answer to the question "What does your father do?" is B: "He's a teacher." Therefore, you should choose answer B.

Please go to the next page. ⇨

16. A. I took it on Friday.
    B. I think I did well on the test.
    C. Yes, I did take it.
    D. At the government testing center.

17. A. No, I'm not old enough.
    B. Yes, I can drive you there.
    C. I've driven there already.
    D. I still do.

18. A. My bike's new, too.
    B. If you are tired, then take the bus.
    C. Did you manage to fix it?
    D. How much is this bike?

19. A. I like my new watch.
    B. Some other time.
    C. It's quarter past eight.
    D. Eight quarters.

20. A. By plane.
    B. Next month.
    C. I'm from Taipei.
    D. Four times.

21. A. I won't.
    B. I will.
    C. Sure.
    D. I'm not.

22. A. I have several.
    B. Only a little.
    C. I have four of them.
    D. Too many.

23. A. Here is the question.
    B. Don't shoot. I'm not wrong.
    C. That's okay. It's just one mistake.
    D. I can't tell you the question.

24. A. Yes, but I don't know him.
    B. Yes, she was with her.
    C. No, he wasn't.
    D. No, she was with him.

25. A. I got soaking wet.
    B. It's been freezing.
    C. It's hard to predict the weather.
    D. Yes, it has.

26. A. Congratulations!
    B. Good for you!
    C. I told Daniel.
    D. No way!

27. A. Don't count on it.
    B. You have?
    C. I don't like betting.
    D. Last chance!

28. A. What do you know about him?
    B. That's fine with me.
    C. How can you tell?
    D. How much does she need?

29. A. Well, I guess we'll have to take it.
    B. I'm only going to tell you once.
    C. I have to choose one or the other.
    D. I haven't seen the other one.

30. A. It's no matter.
    B. Nothing's wrong.
    C. School and family.
    D. My heart is broken.

Part C

In Part C, you will hear 15 conversations between a man and a woman. After each conversation, you will hear a question about the conversation. After you hear the question, read the four possible answers in your test book and choose the best answer to the question you have heard.

Example:

You will hear: (Man)   How do you go to school every
                         day?
               (Woman)   Usually by bus. Sometimes by
                         taxi.
               (Tone)
               Question: How does the woman go to
                         school?

You will read: A. She always goes to school on foot.
               B. She usually rides a bike.
               C. She takes either a bus or a taxi.
               D. She usually goes to school by bus, never
                  by taxi.

The best answer to the question "How does the woman go to school?" is C: "She takes either a bus or a taxi." Therefore, you should choose answer C.

Please go to the next page. ⇨

31. A. She started the report too late.
    B. She didn't finish the report on time.
    C. She didn't pay close attention to the instructions.
    D. She wrote the report carelessly.

32. A. Reduce them.
    B. Put them in the garbage.
    C. Recycle them.
    D. Take them to the man.

33. A. It has a virus.
    B. It has anti-virus software.
    C. It is too old.
    D. It always crashes.

34. A. A hotel.
    B. A doctor's office.
    C. An amusement park.
    D. A bus stop.

35. A. She didn't study for the test.
    B. She usually does well in English.
    C. She failed the test.
    D. She did worse than the man.

36. A. To ask what kind of coffee they want.
    B. To check whether they want sugar in their lattes.
    C. To check whether they want iced or hot lattes.
    D. To ask what type of milk they want in their lattes.

37. A. The mountains.
    B. The coast.
    C. Driving.
    D. A trip route.

38. A. The woman is on
       vacation.
    B. The woman will
       leave on Thursday.
    C. The man and woman
       will visit on
       Wednesday.
    D. The woman has not
       seen the man for a
       long time.

39. A. If he can use the
       microwave.
    B. For how long he
       should put his food in
       the microwave.
    C. If he can put a pot in
       the microwave.
    D. Why he should not
       put his food in the
       microwave.

40. A. Cooking some food.
    B. Cleaning the bathroom.
    C. Putting on clothing.
    D. Talking on the
       telephone.

41. A. Spring.
    B. Hot.
    C. Sunny.
    D. Winter.

42. A. She paid the bill on
       the eleventh.
    B. She forgot to pay the
       bill on time.
    C. She only got the bill
       on the tenth.
    D. She forgot when the
       bill was due.

43. A. He thought they were
       not suitable for each
       other.
    B. He thought they were
       very close.
    C. He thought they were
       angry at each other.
    D. He thought they were
       going to break up.

44. A. He really likes Tom
       Cruise.
    B. He thought the
       woman really liked
       Tom Cruise.
    C. He thought the special
       effects were
       impressive.
    D. We cannot tell.

45. A. He is going to eat
       more vegetables.
    B. He is going to go on
       a diet.
    C. He will do more
       exercise.
    D. He is going to work
       harder.

Listening Test 3 詳解

Part A

For questions number 1 and 2, please look at picture A.

1. (**A**) Question number 1: What is the boy doing?

A. He is shearing the sheep.

B. He is chasing the sheep.

C. He is killing the sheep.

D. He is selling the sheep.

* shear〔ʃɪr〕v. 剪（羊）的毛

sheep〔ʃip〕n. 羊；綿羊

chase〔tʃes〕v. 追趕；追逐

kill〔kɪl〕v. 殺　　sell〔sɛl〕v. 賣；出售

2. (**D**) Question number 2: Please look at picture A again. What does the boy think?

A. He is scared of the sheep.

B. He wonders what the sheep are doing.

C. He is bored with his job.

D. He seems to enjoy his work.

* scared〔skɛrd〕adj. 害怕的　　*be scared of* 怕～

wonder〔'wʌndɚ〕v. 想知道

bored〔bord〕adj. 厭倦的；厭煩的

job〔dʒab〕n. 工作　　seem〔sim〕v. 似乎

enjoy〔ɪn'dʒɔɪ〕v. 喜歡

For questions number 3 and 4, please look at picture B.

3. (**C**)　Question number 3:　What will the boy do after he finishes talking to the girl?

　　　A.　He will wake up.

　　　B.　He will go to work.

　　　C.　He will go to bed.

　　　D.　He will go swimming.

　　　* finish〔ˈfɪnɪʃ〕*v.* 完成；結束

　　　　 wake up 醒來

　　　　 swim〔swɪm〕*v.* 游泳

4. (**B**)　Question number 4:　Please look at picture B again. What is TRUE about this picture?

　　　A.　The girl is at school.

　　　B.　The boy and girl are in different countries.

　　　C.　The boy and girl are from different countries.

　　　D.　The boy is at work.

　　　* different〔ˈdɪfərənt〕*adj.* 不同的

　　　　 country〔ˈkʌntrɪ〕*n.* 國家　　***at work*** 工作中

For questions number 5 to 7, please look at picture C.

5. (**C**)　Question number 5:　What is in the pond?

　　　A.　A fish.　　　　　　　B.　Some grass.

　　　C.　A frog.　　　　　　　D.　A flower.

　　　* pond〔pɑnd〕*n.* 池塘　　grass〔græs〕*n.* 草

　　　　 frog〔frɑg〕*n.* 青蛙

6. (**D**) Question number 6: Please look at picture C again.

How does the rain make the girl feel?

A. It makes her sad.　　B. It makes her hungry.

C. It makes her silent.

D. It makes her feel joyful.

* make〔mek〕*v.* 使　hungry〔'hʌŋgrɪ〕*adj.* 飢餓的
silent〔'saɪlənt〕*adj.* 沉默的
joyful〔'dʒɔɪfəl〕*adj.* 快樂的

7. (**D**) Question number 7: Please look at picture C again.

What is the girl doing?

A. She is afraid of the frog.

B. She is going to school.

C. She is getting very wet.

D. She is singing a song.

* afraid〔ə'fred〕*adj.* 害怕的　*be afraid of* 怕~
frog〔frɑg〕*n.* 青蛙　wet〔wɛt〕*adj.* 濕的
get wet 變濕；淋濕

For questions number 8 to 10, please look at picture D.

8. (**B**) Question number 8: Where are they?

A. They are in the ocean.

B. They are at the beach.

C. They are in a desert.

D. They are in a sandbox.

* ocean〔'oʃən〕*n.* 海洋　desert〔'dɛzət〕*n.* 沙漠
sandbox〔'sænd,bɑks〕*n.* (供兒童在裡面玩耍的) 沙箱；沙場

9. (**B**) Question number 9: Please look at picture D again.
What does the girl want?

A. A new bikini.   B. An ice cream cone.
C. A cold drink.   D. A boyfriend.

* bikini〔bɪˋkini〕 *n.* 比基尼泳裝
ice cream〔ˋaɪsˋkrim〕 *n.* 冰淇淋
cone〔kon〕 *n.* (裝冰淇淋的) 圓錐筒
ice cream cone 蛋捲冰淇淋
cold〔kold〕 *adj.* 冷的；冰過的   drink〔drɪŋk〕 *n.* 飲料

10. (**B**) Question number 10: Please look at picture D again.
What does the boy think?

A. He thinks it is too hot.
B. He thinks the girl is pretty.
C. He wants to go swimming.
D. He wants to sleep all day.

* pretty〔ˋprɪtɪ〕 *adj.* 漂亮的   ***all day*** 整天

For questions number 11 and 12, please look at picture E.

11. (**D**) Question number 11: What are the children doing?

A. They are playing in the water.
B. They are looking at a sandy beach.
C. They are watching the boat.
D. They are building a sand castle.

* sandy〔ˋsændɪ〕 *adj.* 沙質的；多沙的   boat〔bot〕 *n.* 船
build〔bɪld〕 *v.* 建造   sand〔sænd〕 *n.* 沙
castle〔ˋkæsl̩〕 *n.* 城堡

12. (**D**) Question number 12: Please look at picture E again.

What is the girl holding?

A. A spoon and a fork.　B. A knife and a jar.

C. A leaf and a cup.　　D. A shovel and a pail.

* hold〔hold〕*v.* 拿著；握住　　spoon〔spun〕*n.* 湯匙

　fork〔fɔrk〕*n.* 叉子　　knife〔naɪf〕*n.* 刀子

　jar〔dʒɑr〕*n.* 廣口瓶　　leaf〔lif〕*n.* 葉子

　shovel〔'ʃʌvl̩〕*n.* 鏟子　　pail〔pel〕*n.* 水桶

For questions number 13 to 15, please look at picture F.

13. (**C**) Question number 13: Who is singing?

A. The girl on the far left.

B. The girl on the left.

C. The girl on the right.

D. The girl in the front.

* far〔fɑr〕*adv.* 在遠處　　left〔lɛft〕*n.* 左邊

　right〔raɪt〕*n.* 右邊　　front〔frʌnt〕*n.* 前面

14. (**D**) Question number 14: Please look at picture F again.

How is the girl's singing?

A. It is unbelievable.　　B. It is fantastic.

C. It is incredible.　　　D. It is terrible.

* unbelievable〔ˌʌnbə'livəbl̩〕*adj.* 令人難以置信的

　fantastic〔fæn'tæstɪk〕*adj.* 很棒的

　incredible〔ɪn'krɛdəbl̩〕*adj.* 令人難以置信的；極好的

　terrible〔'tɛrəbl̩〕*adj.* 可怕的；很糟的

15. (**C**) Question number 15:　Please look at picture F again.
How many people are there in this picture?

　　　A. Three.　　　　　　B. Four.
　　　C. Five.　　　　　　D. Six.

Part B

16. (**D**) Where did you take the test?

　　　A. I took it on Friday.
　　　B. I think I did well on the test.
　　　C. Yes, I did take it.
　　　D. At the government testing center.

　　　* take〔tek〕v. 接受　　test〔tɛst〕n. 檢查；考試
　　　　do well 考得好　　government〔'gʌvənmənt〕n. 政府
　　　　testing〔'tɛstɪŋ〕adj. 試驗的　　center〔'sɛntə〕n. 中心

17. (**A**) Do you have your driver's license yet?

　　　A. No, I'm not old enough.
　　　B. Yes, I can drive you there.
　　　C. I've driven there already.
　　　D. I still do.

　　　* license〔'laɪsn̩s〕n. 執照　　***driver's license*** 駕照
　　　　yet〔jɛt〕adv. 已經　　enough〔ə'nʌf〕adv. 足夠地
　　　　drive〔draɪv〕v. 用車載（某人）；開車
　　　　already〔ɔl'rɛdɪ〕adv. 已經

18. (**C**) My bike had a flat tire so I had to walk to school.

    A. My bike's new, too.

    B. If you are tired, then take the bus.

    C. Did you manage to fix it?

    D. How much is this bike?

    * bike〔baɪk〕*n.* 腳踏車（= *bicycle*）
      flat〔flæt〕*adj.*（輪胎）洩了氣的　　*flat tire* 洩氣的輪胎
      tired〔taɪrd〕*adj.* 疲倦的　　take〔tek〕*v.* 搭乘
      manage〔'mænɪdʒ〕*v.* 設法　　fix〔fɪks〕*v.* 修理

19. (**C**) Do you have the time?

    A. I like my new watch. B. Some other time.

    C. It's quarter past eight.

    D. Eight quarters.

    * ***Do you have the time?*** 你知道現在幾點嗎？【而 Do you
      have time? 才是「你有時間嗎？」】
      some other time 改天
      quarter〔'kwɔrtɚ〕*n.* 十五分鐘
      past〔pæst〕*prep.* 超過；過了（…分鐘）

20. (**B**) When will you be going back to Taiwan?

    A. By plane.

    B. Next month.

    C. I'm from Taipei.

    D. Four times.

    * plane〔plen〕*n.* 飛機　　time〔taɪm〕*n.* 次數

21. (**C**) Don't you miss your parents?

      A. I won't.   B. I will.

      C. Sure.   D. I'm not.

      * miss〔mɪs〕*v.* 想念   parents〔'pɛrənts〕*n. pl.* 父母

        sure〔ʃur〕*adv.* 當然

22. (**B**) How much do you have left?

      A. I have several.   B. Only a little.

      C. I have four of them. D. Too many.

      * leave〔liv〕*v.* 留下   several〔'sɛvərəl〕*pron.* 幾個

23. (**C**) Shoot! I got this question wrong!

      A. Here is the question.

      B. Don't shoot. I'm not wrong.

      C. That's okay. It's just one mistake.

      D. I can't tell you the question.

      * shoot〔ʃut〕*interj.* 可惡！   *v.* 開槍

        get〔gɛt〕*v.* 使⋯成爲   wrong〔rɔŋ〕*adj.* 錯誤的

        That's okay. 沒關係。

        mistake〔mə'stek〕*n.* 錯誤

24. (**A**) Did you see the boy who was with her?

      A. Yes, but I don't know him.

      B. Yes, she was with her.

      C. No, he wasn't.   D. No, she was with him.

      * with〔wɪθ〕*prep.* 和⋯一起

25. (**B**) How has the weather been recently?

    A. I got soaking wet.   B. It's been freezing.

    C. It's hard to predict the weather.

    D. Yes, it has.

    * weather〔'wɛðɚ〕*n.* 天氣   recently〔'risn̩tlı〕*adv.* 最近
    get〔gɛt〕*v.* 成為；變得   soaking〔'sokıŋ〕*adv.* 濕淋淋地
    wet〔wɛt〕*adj.* 淋濕的   freezing〔'frizıŋ〕*adj.* 極冷的
    hard〔hard〕*adj.* 困難的   predict〔prı'dıkt〕*v.* 預測

26. (**D**) Daniel told me he got 100% on the test.

    A. Congratulations!   B. Good for you!

    C. I told Daniel.   D. No way!

    * congratulations〔kən͵grætʃə'leʃənz〕*n. pl.* 恭喜
    Good for you! 幹得好！   ***No way!*** 不可能！

27. (**A**) I bet school will be cancelled because of this typhoon.

    A. Don't count on it.   B. You have?

    C. I don't like betting.   D. Last chance!

    * bet〔bɛt〕*v.* 打賭；斷定   school〔skul〕*n.* 上課
    cancel〔'kænsl̩〕*v.* 取消   typhoon〔taı'fun〕*n.* 颱風
    count on 指望；期待   betting〔'bɛtıŋ〕*n.* 打賭
    last〔læst〕*adj.* 最後的   chance〔tʃæns〕*n.* 機會

28. (**C**) She seems unhappy lately.

    A. What do you know about him?

    B. That's fine with me.   C. How can you tell?

    D. How much does she need?

    * seem〔sim〕*v.* 似乎   lately〔'letlı〕*adv.* 最近
    That's fine with me. 我沒問題；我沒意見。

29. (**A**) This is the only option.

A. Well, I guess we'll have to take it.

B. I'm only going to tell you once.

C. I have to choose one or the other.

D. I haven't seen the other one.

* option〔'ɑpʃən〕*n.* 選擇　　well〔wɛl〕*interj.* 嗯
guess〔gɛs〕*v.* 猜　　take〔tek〕*v.* 接受
once〔wʌns〕*adv.* 一次　　choose〔tʃuz〕*v.* 選擇

30. (**C**) What matters most to you?

A. It's no matter.

B. Nothing's wrong.

C. School and family.

D. My heart is broken.

* matter〔'mætɚ〕*v.* 重要
It's no matter. 沒關係；無關緊要。
wrong〔rɔŋ〕*adj.* 錯誤的　　heart〔hɑrt〕*n.* 心
broken〔'brokən〕*adj.* 破碎的

Part C

31. (**C**) W : This is impossible—I'm never going to finish the report on time.

M : What's the problem?

W : I didn't read the instructions carefully, and now I have to start over.

(TONE)

Q: What mistake did the woman make?

A. She started the report too late.

B. She didn't finish the report on time.

C. She didn't pay close attention to the instructions.

D. She wrote the report carelessly.

* impossible〔ɪmˈpɑsəbḷ〕 *adj.* 不可能的
  finish〔ˈfɪnɪʃ〕 *v.* 完成
  report〔rɪˈport〕 *n.* 報告　　***on time*** 準時
  instructions〔ɪnˈstrʌkʃənz〕 *n. pl.* 指示；說明書
  start over 重新開始　　mistake〔məˈstek〕 *n.* 錯誤
  late〔let〕 *adv.* 晚　　***pay attention to*** 注意
  close〔klos〕 *adj.* 密切的
  carelessly〔ˈkɛrlɪslɪ〕 *adv.* 不小心地；草率地

32. (**C**)　W: Don't throw those bottles out—we should recycle
　　　　　　　them.

　　　　M: Oh, sorry. Where should I put them?

　　　　W: Over there in the blue bag.

(TONE)

Q: What does the woman want to do with the bottles?

A. Reduce them.　　　B. Put them in the garbage.

C. Recycle them.　　　D. Take them to the man.

* ***throw out*** 丟出；扔掉　　bottle〔ˈbɑtḷ〕 *n.* 瓶子
  recycle〔riˈsaɪkḷ〕 *v.* 再利用　　bag〔bæg〕 *n.* 袋子
  do with 處置　　reduce〔rɪˈdjus〕 *v.* 減少
  garbage〔ˈgɑrbɪdʒ〕 *n.* 垃圾

33. (**D**) W: My computer keeps crashing.

M: Hmm… have you scanned it for viruses?

W: No, I don't have any anti-virus software.

M: Are you serious? You should get some right away.

(TONE)

Q: What's wrong with the woman's computer?

A. It has a virus.

B. It has anti-virus software.

C. It is too old.

D. It always crashes.

* computer〔kəm'pjutɚ〕n. 電腦
  keep〔kip〕v. 持續;一直
  crash〔kræʃ〕v. (電腦)當機 (= *fail*)
  scan〔skæn〕v. 仔細察看;掃描   virus〔'vaɪrəs〕n. 病毒
  anti- 防止   software〔'sɔft,wɛr〕n. 軟體
  serious〔'sɪrɪəs〕adj. 認眞的   get〔gɛt〕v. 買
  right away 立刻   old〔old〕adj. 老舊的

34. (**B**) M: Do you smoke or drink?

W: No, neither.

M: Are you allergic to any medications?

W: Not that I know of.

M: Does your family have a record of heart disease,
high blood pressure or cancer?

(TONE)

Q: Where did this conversation most likely take place?

A. A hotel.

B. A doctor's office.

C. An amusement park.

D. A bus stop.

* smoke〔smok〕v. 抽煙　　drink〔drɪŋk〕v. 喝酒

neither〔'niðɚ〕pron. 兩者皆不

allergic〔ə'lɝdʒɪk〕adj. 過敏的 < to >

medication〔,mɛdɪ'keʃən〕n. 藥物

Not that I know of. 據我所知沒有。

record〔'rɛkɚd〕n. 記錄　　heart〔hɑrt〕n. 心臟

disease〔dɪ'ziz〕n. 疾病　　*heart disease* 心臟病

blood〔blʌd〕n. 血　　pressure〔'prɛʃɚ〕n. 壓力

high blood pressure 高血壓　　cancer〔'kænsɚ〕n. 癌症

conversation〔,kɑnvɚ'seʃən〕n. 對話

likely〔'laɪklɪ〕adv. 可能　　*take place* 發生

hotel〔ho'tɛl〕n. 旅館　　office〔'ɔfɪs〕n. 辦公室；診所

amusement park 遊樂場；遊樂園　　*bus stop* 公車站

35. (**B**)　M: Hey Jessica, how's it going?

W: Oh, not too good.　You?

M: I'm fine, but what's the matter?

W: I only got 70% on the English test.

M: Hey, don't be so hard on yourself.　I hear that
almost half the class failed.

W: Yeah, but that's my best subject.

(TONE)

Q: What do we know about Jessica?

A. She didn't study for the test.

B. She usually does well in English.

C. She failed the test.

D. She did worse than the man.

* ***How's it going?*** 最近如何；你好嗎？

What's the matter? 怎麼了？　　hard〔hɑrd〕*adj.* 嚴厲的

fail〔fel〕*v.* 不及格　　subject〔'sʌbdʒɪkt〕*n.* 科目

do well 考得好　　worse〔wɝs〕*adv.* 較差地

36. (**D**)　W：Can I have two large lattes, one without sugar; two regular coffees, both with milk not cream; and one hot chocolate?

M：Sure. Would you like 2% or whole milk in those lattes?

W：Hold on—I'd better call my coworkers to check.

(TONE)

Q：Why does the woman need to call her coworkers?

A. To ask what kind of coffee they want.

B. To check whether they want sugar in their lattes.

C. To check whether they want iced or hot lattes.

D. To ask what type of milk they want in their lattes.

* latte〔lɑ'te〕*n.* 拿鐵（一種咖啡）　　sugar〔'ʃʊgɚ〕*n.* 糖

regular〔'rɛgjələ〕*adj.* 正常的　　cream〔krim〕*n.* 奶精

sure〔ʃʊr〕*adv.* 好　　whole〔hol〕*adj.* 完全的

whole milk 全脂牛奶　　***hold on*** 稍等一下

had better 最好　　coworker〔ko'wɝkɚ〕*n.* 同事

check〔tʃɛk〕*v.* 確認　　whether〔'hwɛðɚ〕*conj.* 是否

iced〔aɪst〕*adj.* 冰過的

37. (**D**) M：There are only two routes there: the shorter one goes over the mountain, and the longer one goes along the coast.

W：Well, I hate driving on those winding mountain roads—they always make me feel sick.

M：Well, it's up to you, but the longer route will take an extra hour.

W：That's fine.

(TONE)

Q：What are the couple discussing?

A. The mountains.

B. The coast.

C. Driving.

D. A trip route.

* route〔rut〕*n.* 路；路線　　***go over*** 越過

mountain〔'maʊntn̩〕*n.* 山

along〔ə'lɔŋ〕*prep.* 沿著

coast〔kost〕*n.* 海岸　　hate〔het〕*v.* 討厭

winding〔'waɪndɪŋ〕*adj.* 蜿蜒的；彎彎曲曲的

sick〔sɪk〕*adj.* 噁心的；想吐的　　***up to*** 由…決定

take〔tek〕*v.* 花費　　extra〔'ɛkstrə〕*adj.* 額外的

That's fine. 沒關係。

couple〔'kʌpl̩〕*n.* 夫婦；一對男女

discuss〔dɪ'skʌs〕*v.* 討論　　trip〔trɪp〕*n.* 旅行

38. (**D**) W: It's good to be back. I barely remember the last time I saw you!

M: Yeah, it's been ages. It's good to see you, too. How long will you be in town?

W: I'll be here till Friday, but I have business to do tomorrow and on Wednesday.

M: How about Thursday?

W: I'm totally free. Let's do something.

(TONE)

Q: What can we tell from this conversation?

A. The woman is on vacation.

B. The woman will leave on Thursday.

C. The man and woman will visit on Wednesday.

D. The woman has not seen the man for a long time.

　* barely〔'bɛrlɪ〕*adv.* 幾乎不
　remember〔rɪ'mɛmbɚ〕*v.* 記得
　ages〔'edʒɪz〕*n. pl.* 長時間　　till〔tɪl〕*prep.* 直到
　totally〔'totl̩ɪ〕*adv.* 完全地　　free〔fri〕*adj.* 有空的
　tell〔tɛl〕*v.* 知道　　vacation〔ve'keʃən〕*n.* 假期
　on vacation 在休假中；在渡假
　visit〔'vɪzɪt〕*v.* 訪問；拜訪

39. (**C**) M: Do you think I can put this in the microwave?

W: What are you, crazy? That's a metal pot! You can't put metal in the microwave.

M: Yeah, but what if I leave the lid off?

W: I still don't think it's a good idea.

(TONE)

Q: What does the man want to know?

A. If he can use the microwave.

B. For how long he should put his food in the microwave.

C. If he can put a pot in the microwave.

D. Why he should not put his food in the microwave.

* microwave〔'maɪkrə,wev〕 n. 微波爐（= microwave oven）
crazy〔'krezɪ〕 adj. 瘋狂的
What are you, crazy? 你瘋了嗎？（= Are you crazy? ）
metal〔'mɛtl̩〕 adj. 金屬的　 n. 金屬
pot〔pɑt〕 n. 鍋子　 *What if…?* 如果…將會怎麼樣？
leave〔liv〕 v. 使維持（…的狀態）
lid〔lɪd〕 n. 蓋子　 off〔ɔf〕 adj. 拿掉的

40. (**C**) W: Honey, can you help me with this zipper? It's stuck.

M: Oh boy! It really is stuck. Maybe you should wear something else—I don't think it's going to budge.

(TONE)

Q: What is the woman doing?

A. Cooking some food.

B. Cleaning the bathroom.

C. Putting on clothing.

D. Talking on the telephone.

* honey〔'hʌnɪ〕 n. 親愛的　 zipper〔'zɪpɚ〕 n. 拉鍊
stuck〔stʌk〕 adj. 卡住的　 boy〔bɔɪ〕 interj. 哇；咦！
budge〔bʌdʒ〕 v. （稍微）移動
put on 穿上　 clothing〔'kloðɪŋ〕 n. 衣服

41. (**A**)　M：This is my favorite time of year—it's so nice to feel the heat of the sun again.

　　　W：Especially after two months straight of gray, rainy, cold weather.

　　　(TONE)

　　　Q：What season is it?

　　　A. Spring.　　　　　　　B. Hot.

　　　C. Sunny.　　　　　　　D. Winter.

　　　* favorite〔'fevərɪt〕adj. 最喜愛的　　heat〔hit〕n. 熱
　　　　especially〔ə'spɛʃəlɪ〕adv. 特別是
　　　　straight〔stret〕adj. 連續的　　gray〔gre〕adj. 陰沉沉的
　　　　rainy〔'renɪ〕adj. 下雨的　　weather〔'wɛðɚ〕n. 天氣
　　　　season〔'sizṇ〕n. 季節　　sunny〔'sʌnɪ〕adj. 晴朗的

42. (**B**)　M：Did you pay the electricity bill yet?

　　　W：It's not due till the tenth.

　　　M：But it's the eleventh today!

　　　(TONE)

　　　Q：What did the woman do?

　　　A. She paid the bill on the eleventh.

　　　B. She forgot to pay the bill on time.

　　　C. She only got the bill on the tenth.

　　　D. She forgot when the bill was due.

　　　* pay〔pe〕v. 支付　　electricity〔ɪ,lɛk'trɪsətɪ〕n. 電
　　　　bill〔bɪl〕n. 帳單　　yet〔jɛt〕adv. 已經
　　　　due〔dju〕adj. 到期的　　till〔tɪl〕prep. 直到
　　　　on time 準時

43. (**B**)　M：What happened to Mathew?

　　　W：Oh, we broke up last month.

　　　M：Really? I thought you two were joined at the hip.

　　　W：Actually, we didn't have that much in common. He was too serious for me.

(TONE)

Q：What did the man think about the woman and her ex-boyfriend?

A. He thought they were not suitable for each other.

B. He thought they were very close.

C. He thought they were angry at each other.

D. He thought they were going to break up.

* ***break up*** 分手　　join〔dʒɔɪn〕v. 結合；連接
hip〔hɪp〕n. 臀部　　***join at the hip*** 交情深厚
actually〔'æktʃʊəlɪ〕adv. 事實上
in common 共同的　　serious〔'sɪrɪəs〕adj. 嚴肅的
ex- 從前的；前⋯　　suitable〔'sutəbḷ〕adj. 適合的
close〔klos〕adj. 親密的　　angry〔'æŋgrɪ〕adj. 生氣的

44. (**C**)　M：Have you seen the new Tom Cruise movie?

　　　W：I'm not really a big fan of his.

　　　M：Me neither, but you should see it anyway.
　　　　　The special effects are awesome.

(TONE)

Q：Why did the man recommend the movie?

A. He really likes Tom Cruise.

B. He thought the woman really liked Tom Cruise.

C. He thought the special effects were impressive.

D. We cannot tell.

* fan〔fæn〕*n.* 迷　　neither〔'niðɚ〕*adv.* 也不…
anyway〔'ɛnɪ,we〕*adv.* 不管怎麼說；無論如何
special〔'spɛʃəl〕*adj.* 特殊的　　effect〔ə'fɛkt〕*n.* 效果
awesome〔'ɔsəm〕*adj.* 令人嘆爲觀止的；很棒的
recommend〔,rɛkə'mɛnd〕*v.* 推薦
impressive〔ɪm'prɛsɪv〕*adj.* 令人印象深刻的

45. (**C**)　W: You know, you really shouldn't eat that.

　　　M: Why not?

　　　W: Well, didn't you just tell me last week you were
　　　　　on a diet? I thought you wanted to lose weight.

　　　M: Oh, I'm off it already. I decided to work out more
　　　　　instead.

　　(TONE)

　　Q: How does the man plan to lose weight?

A. He is going to eat more vegetables.

B. He is going to go on a diet.

C. He will do more exercise.

D. He is going to work harder.

* diet〔'daɪət〕*n.* 飲食限制　　***be on a diet*** 節食
lose〔luz〕*v.* 減少　　weight〔wet〕*n.* 體重
off〔ɔf〕*prep.* 停止；斷絕　　***work out*** 運動
instead〔ɪn'stɛd〕*adv.* 作爲代替
vegetable〔'vɛdʒətəbl̩〕*n.* 蔬菜　　***go on a diet*** 節食

English Listening Comprehension Test
Test Book No. 4

This listening comprehension test will test your ability to understand spoken English. In this test, each conversation, statement and question will be spoken JUST ONE TIME. They will not be written out for you. There are three parts to this test. Special instructions will be given to you at the beginning of each part.

Part A

In Part A, you will see several pictures in your test book. For each picture, you will be asked 1 to 3 questions. For each question, you will hear four possible answers. Choose the best answer according to what you see in the picture.

Example:

You will see:

You will hear: What is this?
A. This is a table.
B. This is a chair.
C. This is a watch.
D. This is a doll.

The best answer to the question "What is this?" is B: "This is a chair." Therefore, you should choose answer B.

A. <u>Questions 1-2</u>

B. <u>Questions 3-4</u>

C. <u>Questions 5-6</u>

D. <u>Questions 7-8</u>

E. <u>Questions 9-10</u>

F. <u>Questions 11-12</u>

G. Questions 13-14

H. Question 15

Part B

In Part B, you will hear 15 questions. After you hear a question, read the four possible answers in your test book and decide which one is the best answer to the question you have heard.

Example:

<u>You will hear</u>: What does your father do?

<u>You will read</u>: A. He's 50 years old.
                    B. He's a teacher.
                    C. He's hungry.
                    D. He's in Los Angeles.

The best answer to the question "What does your father do?" is B: "He's a teacher." Therefore, you should choose answer B.

Please go to the next page. ⇨

16. A. Of course motorbikes are safe.
    B. Yes. I'll be able to buy one next month.
    C. No, I'll save my motorbike in case I need it again.
    D. Yes, it was a gift.

17. A. It's my new perfume.
    B. Thank you. They're new.
    C. My aunt made me this sweater.
    D. This is my new hat.

18. A. Yes, it's around the corner.
    B. Yes, there's one in a nearby town.
    C. No, he's not a grocer.
    D. No. It's next door.

19. A. Yes, I love the color of the leaves in fall.
    B. That's the leaf of a maple tree.
    C. Yes, it describes the park facilities.
    D. Yes. I'll clean them up later.

20. A. We will meet three times a week.
    B. Yes, it is a required class.
    C. Your grades will be based mostly on two exams.
    D. You will be divided into groups of three.

21. A. We got back at two
       o'clock.
    B. Which one hurts?
    C. Yes, they are.
    D. Why don't you take
       some aspirin?

22. A. Dishes such as liver and
       heart are very popular.
    B. It costs more to grow it
       without chemicals.
    C. These parts would just be
       thrown away otherwise.
    D. Junk food is always
       expensive.

23. A. It's very far from here.
    B. I'm going now. So long.
    C. There was quite a line.
    D. I always go to the bank
       on Mondays.

24. A. Yes, I saw it there a
       minute ago.
    B. The two pieces look
       the same size.
    C. No, I can see the
       whole thing.
    D. Yes. It was too big.

25. A. I get mostly A's
       and B's.
    B. No, I'm not a
       teacher.
    C. Yes, I go there.
    D. Science is my
       favorite subject.

26. A. I keep all the important papers at the bank.
    B. We keep an extra one under the front mat.
    C. Yes, I did keep it in the house.
    D. Indeed, the house is kept clean.

27. A. Those new TVs are the most expensive items in the store.
    B. I spend the most on my mortgage.
    C. I like golf the most.
    D. Mangos — we export several tons every year.

28. A. It was definitely worth the price.
    B. No, this is not the first stereo I've bought.
    C. I preferred the first one.
    D. It was inferior to this one.

29. A. Yes, I know who it is.
    B. I asked them whether they like to sing.
    C. I heard them singing.
    D. I took a poll.

30. A. I like repetitious music.
    B. C sharp is my favorite note.
    C. Repetition will help me play the music better.
    D. Sally is my piano teacher.

Part C

In Part C, you will hear 15 conversations between a man and a woman. After each conversation, you will hear a question about the conversation. After you hear the question, read the four possible answers in your test book and choose the best answer to the question you have heard.

Example:

<u>You will hear</u>: (Man)   How do you go to school every day?

                    (Woman)   Usually by bus. Sometimes by taxi.

                    (Tone)

                    Question: How does the woman go to school?

<u>You will read</u>: A. She always goes to school on foot.
                    B. She usually rides a bike.
                    C. She takes either a bus or a taxi.
                    D. She usually goes to school by bus, never by taxi.

The best answer to the question "How does the woman go to school?" is C: "She takes either a bus or a taxi." Therefore, you should choose answer C.

Please go to the next page. ⇨

31. A. The sun is hidden by clouds.
    B. The man wishes the weather were better.
    C. The man did not see the sun set.
    D. It is still dark outside.

32. A. In 12 hours.
    B. They will travel for the whole day tomorrow.
    C. At night.
    D. They will take a train over to Berlin.

33. A. The man wants the woman to call Mary instead.
    B. The man cannot remember Mary's phone number.
    C. The man can't call Mary because the phone is not working.
    D. The man can't call Mary because it is a long-distance call.

34. A. The beef is not as good today as it usually is.
    B. She may not have a chance to eat lobster again soon.
    C. Lobster is better for her health than beef.
    D. Because lobster is the special today, and it is much cheaper.

35. A. She sells affordable books.
    B. She runs an expensive bookstore.
    C. She delivers books to stores in poor neighborhoods.
    D. She lends books to people in different neighborhoods.

36. A. He needs to be more
        active after his heart
        attack.
    B. It will help him mend
        his broken heart.
    C. He lost his mind when
        Susan left him.
    D. He should find a new
        job because Susan fired
        him.

37. A. Her neighbors play
        music too loudly.
    B. Her neighbors' baby
        cries at night.
    C. In fact, it is her neighbors
        who cannot sleep.
    D. The neighbors' dog is
        very noisy.

38. A. It is not really beautiful.
    B. It is nearly two
        thousand years old.
    C. It is not as nice as it was
        before the dam was built.
    D. It is man-made.

39. A. It is very mature.
    B. It is twice as big as
        the woman's dog.
    C. It is now half of its
        adult size.
    D. It will reach the
        man's waist in two
        years.

40. A. Water is pouring out
        of it.
    B. It is full of mail.
    C. It is open.
    D. It is out of town.

41. A. She hasn't been able
        to do any of the
        reading.
    B. She hasn't finished
        reading chapter three.
    C. She hasn't finished
        chapter four yet.
    D. She hasn't yet read
        the course
        description.

42. A. She may be struck by
   a protester if she rides
   a bus.
   B. The vehicles are not
   reliable enough.
   C. The drivers are going
   to raise the fare
   tomorrow.
   D. The drivers will refuse
   to work tomorrow.

43. A. She does not know
   what happened in the
   meeting.
   B. She was ignored by
   the other people at the
   meeting.
   C. What happened in the
   meeting is a secret.
   D. She does not know
   anything because she
   is uneducated.

44. A. The boss gave Mary a
   birthday party.
   B. It is surprising that the
   boss paid.
   C. Everyone enjoyed the
   company party.
   D. The party was held at
   the home of Mary, the
   boss.

45. A. It is a very hilly road.
   B. It is probably the
   fastest way to
   Bakersville.
   C. It is the most scenic
   route.
   D. It goes only to
   Bakersville.

Listening Test 4 詳解

Part A

For questions number 1 and 2, please look at picture A.

1. (**C**) Question number 1: What happened to the boy?

   A. He missed the early bus.

   B. He was beaten up by a bully.

   C. He neglected to get enough sleep.

   D. He is dizzy from bumping into the sign.

   * happen〔'hæpən〕v. 發生　　miss〔mɪs〕v. 錯過
   beat up 痛打；毒打　　bully〔'bʊlɪ〕n. 惡霸；流氓
   neglect〔nɪ'glɛkt〕v. 忽視；不重視
   dizzy〔'dɪzɪ〕adj. 頭暈的　　***bump into*** 撞到
   sign〔saɪn〕n. 告示牌

2. (**D**) Question number 2: Look at picture A again. What is the cute girl doing?

   A. She's looking at a comic book.

   B. She's moving away from the boy.

   C. She's at the bus stop.

   D. She's reviewing her textbook.

   * cute〔kjut〕adj. 可愛的　　comic〔'kɑmɪk〕adj. 漫畫的
   move away 離開　　***bus stop*** 公車站
   review〔rɪ'vju〕v. 複習
   textbook〔'tɛkst,bʊk〕n. 教科書；課本

For questions number 3 and 4, please look at picture B.

3. (**C**)　Question number 3:　How is the boy behaving?

　　　A.　He's daydreaming.

　　　B.　He feels intelligent.

　　　C.　He has a proud attitude.

　　　D.　He has a new outfit.

　　　* behave〔 bɪˋhev〕v. 行為；舉止；表現得

　　　　daydream〔ˋde͵drim〕v. 作白日夢

　　　　intelligent〔 ɪnˋtɛlədʒənt〕adj. 聰明的

　　　　proud〔 praud〕adj. 驕傲的

　　　　attitude〔ˋætə͵tjud〕n. 態度

　　　　outfit〔ˋaut͵fɪt〕n. 服裝

4. (**D**)　Question number 4:　Look at picture B again.　What
　　　is the reaction of the girls?

　　　A.　She is scratching her head.

　　　B.　They just broke up with him.

　　　C.　She is disappointed in him.

　　　D.　They feel puzzled by him.

　　　* reaction〔 rɪˋækʃən〕n. 反應

　　　　scratch〔 skrætʃ〕v. 搔；抓

　　　　break up with 和～分手

　　　　disappointed〔͵dɪsəˋpɔɪntɪd〕adj. 失望的

　　　　puzzled〔ˋpʌzl̩d〕adj. 困惑的；迷惑的

For questions number 5 and 6, please look at picture C.

5. (**C**) Question number 5: Why is the boy crying?

    A. He misplaced the remote control.

    B. His mom pushed him down.

    C. He wants a robot toy.

    D. He tripped and hurt his hip.

    * misplace〔 mıs'ples 〕v. 將…放錯位置

    remote control 遙控器　　push〔 puʃ 〕v. 推

    robot〔'robɑt 〕n. 機器人　　toy〔 tɔɪ 〕n. 玩具

    trip〔 trɪp 〕v. 跌倒　　hurt〔 hɜt 〕v. 使受傷；弄痛

    hip〔 hɪp 〕n. 臀部；屁股

6. (**B**) Question number 6: Look at picture C again. How
would you describe the boy's behavior?

    A. His mom is spoiled.

    B. Rude and shameful.

    C. His mom took his toy away.

    D. He's mature and too loud.

    * describe〔 dɪ'skraɪb 〕v. 描述

    behavior〔 bɪ'hevjɚ 〕n. 行為

    spoiled〔 spɔɪld 〕adj. 被寵壞的

    rude〔 rud 〕adj. 無禮的

    shameful〔'ʃemfəl 〕adj. 可恥的　　*take away* 拿走

    mature〔 mə'tʃur 〕adj. 成熟的

    oud〔 laud 〕adj. 大聲的

For questions number 7 and 8, please look at picture D.

7. (**C**) Question number 7: How would you describe the boy's actions? What is he actually doing?

    A. He's unlucky.

    B. He's hopeful.

    C. He's pulling.

    D. He's anxious and excited.

    * actually〔'æktʃʊəlɪ〕*adv.* 事實上

      unlucky〔ʌn'lʌkɪ〕*adj.* 不幸的

      hopeful〔'hopfəl〕*adj.* 充滿希望的　　pull〔pʊl〕*v.* 拉

      anxious〔'æŋkʃəs〕*adj.* 焦慮的

      excited〔ɪk'saɪtɪd〕*adj.* 興奮的

8. (**A**) Question number 8: Look at picture D again. According to the picture, what is probably on his mind?

    A. I have a big catch.

    B. The boot is heavy.

    C. He is laboring hard.

    D. The fish are clever and tricky.

    * *according to* 根據　　probably〔'prɑbəblɪ〕*adv.* 可能

      on one's mind 為某人所關心

      catch〔kætʃ〕*n.* 漁獲量　　boot〔but〕*n.* 靴子

      heavy〔'hɛvɪ〕*adj.* 重的　　labor〔'lebɚ〕*v.* 努力；辛勞

      hard〔hɑrd〕*adv.* 拼命地；努力地

      clever〔'klɛvɚ〕*adj.* 聰明的　　tricky〔'trɪkɪ〕*adj.* 狡猾的

For questions number 9 and 10, please look at picture E.

9. (**B**) Question number 9: According to this picture, what is missing?

    A. They are praying.

    B. They are missing sleep.

    C. Their hair is missing.

    D. Only one is making any noise.

    * ***according to*** 根據   missing〔'mɪsɪŋ〕*adj.* 缺少的
    pray〔pre〕*v.* 祈禱；禱告   miss〔mɪs〕*v.* 缺少
    sleep〔slip〕*n.* 睡眠   hair〔hɛr〕*n.* 頭髮
    noise〔nɔɪz〕*n.* 噪音

10. (**B**) Question number 10: Look at picture E again. What are the monks supposed to be doing?

    A. Blessing poor people.

    B. Kneeling and saying prayers.

    C. Praying to remain awake.

    D. Dozing and being drowsy.

    * monk〔mʌŋk〕*n.* 僧侶；和尚
    be supposed to V. 應該   bless〔blɛs〕*v.* 祝福
    poor〔pʊr〕*adj.* 窮的   kneel〔nil〕*v.* 跪下
    prayer〔prɛr〕*n.* 祈禱文   remain〔rɪ'men〕*v.* 保持
    awake〔ə'wek〕*adj.* 醒著的   doze〔doz〕*v.* 打瞌睡
    drowsy〔'draʊzɪ〕*adj.* 想睡的

For questions number 11 and 12, please look at picture F.

11. (**A**) Question number 11: What exactly has happened, according to this picture?

    A. She wrapped on too many bandages.

    B. He exaggerated his injured hand.

    C. The boy cut his little finger.

    D. The nurse is enthusiastic.

    * exactly〔 ɪg'zæktlɪ 〕*adv.* 正確地；精確地

      happen〔'hæpən 〕*v.* 發生　　wrap〔 ræp 〕*v.* 包；裹

      bandage〔'bændɪdʒ 〕*n.* 繃帶

      exaggerate〔 ɪg'zædʒə,ret 〕*v.* 誇大

      injured〔'ɪndʒəd 〕*adj.* 受傷的　　cut〔 kʌt 〕*v.* 切；割

      finger〔'fɪŋgə 〕*n.* 手指　　***little finger*** 小指

      nurse〔 nɝs 〕*n.* 護士

      enthusiastic〔 ɪn,θjuzɪ'æstɪk 〕*adj.* 熱心的

12. (**D**) Question number 12: Please look at picture F again. What is the young man probably feeling?

    A. He feels she's smart.

    B. He feels approval.

    C. He feels that she's cruel.

    D. He is astonished and surprised.

    * probably〔'prabəblɪ 〕*adv.* 可能

      smart〔 smɑrt 〕*adj.* 聰明的

      approval〔 ə'pruvl̩ 〕*n.* 贊成　　cruel〔'kruəl 〕*adj.* 殘忍的

      astonished〔 ə'stɑnɪʃt 〕*adj.* 驚訝的

      surprised〔 sə'praɪzd 〕*adj.* 驚訝的

For questions number 13 and 14, please look at picture G.

13. (**D**) Question number 13: Why is this woman so overdressed?

    A. The forecast predicts rain.

    B. He has a skin disease.

    C. She's trying to scare him.

    D. She is protecting her skin.

    * overdress〔'ovə'drɛs〕 *v.* 過分打扮

       forecast〔'for,kæst〕 *n.* (天氣) 預報

       predict〔prɪ'dɪkt〕 *v.* 預測

       skin〔skɪn〕 *adj.* 皮膚的　　 *n.* 皮膚

       disease〔dɪ'ziz〕 *n.* 疾病　　scare〔skɛr〕 *v.* 驚嚇；使害怕

       protect〔prə'tɛkt〕 *v.* 保護

14. (**C**) Question number 14: Please look at picture G again. What is the woman wearing?

    A. She's wearing an umbrella.

    B. She has long wavy hair.

    C. She's got on a pair of sunglasses.

    D. She's staring at his ice cream.

    * wear〔wɛr〕 *v.* 穿；戴　　umbrella〔ʌm'brɛlə〕 *n.* 雨傘

       wavy〔'wevɪ〕 *adj.* 波浪形的　　***get on*** 戴上

       pair〔pɛr〕 *n.* 一副；一對

       sunglasses〔'sʌn,glæsɪz〕 *n. pl.* 太陽眼鏡

       stare〔stɛr〕 *v.* 盯著看；凝視 < *at* >　　***ice cream*** 冰淇淋

For question number 15, please look at picture H.

15. (**D**)　Question number 15:　What would a detective think happened here?

  A.　The fish is digesting the cat.

  B.　The fish swam away.

  C.　The cat has a whistle in his stomach.

  D.　The cat is guilty.

  * detective〔dɪˋtɛktɪv〕*n.* 偵探

   digest〔daɪˋdʒɛst〕*v.* 消化

   swim〔swɪm〕*v.* 游泳（三態變化為：swim-swam-swum）

   whistle〔ˋhwɪsl̩〕*n.* 哨子　　stomach〔ˋstʌmək〕*n.* 胃

   guilty〔ˋgɪltɪ〕*adj.* 有罪的

Part B

16. (**B**)　Are you saving to buy a motorbike?

  A.　Of course motorbikes are safe.

  B.　Yes.　I'll be able to buy one next month.

  C.　No, I'll save my motorbike in case I need it again.

  D.　Yes, it was a gift.

  * save〔sev〕*v.* 儲蓄；保存

   motorbike〔ˋmotɚˌbaɪk〕*n.* 機車（= *motorcycle*）

   of course 當然　　safe〔sef〕*adj.* 安全的

   be able to V. 能夠～　　***in case*** 以防萬一

   gift〔gɪft〕*n.* 禮物

17. (**A**) What is that lovely scent?

    A. It's my new perfume.

    B. Thank you. They're new.

    C. My aunt made me this sweater.

    D. This is my new hat.

    * lovely〔'lʌvlɪ〕*adj.* 令人愉快的；美好的
      scent〔sɛnt〕*n.* 氣味　　perfume〔'pɝfjum〕*n.* 香水
      aunt〔ænt〕*n.* 阿姨　　sweater〔'swɛtɚ〕*n.* 毛衣

18. (**A**) Is there a grocery store in this neighborhood?

    A. Yes, it's around the corner.

    B. Yes, there's one in a nearby town.

    C. No, he's not a grocer.　　D. No. It's next door.

    * ***grocery store*** 雜貨店
      neighborhood〔'nebɚ͵hud〕*n.* 鄰近地區；附近
      corner〔'kɔrnɚ〕*n.* 轉角　　***around the corner*** 在轉角處
      nearby〔'nɪr͵baɪ〕*adj.* 附近的　　town〔taun〕*n.* 城鎮
      grocer〔'grosɚ〕*n.* 食品雜貨商　　***next door*** 在隔壁的

19. (**C**) Did you see this leaflet from the park service?

    A. Yes, I love the color of the leaves in fall.

    B. That's the leaf of a maple tree.

    C. Yes, it describes the park facilities.

    D. Yes. I'll clean them up later.

    * leaflet〔'liflɪt〕*n.* 傳單　　service〔'sɝvɪs〕*n.*（政府）部門
      park service 公園管理處
      leaf〔lif〕*n.* 葉子（複數為 leaves〔livz〕）
      maple〔'mepl̩〕*n.* 楓樹　　facilities〔fə'sɪlətɪz〕*n. pl.* 設施

20. (**C**)　How will we be evaluated in this class?

　　　A.　We will meet three times a week.

　　　B.　Yes, it is a required class.

　　　C.　Your grades will be based mostly on two exams.

　　　D.　You will be divided into groups of three.

　　　* evaluate〔ɪ'væljʊ,et〕v. 評價　　meet〔mit〕v. 見面
　　　　time〔taɪm〕n. 次數　　required〔rɪ'kwaɪrd〕adj. 必修的
　　　　grade〔gred〕n. 分數；成績　　*be based on* 以…爲基礎
　　　　mostly〔'mostlɪ〕adv. 主要地；大多
　　　　divide〔də'vaɪd〕v. 劃分　　*be divided into* 被分成
　　　　group〔grup〕n. 組；群

21. (**D**)　My legs ache after that run.

　　　A.　We got back at two o'clock.

　　　B.　Which one hurts?

　　　C.　Yes, they are.

　　　D.　Why don't you take some aspirin?

　　　* leg〔lɛg〕n. 腿；腳　　ache〔ek〕v. 疼痛
　　　　run〔rʌn〕n. 跑　　*get back* 回來
　　　　hurt〔hɝt〕v. 受傷；疼痛　　take〔tek〕v. 吃（藥）
　　　　aspirin〔'æsprɪn〕n. 阿斯匹靈

22. (**B**)　Why is organic food more expensive?

　　　A.　Dishes such as liver and heart are very popular.

　　　B.　It costs more to grow it without chemicals.

　　　C.　These parts would just be thrown away otherwise.

　　　D.　Junk food is always expensive.

* organic〔ɔr'gænɪk〕adj. 有機的
  expensive〔ɪk'spɛnsɪv〕adj. 昂貴的　　dish〔dɪʃ〕n. 菜餚
  such as 像是　　liver〔'lɪvɚ〕n. 肝臟
  heart〔hɑrt〕n. 心　　popular〔'pɑpjəlɚ〕adj. 受歡迎的
  cost〔kɔst〕v. 花費　　grow〔gro〕v. 種植
  chemical〔'kɛmɪkḷ〕n. 化學藥品；農藥
  part〔pɑrt〕n. 部份　　**throw away** 丟掉
  otherwise〔'ʌðɚ,waɪz〕adv. 用別的方式；否則
  junk food 垃圾食品

23. (**C**) Why were you in the bank so long?

　　A. It's very far from here.
　　B. I'm going now. So long.
　　C. There was quite a line.
　　D. I always go to the bank on Mondays.

　　* far〔fɑr〕adj. 遠的　　**so long** 再見（= good-bye）
　　　quite a 相當大或多的　　line〔laɪn〕n. 行列
　　　There was quite a line. 排隊排很長。

24. (**D**) Did you saw this piece of wood in half?

　　A. Yes, I saw it there a minute ago.
　　B. The two pieces look the same size.
　　C. No, I can see the whole thing.
　　D. Yes. It was too big.

　　* saw〔sɔ〕v. 鋸；see 的過去式　　piece〔pis〕n. 片；塊
　　　wood〔wʊd〕n. 木頭　　**in half** 成兩半地
　　　ago〔ə'go〕adv. …以前　　same〔sem〕adj. 相同的
　　　size〔saɪz〕n. 大小；尺寸　　whole〔hol〕adj. 全部的

25. (**C**)　Do you study at the academy?

    A.　I get mostly A's and B's.

    B.　No, I'm not a teacher.

    C.　Yes, I go there.

    D.　Science is my favorite subject.

    * academy〔ə'kædəmɪ〕*n.* 學校；學院
　　　mostly〔'mostlɪ〕*adv.* 大多　　　science〔'saɪəns〕*n.* 科學
　　　favorite〔'fevərɪt〕*adj.* 最喜愛的
　　　subject〔'sʌbdʒɪkt〕*n.* 科目

26. (**A**)　Where do you keep the deed for the house?

    A.　I keep all the important papers at the bank.

    B.　We keep an extra one under the front mat.

    C.　Yes, I did keep it in the house.

    D.　Indeed, the house is kept clean.

    * keep〔kip〕*v.* 保存；保持　　　deed〔did〕*n.* 證書；契據
　　　paper〔'pepɚ〕*n.* 文件　　　extra〔'ɛkstrə〕*adj.* 額外的
　　　front〔frʌnt〕*adj.* 前面的　　　mat〔mæt〕*n.* 墊子
　　　indeed〔ɪn'did〕*adv.* 當然；事實上
　　　clean〔klin〕*adj.* 乾淨的

27. (**B**)　What is your biggest expense?

    A.　Those new TVs are the most expensive items in
　　　　the store.

    B.　I spend the most on my mortgage.

    C.　I like golf the most.

    D.　Mangos — we export several tons every year.

* expense〔ɪk'spɛns〕*n.* 花費

item〔'aɪtəm〕*n.* 項目；物品

mortgage〔'mɔrgɪdʒ〕*n.* 抵押貸款

golf〔gɔlf〕*n.* 高爾夫球　　mango〔'mæŋgo〕*n.* 芒果

export〔ɪks'pɔrt〕*v.* 輸出；出口

several〔'sɛvərəl〕*adj.* 幾個的　　ton〔tʌn〕*n.* 噸

28. (**D**) Why didn't you buy the first stereo?

A. It was definitely worth the price.

B. No, this is not the first stereo I've bought.

C. I preferred the first one.

D. It was inferior to this one.

* stereo〔'stɛrɪo〕*n.* 立體音響

definitely〔'dɛfənɪtlɪ〕*adv.* 一定

worth〔wɝθ〕*adj.* 值…的　　price〔praɪs〕*n.* 價格

prefer〔prɪ'fɝ〕*v.* 比較喜歡

inferior〔ɪn'fɪrɪə〕*adj.* 較差的　　***be inferior to*** 比…差

29. (**D**) How do you know who the students' favorite singer is?

A. Yes, I know who it is.

B. I asked them whether they like to sing.

C. I heard them singing.

D. I took a poll.

* favorite〔'fevərɪt〕*adj.* 最喜愛的　　singer〔'sɪŋə〕*n.* 歌手

whether〔'hwɛðə〕*conj.* 是否　　poll〔pol〕*n.* 投票

take a poll 進行投票

30. (**C**)　Why are you playing the same piece of music over and over again?

　　　A.　I like repetitious music.
　　　B.　C sharp is my favorite note.
　　　C.　Repetition will help me play the music better.
　　　D.　Sally is my piano teacher.

　　＊ piece〔pis〕*n.* 一首（曲子）
　　　 over and over again 一再地
　　　 repetitious〔͵rɛpɪˋtɪʃəs〕*adj.* 反覆性的
　　　 sharp〔ʃɑrp〕*n.* 升半音　　***C sharp*** 升 C 的曲調
　　　 note〔not〕*n.* 音；調子
　　　 repetition〔͵rɛpɪˋtɪʃən〕*n.* 重複；重做
　　　 play〔ple〕*v.* 演奏　　piano〔pɪˋæno〕*n.* 鋼琴

Part C

31. (**C**)　M: Where is the sun?
　　　W: It just sank below the horizon.
　　　M: Oh, I missed it.

　　　(TONE)

　　　Q : Which of the following is true?

　　　A.　The sun is hidden by clouds.
　　　B.　The man wishes the weather were better.
　　　C.　The man did not see the sun set.
　　　D.　It is still dark outside.

　　＊ sink〔sɪŋk〕*v.* 下沉；沉落（三態變化為：sink-sank-sunk）
　　　 horizon〔həˋraɪzn̩〕*n.* 地平線　　miss〔mɪs〕*v.* 錯過
　　　 hide〔haɪd〕*v.* 隱藏　　cloud〔klaʊd〕*n.* 雲
　　　 set〔sɛt〕*v.* 下沉　　dark〔dɑrk〕*adj.* 暗的

32. (**C**)　W：How long is the trip to Berlin?

　　　　　M：It takes 12 hours.

　　　　　W：That would waste a whole day.

　　　　　M：Not if we take an overnight train.

　　　　　(TONE)

　　　　　Q：When will they travel to Berlin?

　　　　　A. In 12 hours.

　　　　　B. They will travel for the whole day tomorrow.

　　　　　C. At night.

　　　　　D. They will take a train over to Berlin.

　　　* trip〔trɪp〕n. 行程；走一趟
　　　　Berlin〔bɝˈlɪn〕n. 柏林
　　　　take〔tek〕v. 花費　　waste〔west〕v. 浪費
　　　　whole〔hol〕adj. 整個的
　　　　overnight〔ˈovɚˈnaɪt〕adj. 過夜的；通宵的
　　　　travel to 前往
　　　　take…over 把…從一地運送到另一地

33. (**B**)　M：I should call Mary.

　　　　　W：Do you know her phone number?

　　　　　M：I can't recall it.

　　　　　(TONE)

　　　　　Q：Which of the following is true?

　　　　　A. The man wants the woman to call Mary instead.

　　　　　B. The man cannot remember Mary's phone number.

C. The man can't call Mary because the phone is not working.

D. The man can't call Mary because it is a long-distance call.

* call〔kɔl〕*v.* 打電話給　*n.* 打電話
recall〔rɪˈkɔl〕*v.* 想起
instead〔ɪnˈstɛd〕*adv.* 作為代替
work〔wɝk〕*v.*（機器等）運作；運轉
a long-distance call 長途電話

34. (**B**)　W：Would you recommend the roast beef?

M：Normally I would, but today we have something even better.

W：What's that?

M：Fresh lobster, and we don't usually have it, but roast beef is always on the menu.

W：I'll have the lobster then.

(TONE)

Q：Why didn't the woman order roast beef?

A. The beef is not as good today as it usually is.

B. She may not have a chance to eat lobster again soon.

C. Lobster is better for her health than beef.

D. Because lobster is the special today, and it is much cheaper.

* recommend〔͵rɛkə'mɛnd〕v. 推薦

roast〔rost〕adj. 烤過的　　　beef〔bif〕n. 牛肉

normally〔'nɔrml̩ɪ〕adv. 通常　　fresh〔frɛʃ〕adj. 新鮮的

lobster〔'lɑbstɚ〕n. 龍蝦　　　menu〔'mɛnju〕n. 菜單

have〔hæv〕v. 吃　　　then〔ðɛn〕adv. 那麼

order〔'ɔrdɚ〕v. 點 (菜)　　chance〔tʃæns〕n. 機會

soon〔sun〕adv. 很快地　　　health〔hɛlθ〕n. 健康

special〔'spɛʃəl〕n. (餐館菜單上的) 特色菜

cheap〔tʃip〕adj. 便宜的

35. (**D**)　M: Why do you have so many books in your van?

　　　W: This is a mobile library.

　　　M: Really?　Where do you go?

　　　W: I go to neighborhoods where families can't afford
　　　　　to buy their kids books.

　　(TONE)

　　　Q : What does the woman do in her job?

　　　A.　She sells affordable books.

　　　B.　She runs an expensive bookstore.

　　　C.　She delivers books to stores in poor neighborhoods.

　　　D.　She lends books to people in different
　　　　　neighborhoods.

* van〔væn〕n. 貨車　　mobile〔'mobl̩, 'mobil〕adj. 流動的

library〔'laɪ͵brɛrɪ〕n. 圖書館

afford〔ə'ford〕v. 負擔得起　　kid〔kɪd〕n. 小孩

affordable〔ə'fordəbl̩〕adj. 負擔得起的

run〔rʌn〕v. 經營　　expensive〔ɪk'spɛnsɪv〕adj. 昂貴的

bookstore〔'bʊk͵stor〕n. 書店　　deliver〔dɪ'lɪvɚ〕v. 遞送

poor〔pʊr〕adj. 貧窮的　　lend〔lɛnd〕v. 借 (出)

different〔'dɪfərənt〕adj. 不同的

36. (**B**) M: I've felt so bad since Susan broke up with me.

W: You should get involved in some new activities.

M: How will that help?

W: It will take your mind off it and help you get over your heartbreak.

(TONE)

Q : Why should the man do something new?

A. He needs to be more active after his heart attack.

B. It will help him mend his broken heart.

C. He lost his mind when Susan left him.

D. He should find a new job because Susan fired him.

* ***break up*** 分手　　involved〔ɪn'vɑlvd〕*adj.* 參與的
  get involved in 參與
  take *one's **mind off*** ⋯ 使人忘記⋯
  get over 自(打擊、創傷中)復原
  heartbreak〔'hɑrt,brek〕*n.* 悲傷；心碎
  active〔'æktɪv〕*adj.* 活躍的；積極的
  heart attack 心臟病發作　　mend〔mɛnd〕*v.* 修補
  broken〔'brokən〕*adj.* 破碎的　　***lose*** *one's **mind*** 發瘋
  fire〔faɪr〕*v.* 開除

37. (**B**) M: You look tired.

W: I haven't been getting much sleep.

M: Why not?

W: My neighbors' infant is keeping me awake.

(TONE)

Q : Why can't the woman sleep?

A. Her neighbors play music too loudly.

B. Her neighbors' baby cries at night.

C. In fact, it is her neighbors who cannot sleep.

D. The neighbors' dog is very noisy.

* neighbor〔'nebɚ〕 *n.* 鄰居　　infant〔'ɪnfənt〕 *n.* 嬰兒
  awake〔ə'wek〕 *adj.* 醒著的
  loudly〔'laʊdlɪ〕 *adv.* 大聲地
  noisy〔'nɔɪzɪ〕 *adj.* 吵雜的

38.（ **D** ）W：This lake is one of the nicest attractions in the area.

M：It's a beautiful, natural place.

W：Well, it's not exactly natural.　It didn't exist before
　the dam was built in 1970.

(TONE)

Q：What is true about the lake?

A. It is not really beautiful.

B. It is nearly two thousand years old.

C. It is not as nice as it was before the dam was built.

D. It is man-made.

* lake〔lek〕 *n.* 湖
  attraction〔ə'trækʃən〕 *n.* 具有吸引力的事物；觀光勝地
  area〔'ɛrɪə〕 *n.* 地區　　natural〔'nætʃərəl〕 *adj.* 自然的
  exactly〔ɪg'zæktlɪ〕 *adv.* 完全地；全然
  exist〔ɪg'zɪst〕 *v.* 存在　　dam〔dæm〕 *n.* 水壩
  nearly〔'nɪrlɪ〕 *adv.* 將近
  man-made〔'mæn,med〕 *adj.* 人造的；人工的

39. (**C**)　W：What a big dog!

M：And he's just a puppy.

W：How big will he be when he reaches maturity?

M：About twice this size.

(TONE)

Q：What is true about the man's dog?

A.　It is very mature.

B.　It is twice as big as the woman's dog.

C.　It is now half of its adult size.

D.　It will reach the man's waist in two years.

* puppy〔'pʌpɪ〕 *n.* 小狗　　reach〔ritʃ〕 *v.* 達到
maturity〔mə'tjurətɪ〕 *n.* 成熟
twice〔twaɪs〕 *adv.* 兩倍地　　size〔saɪz〕 *n.* 大小；尺寸
mature〔mə'tʃur〕 *adj.* 成熟的　　half〔hæf〕 *n.* 一半
adult〔ə'dʌlt〕 *adj.* 成年的　　waist〔west〕 *n.* 腰部

40. (**B**)　W：The Jacksons must be out of town.

M：Why do you say that?

W：Their mailbox is overflowing.

(TONE)

Q：What has happened to the Jacksons' mailbox?

A.　Water is pouring out of it.

B.　It is full of mail.

C.　It is open.　　　　　　D.　It is out of town.

* ***the Jacksons*** 傑克森一家人　　must〔mʌst〕 *aux.* 一定
out of town 出城　　mailbox〔'mel,bɑks〕 *n.* 信箱
overflow〔,ovə'flo〕 *v.* 滿出
pour〔por〕 *v.* (水等) 流出來　　***be full of*** 充滿

41. (**B**) M: Did you read chapter four?

W: Yes, but I still haven't finished the previous one.

M: Well, the course description did say there would be a lot of reading.

W: I don't know how I'll ever finish it all.

(TONE)

Q : What hasn't the woman read yet?

A. She hasn't been able to do any of the reading.

B. She hasn't finished reading chapter three.

C. She hasn't finished chapter four yet.

D. She hasn't yet read the course description.

* chapter〔'tʃæptɚ〕*n.*（書籍的）章；篇

finish〔'fınıʃ〕*v.* 完成

previous〔'privıəs〕*adj.* 之前的

course〔kors〕*n.* 課程

description〔dı'skrıpʃən〕*n.* 說明

ever〔'ɛvɚ〕*adv.* 究竟；到底

yet〔jɛt〕*adv.* 尚（未）

42. (**D**) M: Do you rely on the bus to get to work?

W: Yes, I take it every day.

M: You had better find another way tomorrow.

W: Why?

M: The drivers are going on strike.

(TONE)

Q：Why can't the woman take the bus tomorrow?

A. She may be struck by a protester if she rides a bus.

B. The vehicles are not reliable enough.

C. The drivers are going to raise the fare tomorrow.

D. The drivers will refuse to work tomorrow.

* ***rely on*** 依賴　　take〔tek〕*v.* 搭乘

had better V. 最好…　　way〔we〕*n.* 方式

strike〔straɪk〕*n.* 罷工　*v.* 打；毆打（過去式及過去分

詞為 struck）　***go on strike*** 進行罷工

protester〔prəˈtɛstɚ〕*n.* 抗議者

ride〔raɪd〕*v.* 搭乘

vehicle〔ˈviɪkl̩〕*n.* 車輛；交通工具

reliable〔rɪˈlaɪəbl̩〕*adj.* 可靠的

raise〔rez〕*v.* 提高　　fare〔fɛr〕*n.* 車費

refuse〔rɪˈfjuz〕*v.* 拒絕

43. (**A**) M：Can you tell me what happened in the meeting?

W：Sorry.　I can't.

M：Is it a secret?

W：No, but I wasn't there so I'm ignorant of the facts.

(TONE)

Q：What does the woman mean?

A. She does not know what happened in the meeting.

B. She was ignored by the other people at the meeting.

C. What happened in the meeting is a secret.

D. She does not know anything because she is uneducated.

* meeting〔'mitɪŋ〕*n.* 會議　　secret〔'sikrɪt〕*n.* 秘密

ignorant〔'ɪgnərənt〕*adj.* 不知道的

be ignorant of 不知道　　fact〔fækt〕*n.* 事實

ignore〔ɪg'nor〕*v.* 忽視

uneducated〔ʌn'ɛdʒə,ketɪd〕*adj.* 未受教育的

44. (**C**)　W: How was the party last night?

M: Great. Everyone was in a merry mood.

W: That's no surprise when the boss pays for the party.

(TONE)

Q: Which of the following is true?

A. The boss gave Mary a birthday party.

B. It is surprising that the boss paid.

C. Everyone enjoyed the company party.

D. The party was held at the home of Mary, the boss.

* great〔gret〕*adj.* 很棒的　　merry〔'mɛrɪ〕*adj.* 快樂的

mood〔mud〕*n.* 心情　　surprise〔sə'praɪz〕*n.* 驚訝

boss〔bɔs〕*n.* 老闆　　***pay for*** 付～的錢

surprising〔sə'praɪzɪŋ〕*adj.* 令人驚訝的

enjoy〔ɪn'dʒɔɪ〕*v.* 喜歡　　company〔'kʌmpənɪ〕*n.* 公司

hold〔hold〕*v.* 舉辦

45. (**B**)　M: What's the best way to get to Bakersville?

W: There are multiple routes, but I think the best one is highway 5.

M: Why is that?

W: It's not mountainous like the others, so it's more direct.

(TONE)

Q: What is true about highway 5?

A. It is a very hilly road.

B. It is probably the fastest way to Bakersville.

C. It is the most scenic route.

D. It goes only to Bakersville.

* ***get to*** 到達　　multiple〔'mʌltəpļ〕*adj.* 許多的
route〔rut〕*n.* 路線　　highway〔'haɪ,we〕*n.* 公路
mountainous〔'mauntn̩əs〕*adj.* 多山的
direct〔də'rɛkt〕*adj.* 筆直的；最近的
hilly〔'hɪlɪ〕*adj.* 陡峭的；多山丘的
probably〔'prɑbəblɪ〕*adv.* 可能
scenic〔'sinɪk〕*adj.* 風景優美的
go to 延伸到；通往

English Listening Comprehension Test
Test Book No. 5

This listening comprehension test will test your ability to understand spoken English. In this test, each conversation, statement and question will be spoken JUST ONE TIME. They will not be written out for you. There are three parts to this test. Special instructions will be given to you at the beginning of each part.

Part A

In Part A, you will see several pictures in your test book. For each picture, you will be asked 1 to 3 questions. For each question, you will hear four possible answers. Choose the best answer according to what you see in the picture.

Example:

<u>You will see</u>:

<u>You will hear</u>: What is this?

  A. This is a table.
  B. This is a chair.
  C. This is a watch.
  D. This is a doll.

The best answer to the question "What is this?" is B: "This is a chair." Therefore, you should choose answer B.

A. <u>Questions 1-2</u>

B. <u>Questions 3-4</u>

C. <u>Questions 5-6</u>

D. Questions 7-8

E. Questions 9-10

F. Questions 11-12

G. Questions 13-14

H. Question 15

Part B

In Part B, you will hear 15 questions. After you hear a question, read the four possible answers in your test book and decide which one is the best answer to the question you have heard.

Example:

<u>You will hear</u>: What does your father do?

<u>You will read</u>: A. He's 50 years old.
B. He's a teacher.
C. He's hungry.
D. He's in Los Angeles.

The best answer to the question "What does your father do?" is B: "He's a teacher." Therefore, you should choose answer B.

Please go to the next page. ⇨

16. A. She's feeling better.
    B. No, I don't.
    C. She's an acquaintance
       of mine.
    D. I acquired her 10
       years ago.

17. A. Yes, I always have a
       big supper.
    B. No, I always have a
       light lunch.
    C. No. It's not good to
       eat a lot late at night.
    D. No. I prefer to eat at
       noon.

18. A. There are two pillows
       on your bed already.
    B. You should take them
       now.
    C. The usual dosage is
       two.
    D. Yes, help yourself.

19. A. The second one
       produces a better sound.
    B. The first one is more
       qualified.
    C. This one is much more
       expensive.
    D. They're exactly the
       same color.

20. A. I think it's two hours
       long.
    B. Why don't we see Star
       Wars?
    C. No, I didn't think so.
    D. I thought it was quite
       entertaining.

21. A. Yes, but I took some
       medicine for it.
    B. No, it's not broken.
    C. It hurt a little at the
       time.
    D. Yes, he was badly hurt.

22. A. No. I don't like to stay
      up late.
    B. Yes. In fact, we had
      some guests last night.
    C. Only after watching a
      scary movie.
    D. It's upstairs in the
      bedroom.

24. A. It is. I wish the
      humidity would
      drop.
    B. Yes, the sky is
      really black.
    C. I'm bored, too.
    D. Really? I don't
      feel hot at all.

23. A. We are a big producer
      of steel.
    B. Yes, industry is quite
      important.
    C. Most industry is found
      in the south of the
      country.
    D. About 60% of the
      population is
      employed by factories.

25. A. No, thank you.
    B. Yes, it's perfect.
    C. Yes, it needs a bit
      more salt.
    D. No, it's not too
      salty.

26. A. Yes, I informed everyone.
    B. Yes. Just wear jeans.
    C. No. I don't know anyone here.
    D. No, it's tomorrow.

27. A. It's 10 meters square.
    B. It's the living room.
    C. There are seven people in there.
    D. Yes, it's a really large room.

28. A. No. It's 35 degrees.
    B. No, I don't like it.
    C. Yes, I think it is.
    D. Yes. It's so refreshing.

29. A. I think she's capable of doing the job.
    B. Don't worry. She'll recommend you for the job.
    C. Yes, I think she would like to have your job.
    D. She approves of how you are doing the job.

30. A. There is a lot of information in this brochure.
    B. Here is my driver's license.
    C. You can find what you want in the index.
    D. Do you have a passport?

Part C

In Part C, you will hear 15 conversations between a man and a woman. After each conversation, you will hear a question about the conversation. After you hear the question, read the four possible answers in your test book and choose the best answer to the question you have heard.

Example:

<u>You will hear</u>: (Man)   How do you go to school every day?

(Woman) Usually by bus. Sometimes by taxi.

(Tone)

Question: How does the woman go to school?

<u>You will read</u>: A. She always goes to school on foot.

B. She usually rides a bike.

C. She takes either a bus or a taxi.

D. She usually goes to school by bus, never by taxi.

The best answer to the question "How does the woman go to school?" is C: "She takes either a bus or a taxi." Therefore, you should choose answer C.

Please go to the next page. ⇨

31. A. Prices are rising.
    B. His salary is high.
    C. He cannot accept the new car models.
    D. Today's cars are too large.

32. A. They have lost their key.
    B. The door is easy to open without a key.
    C. The door shakes when it is opened.
    D. The door might not open.

33. A. It is a recent addition.
    B. It is not movable.
    C. The woman built it herself.
    D. It belongs to the building's owner.

34. A. It will be three times as much.
    B. It varies with the price of the ticket.
    C. It will be cheaper to post it.
    D. It depends on how it is sent.

35. A. Gayle is not able to type such a long report.
    B. The report is not ready to be typed yet.
    C. Gayle would type the report willingly.
    D. Gayle will be reluctant to type the report.

36. A. She understands
       Helen's reason.
    B. She doesn't know
       why Helen won't
       come.
    C. She often cannot
       understand Helen's
       speech.
    D. Helen misunderstood
       her description of the
       outing.

37. A. They let a suspect go
       free for lack of
       evidence.
    B. They arrested the
       robber, but he
       escaped.
    C. They let the robber
       go after he returned
       what he stole.
    D. They kept the robber
       in jail until they
       could prove their
       case.

38. A. He was the fifth runner
       to cross the line.
    B. He won five
       competitions.
    C. He finished his fifth
       management project.
    D. He was the greatest
       competitor.

39. A. Yes, because he has too
       many bags.
    B. No, because he does not
       have two bags.
    C. Yes, because his luggage
       is not heavy enough.
    D. No, because his luggage
       is not too heavy.

40. A. Because she
       misunderstood him.
    B. Sixty dollars.
    C. She expected the man
       to ask for too much.
    D. Thirty-two dollars.

41. A. The train will not stop
       in Chicago.
    B. The train will stop every
       hour.
    C. She doesn't know her
       location.
    D. She doesn't know how
       long the trip will take.

42. A. The story in the movie
       was not believable.
    B. He really disliked the
       whole movie.
    C. He liked the story most
       of all.
    D. He liked the movie more
       than the woman did.

43. A. She must replace the
       roof.
    B. She must replace
       everything but the roof.
    C. She must build a new
       house.
    D. She must make the
       house stronger before
       the next typhoon.

44. A. They need to listen to
       some more concerts
       first.
    B. They need to practice
       before the concert.
    C. They need more time
       to get ready for the
       concert.
    D. They must be ready
       for even more
       concerts in the
       future.

45. A. His party consists of
       two people.
    B. There are at least
       four people with him.
    C. Everyone in his group
       may go except him.
    D. Two people in his
       group do not want to
       go.

Listening Test 5 詳解

Part A

For questions number 1 and 2, please look at picture A.

1. (**C**) Question number 1: What is happening in the aquarium?

   A. The cat is getting revenge on the fish.
   B. The fish are drinking water.
   C. The cat is enduring an attack.
   D. Five fish are thirsty.

   * aquarium〔ə'kwɛrɪəm〕 *n.* 水族館
   revenge〔rɪ'vɛndʒ〕 *n.* 報仇;報復
   get revenge on 向…報復
   endure〔ɪn'djʊr〕 *v.* 忍耐;忍受　　attack〔ə'tæk〕 *n.* 攻擊
   thirsty〔'θɝstɪ〕 *adj.* 口渴的

2. (**A**) Question number 2: Describe the aquarium picture. Which is NOT true?

   A. The tank is half full of water.
   B. The cat is jumping on one leg.
   C. Some fish have sharp teeth.
   D. Six fish inhabit it.

   * describe〔dɪ'skraɪb〕 *v.* 描述　　tank〔tæŋk〕 *n.* 水槽
   half〔hæf〕 *adv.* 一半地　　***be full of*** 充滿
   jump on one leg 用單腳跳　　sharp〔ʃɑrp〕 *adj.* 尖銳的
   teeth〔tiθ〕 *n. pl.* 牙齒 (單數為 tooth〔tuθ〕)
   inhabit〔ɪn'hæbɪt〕 *v.* 居住於

For questions number 3 and 4, please look at picture B.

3. (**A**) Question number 3: What is happening in this picture?

    A. One girl is refusing a piece of cake.

    B. One girl is sharing an apple.

    C. Both girls are offering food.

    D. Both are showing generosity.

    * refuse〔rɪˈfjuz〕v. 拒絕　　piece〔pis〕n. 片；塊
      share〔ʃɛr〕v. 分享；共享　　offer〔ˈɔfɚ〕v. 提供
      show〔ʃo〕v. 表現出　　generosity〔ˌdʒɛnəˈrɑsətɪ〕n. 慷慨

4. (**D**) Question number 4: Look at picture B again. Which statement about this picture is true?

    A. One girl is waving good-bye.

    B. Only one girl is wearing a skirt.

    C. Both girls are eating.　　D. One girl is very thin.

    * ***wave good-bye*** 揮手告別　　wear〔wɛr〕v. 穿；戴

For questions number 5 and 6, please look at picture C.

5. (**C**) Question number 5: What is the cat doing?

    A. Trying to chase a mouse.

    B. The cat is exhausted.

    C. Playing with a ball of string.

    D. Dancing in an energetic way.

    * chase〔tʃes〕v. 追捕
      exhausted〔ɪgˈzɔstɪd〕adj. 筋疲力竭的
      ball〔bɔl〕n. 球狀物　　string〔strɪŋ〕n. 繩子；線
      energetic〔ˌɛnɚˈdʒɛtɪk〕adj. 充滿活力的

6. (**B**) Question number 6: Where is the mouse located in this picture?

    A. Crawling on the floor.   B. In the corner, in a hole.

    C. On the horizon.

    D. Laughing on top of the cat.

    * ***be located in*** 位於⋯   crawl〔krɔl〕*v.* 爬行

    floor〔flor〕*n.* 地板   corner〔'kɔrnɚ〕*n.* 角落

    hole〔hol〕*n.* 洞   horizon〔hə'raɪzn̩〕*n.* 地平線

    on the horizon 在地平線上   ***on top of*** 在⋯的上面

For questions number 7 and 8, please look at picture D.

7. (**D**) Question number 7: What does the desperate boy need most?

    A. A piece of cake.   B. A swimming pool.

    C. A book.   D. A nice drink of water.

    * desperate〔'dɛspərɪt〕*adj.* 不顧一切的;飢渴的;渴望的

    swimming pool 游泳池   drink〔drɪŋk〕*n.* 一杯;一口

8. (**D**) Question number 8: Which of the following statements is NOT TRUE?

    A. He is suffering.   B. He is thirsty.

    C. He's very uncomfortable.

    D. He's icy.

    * suffer〔'sʌfɚ〕*v.* 受苦   thirsty〔'θɝstɪ〕*adj.* 口渴的

    uncomfortable〔ʌn'kʌmfɚtəbl̩〕*adj.* 不舒服的

    icy〔'aɪsɪ〕*adj.* 冷漠的

For questions number 9 and 10, please look at picture E.

9. (**C**) Question number 9: What might the boy be saying to the girl?

    A. Are you going outside?

    B. You flatter the floor!

    C. What happened to you?

    D. What is tomorrow's forecast?

    * flatter〔'flætɚ〕v. 奉承；諂媚   floor〔flor〕n. 地板
     forecast〔'for‚kæst〕n.（天氣）預報

10. (**B**) Question number 10: How is the girl probably feeling?

    A. Messy and overweight.

    B. Miserable and upset.

    C. Sleepy and misunderstood.

    D. Raining cats and dogs.

    * probably〔'prɑbəblɪ〕adv. 可能
     messy〔'mɛsɪ〕adj. 雜亂的
     overweight〔'ovɚ'wet〕adj. 超重的；太胖的
     miserable〔'mɪzərəbḷ〕adj. 悲慘的
     upset〔ʌp'sɛt〕adj. 不高興的
     sleepy〔'spipɪ〕adj. 想睡的
     misunderstood〔‚mɪsʌndɚ'stud〕adj. 被誤解的
     rain cats and dogs 下傾盆大雨

For questions number 11 and 12, please look at picture F.

11. (**A**) Question number 11: What is most likely true about this picture?

    A. The man is imagining something not true.

    B. The man is looking for his lost wife.

    C. A sea gull thinks he's sexy.

    D. The seaside weather is foggy.

    * imagine〔ɪˈmædʒɪn〕v. 想像　　***look for*** 尋找
    lost〔lɔst〕adj. 失蹤的　　　gull〔gʌl〕n.（海）鷗
    sea gull 海鷗　　sexy〔ˈsɛksɪ〕adj. 性感的
    seaside〔ˈsiˌsaɪd〕adj. 海邊的　　weather〔ˈwɛðɚ〕n. 天氣
    foggy〔ˈfɑgɪ〕adj. 有濃霧的

12. (**A**) Question number 12: According to the picture, what do you think is the reality of the situation?

    A. It's a seal sitting on a rock.

    B. It's a girl sunbathing on a rock.

    C. The man wants to go surfing.

    D. A magic fish is confusing him.

    * reality〔rɪˈælətɪ〕n. 事實
    situation〔ˌsɪtʃʊˈeʃən〕n. 情況
    seal〔sil〕n. 海豹；海獅；海狗　　rock〔rɑk〕n. 岩石
    sunbathe〔ˈsʌnˌbeð〕v. 做日光浴　　surf〔sɝf〕v. 衝浪
    magic〔ˈmædʒɪk〕adj. 神奇的；魔法的
    confuse〔kənˈfjuz〕v. 使困惑

For questions number 13 and 14, please look at picture G.

13. (**C**) Question number 13: What can we conclude about the picture?

    A. Their skirts are skating.

    B. Their sleeves are flying.

    C. The wind is really blowing hard.

    D. Two girls feel slippery.

* conclude〔kən'klud〕*v.* 推斷 skirt〔skɝt〕*n.* 裙子

    skate〔sket〕*v.* 溜冰 sleeve〔sliv〕*n.* 袖子

    fly〔flaɪ〕*v.* 隨風飄揚 wind〔wɪnd〕*n.* 風

    blow〔blo〕*v.* (風)吹；刮 hard〔hɑrd〕*adv.* 猛烈地

    slippery〔'slɪpərɪ〕*adj.* 滑的

14. (**B**) Question number 14: What can you actually see happening in this picture?

    A. A hurricane is whistling.

    B. Things are being blown around.

    C. A thunderstorm has struck.

    D. The wind is terrifying the boy.

* actually〔'æktʃʊəlɪ〕*adv.* 實際上

    happen〔'hæpən〕*v.* 發生

    hurricane〔'hɝɪˌken〕*n.* 颶風；暴風雨

    whistle〔'hwɪsl̩〕*v.* (風)颼颼作響

    around〔ə'raʊnd〕*adv.* 到處

    thunderstorm〔'θʌndɚˌstɔrm〕*n.* 雷雨

    strike〔straɪk〕*v.* (雷電、暴風雨等)襲擊(過去式及過去分詞爲 struck) terrify〔'tɛrəˌfaɪ〕*v.* 使恐懼

For question number 15, please look at picture H.

15. (**B**) Question number 15: What is this picture depicting?

A. A girl causing mischief.

B. A student pulling another's hair.

C. A pupil admitting guilt.

D. A boy showing boastful behavior.

* depict〔dɪ'pɪkt〕v. 描繪

cause〔kɔz〕v. 造成   mischief〔'mɪstʃɪf〕n. 損害;危害

pull〔pul〕v. 拉   pupil〔'pjupḷ〕n. 學生

admit〔əd'mɪt〕v. 承認   guilt〔gɪlt〕n. 有罪;犯罪

show〔ʃo〕v. 表現   boastful〔'bostfəl〕adj. 自誇的

behavior〔bɪ'hevjɚ〕n. 行為

Part B

16. (**C**) How well do you know Isabel?

A. She's feeling better.   B. No, I don't.

C. She's an acquaintance of mine.

D. I acquired her 10 years ago.

* acquaintance〔ə'kwentəns〕n. 認識的人;熟人

acquire〔ə'kwaɪr〕v. 獲得   ago〔ə'go〕adv. …以前

17. (**B**) Do you usually have a big meal at midday?

A. Yes, I always have a big supper.

B. No, I always have a light lunch.

C. No. It's not good to eat a lot late at night.

D. No. I prefer to eat at noon.

     * have〔hæv〕v. 吃　　meal〔mil〕n. 餐
     midday〔'mɪd,de〕n. 中午　　supper〔'sʌpɚ〕n. 晚餐
     light〔laɪt〕adj. 清淡的；不油膩的　　late〔let〕adv. 晚
     prefer〔prɪ'fɝ〕v. 比較喜歡

18.（**C**）How many pills should I take?

    A. There are two pillows on your bed already.

    B. You should take them now.

    C. The usual dosage is two.

    D. Yes, help yourself.

    * pill〔pɪl〕n. 藥丸　　take〔tek〕v. 吃（藥）
    pillow〔'pɪlo〕n. 枕頭　　usual〔'juʒʊəl〕adj. 平常的
    dosage〔'dosɪdʒ〕n. 劑量　　***help** oneself* (**to**) 自行取用

19.（**A**）How does the quality of these two stereos compare?

    A. The second one produces a better sound.

    B. The first one is more qualified.

    C. This one is much more expensive.

    D. They're exactly the same color.

    * quality〔'kwɑlətɪ〕n. 品質　　stereo〔'stɛrɪo〕n. 立體音響
    compare〔kəm'pɛr〕v. 比較
    produce〔prə'djus〕v. 製造；產生
    sound〔saʊnd〕n. 聲音
    qualified〔'kwɑlə,faɪd〕adj. 適合的；合格的
    exactly〔ɪg'zæktlɪ〕adv. 完全地
    same〔sem〕adj. 相同的

20. (**D**) What did you think of the movie?

    A. I think it's two hours long.

    B. Why don't we see Star Wars?

    C. No, I didn't think so.

    D. I thought it was quite entertaining.

    * war〔wɔr〕*n.* 戰爭　　quite〔kwaɪt〕*adv.* 非常

      entertaining〔͵ɛntɚˈtenɪŋ〕*adj.* 令人愉快的；有趣的

21. (**C**) Was the injection painful?

    A. Yes, but I took some medicine for it.

    B. No, it's not broken.

    C. It hurt a little at the time.

    D. Yes, he was badly hurt.

    * injection〔ɪnˈdʒɛkʃən〕*n.* 注射；打針

      painful〔ˈpenfəl〕*adj.* 疼痛的　　medicine〔ˈmɛdəsn̩〕*n.* 藥

      broken〔ˈbrokən〕*adj.* 損壞的；破裂的

      hurt〔hɝt〕*v.* 弄痛；使受傷　　badly〔ˈbædlɪ〕*adv.* 嚴重地

22. (**C**) Do you ever have nightmares?

    A. No. I don't like to stay up late.

    B. Yes. In fact, we had some guests last night.

    C. Only after watching a scary movie.

    D. It's upstairs in the bedroom.

    * nightmare〔ˈnaɪt͵mɛr〕*n.* 惡夢　　***stay up*** 熬夜

      in fact 事實上　　guest〔gɛst〕*n.* 客人

      scary〔ˈskɛrɪ〕*adj.* 恐怖的

      upstairs〔ˈʌpˈstɛrz〕*adv.* 在樓上

23. (**A**) What is the major industry of your country?

　　　A. We are a big producer of steel.

　　　B. Yes, industry is quite important.

　　　C. Most industry is found in the south of the country.

　　　D. About 60% of the population is employed by factories.

　　　* major〔ˋmedʒɚ〕 adj. 主要的
　　　　industry〔ˋɪndəstrɪ〕 n. 產業；工業
　　　　producer〔prəˋdjusɚ〕 n. 生產者；製造者
　　　　steel〔stil〕 n. 鋼鐵　　quite〔kwaɪt〕 adv. 非常
　　　　south〔sauθ〕 n. 南方　　population〔͵papjəˋleʃən〕 n. 人口
　　　　employ〔ɪmˋplɔɪ〕 v. 雇用　　factory〔ˋfæktrɪ〕 n. 工廠

24. (**A**) It's so damp today.

　　　A. It is. I wish the humidity would drop.

　　　B. Yes, the sky is really black.

　　　C. I'm bored, too.

　　　D. Really? I don't feel hot at all.

　　　* damp〔dæmp〕 adj. 潮濕的
　　　　humidity〔hjuˋmɪdətɪ〕 n. 濕氣；溼度
　　　　drop〔drap〕 v. 下降　　 ***not…at all*** 一點也不

25. (**B**) Is the soup salty enough?

　　　A. No, thank you.　　　B. Yes, it's perfect.

　　　C. Yes, it needs a bit more salt.

　　　D. No, it's not too salty.

　　　* soup〔sup〕 n. 湯　　salty〔ˋsɔltɪ〕 adj. 鹹的
　　　　a bit 稍微　　salt〔sɔlt〕 n. 鹽

26. (**B**) Is the party informal?

A. Yes, I informed everyone.

B. Yes. Just wear jeans.

C. No. I don't know anyone here.

D. No, it's tomorrow.

* informal〔ɪnˋfɔrml̩〕*adj.* 非正式的

inform〔ɪnˋfɔrm〕*v.* 通知　　jeans〔dʒinz〕*n. pl.* 牛仔褲

27. (**A**) What is the actual size of the room?

A. It's 10 meters square.

B. It's the living room.

C. There are seven people in there.

D. Yes, it's a really large room.

* actual〔ˋæktʃʊəl〕*adj.* 實際的　　size〔saɪz〕*n.* 尺寸；大小

meter〔ˋmitɚ〕*n.* 公尺

square〔skwɛr〕*adj.* 平方的；見方的；等邊的

10 meters square 十公尺見方【即每邊十公尺】

28. (**D**) Do you feel that breeze?

A. No. It's 35 degrees.

B. No, I don't like it.

C. Yes, I think it is.

D. Yes. It's so refreshing.

* breeze〔briz〕*n.* 微風　　degree〔dɪˋgri〕*n.* 度

refreshing〔rɪˋfrɛʃɪŋ〕*adj.* 提神的；涼爽的

29. (**C**)　Do you think Marsha is envious of my job?

    A.　I think she's capable of doing the job.

    B.　Don't worry.　She'll recommend you for the job.

    C.　Yes, I think she would like to have your job.

    D.　She approves of how you are doing the job.

    * envious〔'ɛnvɪəs〕*adj.* 嫉妒的；羨慕的 < *of* >

    capable〔'kepəbḷ〕*adj.* 能夠的

    recommend〔,rɛkə'mɛnd〕*v.* 推薦

    approve〔ə'pruv〕*v.* 贊成；同意

30. (**B**)　Please show me some identification.

    A.　There is a lot of information in this brochure.

    B.　Here is my driver's license.

    C.　You can find what you want in the index.

    D.　Do you have a passport?

    * show〔ʃo〕*v.* 出示；給～看

    identification〔aɪ,dɛntəfə'keʃən〕*n.* 身分證件

    information〔,ɪnfə'meʃən〕*n.* 資訊

    brochure〔bro'ʃʊr〕*n.* 小冊子　　license〔'laɪsn̩s〕*n.* 執照

    driver's license 駕照　　index〔'ɪndɛks〕*n.* 索引

    passport〔'pæs,pɔrt〕*n.* 護照

Part C

31. (**A**)　M: I wish I could buy a new car.

    W: Why don't you?

    M: With this high inflation, I just can't afford it.

(TONE)

Q：Why can't the man buy a new car?

A. Prices are rising.

B. His salary is high.

C. He cannot accept the new car models.

D. Today's cars are too large.

＊ wish〔wɪʃ〕v. 希望　　inflation〔ɪnˈfleʃən〕n. 通貨膨脹

afford〔əˈfɔrd〕v. 負擔得起；買得起

price〔praɪs〕n. 價格　　rise〔raɪz〕v.（物價等）上漲

salary〔ˈsælərɪ〕n. 薪水　　accept〔əkˈsɛpt〕v. 接受

model〔ˈmɑdḷ〕n. 型；款式

today〔təˈde〕n. 現在；現代

32.（ **B** ）M：How did you get in without a key?

W：I just gave the door a mighty shake.

M：Really! I guess we'll have to get a stronger door.

(TONE)

Q：Why should they get a new door?

A. They have lost their key.

B. The door is easy to open without a key.

C. The door shakes when it is opened.

D. The door might not open.

＊ mighty〔ˈmaɪtɪ〕adj. 強有力的　　shake〔ʃek〕n. 搖動

guess〔gɛs〕v. 猜測　　get〔gɛt〕v. 買

lose〔luz〕v. 遺失

33. (**B**) M: Let's move that bookcase to the other wall.

W: We can't do that.

M: Why not?

W: It's built-in.

(TONE)

Q: What is true about the bookcase?

A. It is a recent addition.

B. It is not movable.

C. The woman built it herself.

D. It belongs to the building's owner.

* move〔muv〕*v.* 移動

bookcase〔'bʊk͵kes〕*n.* 書櫃　　wall〔wɔl〕*n.* 牆壁

built-in〔'bɪlt'ɪn〕*adj.* 嵌入的；固定的

recent〔'risn̩t〕*adj.* 新的；最近的

addition〔ə'dɪʃən〕*n.* 增建（物）；附加物

movable〔'muvəbl̩〕*adj.* 可移動的

belong to 屬於　　building〔'bɪldɪŋ〕*n.* 建築物

owner〔'onɚ〕*n.* 擁有者

34. (**D**) M: What's the postage for this box?

W: Do you want to send it by air or by land?

M: Which is better?

W: Airmail is much faster, but it's three times as
expensive.

(TONE)

Q: How much will it cost to send the box?

A. It will be three times as much.

B. It varies with the price of the ticket.

C. It will be cheaper to post it.

D. It depends on how it is sent.

* postage〔'postɪdʒ〕n. 郵資　　send〔sɛnd〕v. 寄；送
  by air 以航空郵件　　land〔lænd〕n. 陸地
  by land 經由陸路　　airmail〔'ɛr,mel〕n. 航空郵件
  three times as expensive 貴三倍　　**as much** 一樣多
  vary〔'vɛrɪ〕v. 不同；有差異　　price〔praɪs〕n. 價格
  ticket〔'tɪkɪt〕n. 票　　cheap〔tʃip〕adj. 便宜的
  post〔post〕v. 郵寄　　**depend on** 視…而定

35. (**D**)　M: Did you ask Gail to type the report?

W: No, I didn't.

M: Why not?

W: I don't think she will readily agree.

(TONE)

Q : What does the woman mean?

A. Gayle is not able to type such a long report.

B. The report is not ready to be typed yet.

C. Gayle would type the report willingly.

D. Gayle will be reluctant to type the report.

* type〔taɪp〕v. 打字　　report〔rɪ'port〕n. 報告
  readily〔'rɛdɪlɪ〕adv. 輕易地；爽快地
  agree〔ə'gri〕v. 同意；答應
  willingly〔'wɪlɪŋlɪ〕adv. 自動地；樂意地
  reluctant〔rɪ'lʌktənt〕adj. 不情願的

36. (**B**)　W : I guess Helen is not going to go on the outing with us.

　　　　　　M : No, she's not.

　　　　　　W : I just can't understand her refusal.

　　　　　　(TONE)

　　　　　　Q : What does the woman mean?

　　　　　　A.　She understands Helen's reason.

　　　　　　B.　She doesn't know why Helen won't come.

　　　　　　C.　She often cannot understand Helen's speech.

　　　　　　D.　Helen misunderstood her description of the outing.

　　　　*　guess〔gɛs〕v. 猜　　**go on** 爲（某一目的）而去
　　　　　outing〔'aʊtɪŋ〕n. 郊遊　　refusal〔rɪ'fjuzl̩〕n. 拒絕
　　　　　reason〔'rizn̩〕n. 理由　　speech〔spitʃ〕n. 演說；說話
　　　　　misunderstand〔͵mɪsʌndɚ'stænd〕v. 誤解
　　　　　description〔dɪ'skrɪpʃən〕n. 敘述

37. (**A**)　W : Did they catch the robber?

　　　　　　M : The police arrested a man, but then they released him.

　　　　　　W : Why?

　　　　　　M : I guess they couldn't prove their case.

　　　　　　(TONE)

　　　　　　Q : What did the police do?

　　　　　　A.　They let a suspect go free for lack of evidence.

　　　　　　B.　They arrested the robber, but he escaped.

　　　　　　C.　They let the robber go after he returned what he stole.

　　　　　　D.　They kept the robber in jail until they could prove their case.

* catch〔kætʃ〕v. 抓到　　robber〔'rɑbɚ〕n. 強盜

police〔pə'lis〕n. 警察　　**the police** 警方

arrest〔ə'rɛst〕v. 逮捕　　then〔ðɛn〕adv. 之後

release〔rɪ'lis〕v. 釋放　　guess〔gɛs〕v. 猜測

prove〔pruv〕v. 證明　　case〔kes〕n. 案件

they couldn't prove their case 他們無法證明那名男

　　子是強盜。　　let〔lɛt〕v. 讓

suspect〔'sʌspɛkt〕n. 嫌疑犯

free〔fri〕adj. 自由的　　**let sb. go free** 放某人自由

lack〔læk〕n. 缺乏　　**for lack of** 因為缺乏

evidence〔'ɛvədəns〕n. 證據

escape〔ə'skep〕v. 逃走　　return〔rɪ't3n〕v. 歸還

steal〔stil〕v. 偷竊（三態變化為：steal-stole-stolen）

jail〔dʒel〕n. 監獄

38. (**A**)　W：How did you do in the marathon?

　　M：I finished in 5th place.

　　W：That's great!

(TONE)

Q：What did the man do?

A. He was the fifth runner to cross the line.

B. He won five competitions.

C. He finished his fifth management project.

D. He was the greatest competitor.

* marathon〔'mærə,θan〕*n.* 馬拉松
  finish〔'fɪnɪʃ〕*v.* 以…結束　　fifth〔fɪfθ〕*adj.* 第五的
  place〔ples〕*n.* 先到達的順序；得獎的順序
  finish in 5th place 最後得第五名
  runner〔'rʌnɚ〕*n.* 跑者　　***cross the line*** 越過終點線
  competition〔,kampə'tɪʃən〕*n.* 比賽
  management〔'mænɪdʒmənt〕*n.* 經營；管理
  project〔'pradʒɛkt〕*n.* 計畫
  competitor〔kəm'pɛtətɚ〕*n.* 競爭者；對手

39. (**D**)　W: I'll have to weigh your luggage, sir.

　　　　　M: But I'm allowed to take two bags free, aren't I?

　　　　　W: Yes, sir, but if the total weight exceeds 20kg,
　　　　　　　you'll have to pay extra.

　　　　　M: And what is the weight?

　　　　　W: 17 kilos.

　　　　　(TONE)

　　　　　Q: Does the man have to pay for his luggage?

　　　　　A. Yes, because he has too many bags.

　　　　　B. No, because he does not have two bags.

　　　　　C. Yes, because his luggage is not heavy enough.

　　　　　D. No, because his luggage is not too heavy.

* weigh〔we〕*v.* 稱…的重量　　luggage〔'lʌgɪdʒ〕*n.* 行李
  allow〔ə'lau〕*v.* 允許　　bag〔bæg〕*n.* 行李
  weight〔wet〕*n.* 重量　　exceed〔ɪk'sid〕*v.* 超過
  extra〔'ɛkstrə〕*adv.* 額外地
  kilo〔'kɪlo〕*n.* 公斤（ = *kilogram* = *kg* ）
  heavy〔'hɛvɪ〕*adj.* 重的

40. (**D**) M: That'll be 120 dollars.

W: Why so much?

M: They're sixty dollars each and you have two.

W: Oh, I thought you said sixteen.

(TONE)

Q : How much did the woman expect to pay?

A. Because she misunderstood him.

B. Sixty dollars.

C. She expected the man to ask for too much.

D. Thirty-two dollars.

* expect 〔 ɪk'spɛkt 〕 v. 預期
  misunderstand 〔,mɪsʌndə-'stænd 〕 v. 誤會

41. (**D**) W: Is this the train to Chicago?

M: Yes, it is.

W: Do you know how long it will take?

M: It's a nonstop, so we should be there in an hour.

(TONE)

Q : What does the woman mean?

A. The train will not stop in Chicago.

B. The train will stop every hour.

C. She doesn't know her location.

D. She doesn't know how long the trip will take.

* Chicago 〔 ʃɪ'kɑgo 〕 n. 芝加哥   take 〔 tek 〕 v. 花費
  nonstop 〔'nɑn'stɑp 〕 n. 直達火車
  location 〔 lo'keʃən 〕 n. 所在地；位置

42. (**A**)　M: Did you like the movie?

W: Yes, how about you?

M: I liked it, but the story wasn't very realistic.

(TONE)

Q : What does the man mean?

A. The story in the movie was not believable.

B. He really disliked the whole movie.

C. He liked the story most of all.

D. He liked the movie more than the woman did.

* realistic〔ˌriə'lɪstɪk〕*adj.* 實際的

believable〔bə'livəbḷ〕*adj.* 可信的

dislike〔dɪs'laɪk〕*v.* 不喜歡　　whole〔hol〕*adj.* 整個的

most of all 特別；尤其

43. (**C**)　M: Was your home damaged by the typhoon?

W: Unfortunately, it was.

M: That's too bad.　Do you have to replace the roof?

W: Actually, we need to rebuild the house.

(TONE)

Q : What must the woman do to repair her house?

A. She must replace the roof.

B. She must replace everything but the roof.

C. She must build a new house.

D. She must make the house stronger before the next typhoon.

* damage〔'dæmɪdʒ〕v. 損害；破壞
  typhoon〔taɪ'fun〕n. 颱風
  unfortunately〔ʌn'fɔrtʃənɪtlɪ〕adv. 不幸地
  replace〔rɪ'ples〕v. 更換　　roof〔ruf〕n. 屋頂
  actually〔'æktʃʊəlɪ〕adv. 實際上
  rebuild〔ri'bɪld〕v. 重建　　repair〔rɪ'pɛr〕v. 修理
  but〔bʌt〕prep. 除了

44. (**B**) W: I can't believe the concert is in three days.

M: Me neither.

W: Do you think we'll be ready?

M: We will if we rehearse some more.

(TONE)

Q: What does the man mean?

A. They need to listen to some more concerts first.

B. They need to practice before the concert.

C. They need more time to get ready for the concert.

D. They must be ready for even more concerts in the future.

* concert〔'kɑnsɝt〕n. 音樂會
  neither〔'niðɚ〕adv. 也不
  ready〔'rɛdɪ〕adj. 準備好的
  rehearse〔rɪ'hɝs〕v. 排演；練習
  practice〔'præktɪs〕v. 練習　　*get ready* 做好準備
  even〔'ivən〕adv. 更加　　*in the future* 未來

45. (**A**) M: We'd like to take a tour of the castle.

W: I'm sorry, sir, but there must be a minimum of four people in your party.

M: Couldn't you make an exception for us?

W: No, but I think it will be easy for you to find another two people to join you.

(TONE)

Q: Why can't the man take a tour now?

A. His party consists of two people.

B. There are at least four people with him.

C. Everyone in his group may go except him.

D. Two people in his group do not want to go.

* tour〔tur〕n. 旅行;遊覽   castle〔'kæsl〕n. 城堡
minimum〔'mınəməm〕n. 最小量
party〔'parti〕n. 一行人
exception〔ık'sɛpʃən〕n. 例外
make an exception 把…作爲例外;對…特別看待
join〔dʒɔɪn〕v. 加入   **consist of** 由…組成
at least 至少   group〔grup〕n. 團體
except〔ık'sɛpt〕prep. 除了

English Listening Comprehension Test
Test Book No. 6

This listening comprehension test will test your ability to understand spoken English. In this test, each conversation, statement and question will be spoken JUST ONE TIME. They will not be written out for you. There are three parts to this test. Special instructions will be given to you at the beginning of each part.

Part A

In Part A, you will see several pictures in your test book. For each picture, you will be asked 1 to 3 questions. For each question, you will hear four possible answers. Choose the best answer according to what you see in the picture.

Example:

<u>You will see</u>:

<u>You will hear</u>: What is this?
   A. This is a table.
   B. This is a chair.
   C. This is a watch.
   D. This is a doll.

The best answer to the question "What is this?" is B: "This is a chair." Therefore, you should choose answer B.

A. Questions 1-2

B. Questions 3-4

C. Questions 5-6

D. Questions 7-8

E. Questions 9-10

F. Questions 11-12

G. <u>Questions 13-14</u>

H. <u>Question 15</u>

Part B

In Part B, you will hear 15 questions. After you hear a question, read the four possible answers in your test book and decide which one is the best answer to the question you have heard.

Example:

<u>You will hear</u>: What does your father do?

<u>You will read</u>: A. He's 50 years old.
B. He's a teacher.
C. He's hungry.
D. He's in Los Angeles.

The best answer to the question "What does your father do?" is B: "He's a teacher." Therefore, you should choose answer B.

Please go to the next page. ⇨

16. A. Airfares are too expensive now.
    B. I've already been to Japan.
    C. Yes, let's get on.
    D. No, I'm not at all bored.

17. A. We take cash or credit cards.
    B. The total is NT$590.
    C. At the back of the store.
    D. Kelly is working today.

18. A. Yes, she said you plan to do it tomorrow.
    B. No, she just gave us an outline of what you plan to do.
    C. She will give us all the materials tomorrow.
    D. No, she gave us all the specifics.

19. A. No one sent any of the dishes back.
    B. No. The back dining room is closed.
    C. Yes, there were a few comments in the suggestion-box.
    D. Yes. We recalled the product yesterday.

20. A. Me, too. The author writes very clearly.
    B. I thought they were too short.
    C. Yes, they're very artistic.
    D. Not me. The vocabulary is too difficult.

21. A. Yes. You should wash
    them.
    B. No, they're mine.
    C. No. They are too
    expensive.
    D. Yes. You should
    lengthen them.

22. A. Yes, I took the eye test.
    B. Yes, he will fix my
    teeth next week.
    C. No, my heart is fine.
    D. No, my arm is only
    sprained, not broken.

23. A. Because two people
    couldn't attend.
    B. Yes, until next week.
    C. Yes, it was very fruitful.
    D. Mr. Thomas called the
    meeting.

24. A. No. He even cried.
    B. No, he only shouted
    at us and punished
    us.
    C. Yes, he was in a rage.
    D. Yes, he didn't mind
    at all.

25. A. There is a lot of dust
    in the air today.
    B. It was stolen last
    week.
    C. I often left it out in
    the rain.
    D. I just polished it.

26. A. I'd like it well-done, please.
    B. Just lettuce and tomato.
    C. I'll have a large order of fries and a Coke.
    D. I'll have it on a bun.

27. A. He is waiting for his uncle to arrive.
    B. He thinks it will be good for business.
    C. He is worried about the noise.
    D. The street is too busy to cross.

28. A. It's only about three years old.
    B. I will need it until next week.
    C. I can keep it for you until Friday.
    D. We'll replace it for any reason within six months.

29. A. I thought he was hilarious.
    B. I don't often go to the movies.
    C. No, I'd rather be a singer.
    D. It sounds great.

30. A. I can catch it.
    B. It already bit me.
    C. But it itches.
    D. Where did it go?

Part C

In Part C, you will hear 15 conversations between a man and a woman. After each conversation, you will hear a question about the conversation. After you hear the question, read the four possible answers in your test book and choose the best answer to the question you have heard.

Example:

<u>You will hear</u>: (Man)　　　How do you go to school every day?

(Woman)　Usually by bus. Sometimes by taxi.

(Tone)

Question:　How does the woman go to school?

<u>You will read</u>:　A. She always goes to school on foot.

B. She usually rides a bike.

C. She takes either a bus or a taxi.

D. She usually goes to school by bus, never by taxi.

The best answer to the question "How does the woman go to school?" is C: "She takes either a bus or a taxi." Therefore, you should choose answer C.

Please go to the next page. ⇨

31. A. They will take a test
    next week.
   B. They will have two tests
      every week.
   C. They are tested every
      other week.
   D. There will be no more
      tests after next week.

32. A. She wants the man to
      prove that he made
      the pie.
   B. She wants to take a
      piece of pie home.
   C. She wants to know how
      to make the pie.
   D. She wants the man to
      make another pie for her.

33. A. The man does not like
      little dogs.
   B. The man's dog had one
      little baby.
   C. The man's dog had
      many puppies.
   D. The man wants to give
      away his dog because
      it is too big.

34. A. He expects the
      economy to improve
      soon.
   B. The victims of the
      crisis will recover
      soon.
   C. The economy is
      booming, but may slow
      down soon.
   D. The economy must be
      reformed to prevent a
      recession.

35. A. Warn the car owner
      that his lights are still
      on.
   B. Shout at people who
      leave their lights on.
   C. Turn the lights on so
      that he can find his
      car.
   D. Tell his friends that
      he is lost.

36. A. She doesn't like Japanese food.
    B. She can't stand the smell of fish.
    C. She doesn't like uncooked food.
    D. She already ate lunch.

37. A. They like the play very much.
    B. They didn't like the show.
    C. They could have played better themselves.
    D. They cannot agree.

38. A. The vase is bigger than the catalog.
    B. The woman looked at the wrong picture when she ordered the vase.
    C. The picture makes the vase look bigger than it really is.
    D. The woman should have bought the vase in the catalog picture instead.

39. A. Baker will be happy if they both work on the project.
    B. Everyone is interested in the Baker project.
    C. Finishing the Baker project will benefit both of them.
    D. The Baker project is the most interesting project.

40. A. She does not live with her parents.
    B. They do not know where she was born.
    C. She does not look Japanese.
    D. She may not speak Japanese.

41. A. They may have to work tomorrow.
    B. Tomorrow is not a national holiday.
    C. The typhoon may jump over the island.
    D. It is never necessary to work during a typhoon.

42. A. He cannot remember where he went.
    B. He went to a new place yesterday.
    C. He did not have a holiday yesterday.
    D. He stayed at home on the holiday.

43. A. The company has moved its office from Taipei to Kaohsiung.
    B. The man will work at the Kaohsiung office from now on.
    C. His permanent home is in Taipei.
    D. The company has forced him to move to Kaohsiung.

44. A. The Jets might become the champions.
    B. She is afraid that the Jets will win the game.
    C. Their team will probably lose the game.
    D. It's possible that neither team will win.

45. A. The woman will be surprised by her friends.
    B. The woman will do her best to surprise her friends.
    C. The woman will pretend to be surprised.
    D. Everyone will be surprised to see the woman.

Listening Test 6 詳解

Part A

For questions number 1 and 2, please look at picture A.

1. (**C**) Question number 1: What is the lady on the left most likely saying?

 A. Ouch! It really hurts me!

 B. Honey, you can only have one piece of candy.

 C. No more sweets or junk food for you.

 D. I don't want any more, thank you.

 * left〔lɛft〕*n.* 左邊　　likely〔'laɪklɪ〕*adv.* 可能地

 ouch〔aʊtʃ〕*interj.* 哎唷！

 hurt〔hɝt〕*v.* 使受傷；弄痛　　honey〔'hʌnɪ〕*n.* 親愛的人

 have〔hæv〕*v.* 吃　　piece〔pis〕*n.* 片；個

 sweets〔swits〕*n. pl.* 糖果　　***junk food*** 垃圾食品

2. (**A**) Question number 2: Why does the longhaired girl have her hands clasped together?

 A. She is in pain.

 B. She is pleading and begging for sweets.

 C. She's trying to calm her down.

 D. She is offering her some candy.

 * longhaired〔'lɔŋˌhɛrd〕*adj.* 長髮的

 clasp〔klæsp〕*v.* 握緊　　pain〔pen〕*n.* 痛苦

 be in pain 在疼痛；在痛苦中　　plead〔plid〕*v.* 懇求

 beg〔bɛg〕*v.* 乞求　　calm〔kɑm〕*v.* 使平靜

 calm sb. down 使某人平靜下來　　offer〔'ɔfɚ〕*v.* 提供

For questions number 3 and 4, please look at picture B.

3. (**C**) Question number 3: What is the place being depicted in the picture?

      A. It's a fish.

      B. It's not a picture.

      C. A kindergarten classroom.

      D. He thinks it is a poor picture.

    * depict〔dɪ'pɪkt〕v. 描繪

      kindergarten〔'kɪndə‚gɑrtn̩〕n. 幼稚園

      poor〔pʊr〕adj. 差勁的

4. (**C**) Question number 4: Why is the man a little upset?

      A. Because the little girl was sleeping.

      B. She is embarrassed.

      C. The girl didn't write the word.

      D. She cannot draw well.

    * upset〔ʌp'sɛt〕adj. 不高興的

      embarrassed〔ɪm'bærəst〕adj. 尷尬的

      draw〔drɔ〕v. 畫

For questions number 5 and 6, please look at picture C.

5. (**D**) Question number 5: What is the girl's mother doing?

      A. She's telling a joke.

      B. She's shopping for fruit.

      C. She's thinking about eating a banana.

      D. She's holding the girl's hand.

    * joke〔dʒok〕n. 笑話   ***shop for*** 購買

      banana〔bə'nænə〕n. 香蕉   hold〔hold〕v. 握著

6. (**B**) Question number 6: Look at picture C again. What is the little girl probably saying?

    A. She is pointing.

    B. His face is shaped like a banana.

    C. She will probably be punished.

    D. She's hungry for a banana.

    * probably (ˈprɑbəblɪ) adv. 可能　　point (pɔɪnt) v. 指著
    shape (ʃep) v. 使成形；塑造　**be shaped like** 形狀像是
    punish (ˈpʌnɪʃ) v. 處罰　　hungry (ˈhʌŋgrɪ) adj. 渴望的

For questions number 7 and 8, please look at picture D.

7. (**B**) Question number 7: What is the problem with the baby?

    A. He has a bottle.

    B. The baby has a dirty diaper.

    C. The older boy is making the baby cry.

    D. The baby's mother is with him.

    * problem (ˈprɑbləm) n. 問題　　bottle (ˈbɑtḷ) n. 瓶子
    dirty (ˈdɝtɪ) adj. 髒的　　diaper (ˈdaɪəpɚ) n. 尿布

8. (**D**) Question number 8: Why does the boy on the left look so upset?

    A. He wants the bottle.

    B. No. It is the baby that is upset.

    C. He can't find a bathroom.

    D. The baby is driving him crazy.

    * bathroom (ˈbæθ,rum) n. 浴室；洗手間
    drive (draɪv) v. 使　　crazy (ˈkrezɪ) adj. 發瘋的

For questions number 9 and 10, please look at picture E.

9. (**A**) Question number 9: What is happening in this picture?

    A. The boy is choking on a fish bone.

    B. The boy is too shy to talk.

    C. The girl wants to introduce herself to him.

    D. The boy feels very chilly.

    * happen〔'hæpən〕v. 發生　　choke〔tʃok〕v. 噎到；哽住
    bone〔bon〕n. 骨頭　　shy〔ʃaɪ〕adj. 害羞的
    introduce〔͵ɪntrə'djus〕v. 介紹　　chilly〔'tʃɪlɪ〕adj. 寒冷的

10. (**C**) Question number 10: What can we assume from this picture?

    A. He is refusing the glass of water.

    B. He has choked to death.

    C. She is trying to help him.

    D. They are both very thirsty.

    * assume〔ə'sum〕v. 認定；推測　　refuse〔rɪ'fjuz〕v. 拒絕
    death〔dɛθ〕n. 死亡　　thirsty〔'θɝstɪ〕adj. 口渴的

For questions number 11 and 12, please look at picture F.

11. (**C**) Question number 11: Why is the boy in so much pain?

    A. Yes, he is in a lot of pain.

    B. She kicked him.

    C. He stepped on a sharp tack.

    D. His foot.

    * pain〔pen〕n. 痛苦　　**be in pain** 在疼痛；在痛苦中
    kick〔kɪk〕v. 踢　　step〔stɛp〕v. 踩
    sharp〔ʃɑrp〕adj. 尖銳的　　tack〔tæk〕n. 圖釘
    foot〔fʊt〕n. 腳（複數形為 feet〔fit〕）

12. (**C**)　Question number 12: Why is the girl holding up two fingers?

    A. She wants to hurt him twice.

    B. No, there is only one tack.

    C. She feels happy that he is in pain.

    D. He cannot stand on two feet.

    * **hold up** 舉起　　finger〔ˈfɪŋgɚ〕 n. 手指

    hurt〔hɝt〕 v. 傷害　　twice〔twaɪs〕 adv. 兩次

    stand on two feet 用兩隻腳站著

For questions number 13 and 14, please look at picture G.

13. (**B**)　Question number 13: What can we conclude from this picture?

    A. The weather is extremely hot.

    B. Someone dropped the ice cream cone.

    C. The little girl loves to eat candy.

    D. The lady is her aunt.

    * conclude〔kənˈklud〕 v. 下結論　weather〔ˈwɛðɚ〕 n. 天氣

    extremely〔ɪkˈstrimlɪ〕 adv. 非常　drop〔drɑp〕 v. 掉落

    ice cream cone 蛋捲冰淇淋　aunt〔ænt〕 n. 阿姨

14. (**B**)　Question number 14: What is the woman trying to do?

    A. She's angry.

    B. She's offering the girl another treat.

    C. She's crossing her arms.

    D. She's inviting the girl to play.

    * angry〔ˈæŋgrɪ〕 adj. 生氣的　offer〔ˈɔfɚ〕 v. 提供

    treat〔trit〕 n. 美食；甜點　cross〔krɔs〕 v. 使交叉

    arm〔ɑrm〕 n. 手臂　invite〔ɪnˈvaɪt〕 v. 邀請

For question number 15, please look at picture H.

15. (**B**) Question number 15: What are the two girls doing?

    A. Listening carefully.   B. Whispering.

    C. They are offended.   D. She is angry with them.

    * whisper ('hwɪspɚ) v. 說悄悄話；小聲說

      offend (ə'fɛnd) v. 冒犯；觸怒

Part B

16. (**C**) Shall we all go aboard now?

    A. Airfares are too expensive now.

    B. I've already been to Japan.

    C. Yes, let's get on.

    D. No, I'm not at all bored.

    * aboard (ə'bord) adv. 搭乘（車、船、飛機等）

      go aboard 上車（船等）   airfare ('ɛr,fɛr) n. 飛機票價

      expensive (ɪk'spɛnsɪv) adj. 昂貴的

      Japan (dʒə'pæn) n. 日本

      get on 上（車、船、飛機等）   ***not…at all*** 一點也不

      bored (bord) adj. 無聊的

17. (**C**) Where is the cashier?

    A. We take cash or credit cards.

    B. The total is NT$590.

    C. At the back of the store.

    D. Kelly is working today.

    * cashier (kæ'ʃɪr) n. （旅館等的）櫃檯；出納員

      cash (kæʃ) n. 現金   ***credit card*** 信用卡

      total ('totḷ) n. 總額   back (bæk) n. 後面

18. (**B**) Did Angela give you the details of our plan for tomorrow?

    A. Yes, she said you plan to do it tomorrow.

    B. No, she just gave us an outline of what you plan to do.

    C. She will give us all the materials tomorrow.

    D. No, she gave us all the specifics.

    * detail (ˈditel) n. 細節　　plan (plæn) n. v. 計畫
      outline (ˈaʊt‚laɪn) n. 大綱；概要
      material (məˈtɪrɪəl) n. 資料
      specifics (spɪˈsɪfɪks) n. pl. 細節

19. (**C**) Have you got any feedback from the customers?

    A. No one sent any of the dishes back.

    B. No.　The back dining room is closed.

    C. Yes, there were a few comments in the suggestion-box.

    D. Yes.　We recalled the product yesterday.

    * feedback (ˈfid‚bæk) n. 反應；意見；看法
      customer (ˈkʌstəmɚ) n. 顧客　　send (sɛnd) v. 送
      dish (dɪʃ) n. 盤子　　back (bæk) adv. 返還 adj. 後方的
      dining room 餐廳
      closed (klozd) adj. 關閉的；停止營業的
      a few 一些　　comment (ˈkamɛnt) n. 評論
      suggestion (səˈdʒɛstʃən) n. 建議
      suggestion-box 意見箱　　recall (rɪˈkɔl) v. 收回
      product (ˈpradʌkt) n. 產品

20. (**C**) I love the illustrations in this book.

    A. Me, too. The author writes very clearly.

    B. I thought they were too short.

    C. Yes, they're very artistic.

    D. Not me. The vocabulary is too difficult.

    * illustration〔͵ɪləs'treʃən〕 n. 插圖　author〔'ɔθɚ〕 n. 作者
    clearly〔'klɪrlɪ〕 adv. 清楚地
    artistic〔ɑr'tɪstɪk〕 adj. 富有藝術性的；精美的
    vocabulary〔və'kæbjə͵lɛrɪ〕 n. 字彙
    difficult〔'dɪfə͵kʌlt〕 adj. 困難的

21. (**D**) Are these pants too short?

    A. Yes. You should wash them.

    B. No, they're mine.

    C. No. They are too expensive.

    D. Yes. You should lengthen them.

    * pants〔pænts〕 n. pl. 褲子　wash〔wɑʃ〕 v. 清洗
    lengthen〔'lɛŋθən〕 v. 放長；加長

22. (**B**) Did you go to see the dentist?

    A. Yes, I took the eye test.

    B. Yes, he will fix my teeth next week.

    C. No, my heart is fine.

    D. No, my arm is only sprained, not broken.

    * dentist〔'dɛntɪst〕 n. 牙醫　take〔tek〕 v. 做
    test〔tɛst〕 n. 測試　fix〔fɪks〕 v. 修理；使固定
    heart〔hɑrt〕 n. 心臟　arm〔ɑrm〕 n. 手臂
    sprained〔sprend〕 adj. 扭傷的
    broken〔'brokən〕 adj. 骨折的；折斷的

23. (**B**) Was the meeting postponed?

    A. Because two people couldn't attend.

    B. Yes, until next week.

    C. Yes, it was very fruitful.

    D. Mr. Thomas called the meeting.

    * meeting ('mitɪŋ) *n.* 會議   postpone (post'pon) *v.* 延期
    attend (ə'tɛnd) *v.* 出席；參加
    fruitful ('frutfəl) *adj.* 成果豐碩的   call (kɔl) *v.* 召開

24. (**C**) Was Mr. Weiss upset about the broken window?

    A. No. He even cried.

    B. No, he only shouted at us and punished us.

    C. Yes, he was in a rage.

    D. Yes, he didn't mind at all.

    * upset (ʌp'sɛt) *adj.* 不高興的
    broken ('brokən) *adj.* 破碎的   shout (ʃaut) *v.* 吼叫
    punish ('pʌnɪʃ) *v.* 處罰   rage (redʒ) *n.* 憤怒
    in a rage 在盛怒之中   mind (maɪnd) *v.* 介意
    not…at all 一點也不…

25. (**C**) How did the bike get so rusty?

    A. There is a lot of dust in the air today.

    B. It was stolen last week.

    C. I often left it out in the rain.

    D. I just polished it.

    * bike (baɪk) *n.* 腳踏車   rusty ('rʌstɪ) *adj.* 生銹的
    dust (dʌst) *n.* 灰塵   air (ɛr) *n.* 空氣
    steal (stil) *v.* 偷 (三態變化為：steal-stole-stolen)
    leave (liv) *v.* 遺留   polish ('palɪʃ) *v.* 擦亮

26. (**B**) What would you like on your burger?

　　A. I'd like it well-done, please.

　　B. Just lettuce and tomato.

　　C. I'll have a large order of fries and a Coke.

　　D. I'll have it on a bun.

　　* burger〔'bɝgə·〕n. 漢堡
　　　well-done〔'wɛl'dʌn〕adj. 全熟的
　　　lettuce〔'lɛtɪs〕n. 萵苣　　tomato〔tə'meto〕n. 番茄
　　　order〔'ɔrdə·〕n. 所點的（一客）食物
　　　fries〔fraɪz〕n. pl. 薯條　　Coke〔kok〕n. 可口可樂
　　　bun〔bʌn〕n. 小圓麵包

27. (**C**) Why is Tim opposed to the new airport?

　　A. He is waiting for his uncle to arrive.

　　B. He thinks it will be good for business.

　　C. He is worried about the noise.

　　D. The street is too busy to cross.

　　* oppose〔ə'poz〕v. 反對　　***be opposed to*** 反對
　　　airport〔'ɛr,port〕n. 機場　　uncle〔'ʌŋkḷ〕n. 叔叔
　　　arrive〔ə'raɪv〕v. 抵達　　***be worried about*** 擔心
　　　noise〔nɔɪz〕n. 噪音　　busy〔'bɪzɪ〕adj. 熱鬧的；繁忙的
　　　cross〔krɔs〕v. 橫越

28. (**D**) For how long will you guarantee the machine?

　　A. It's only about three years old.

　　B. I will need it until next week.

　　C. I can keep it for you until Friday.

　　D. We'll replace it for any reason within six months.

* guarantee〔͵gærən'ti〕v. 保證
  machine〔mə'ʃin〕n. 機器　　keep〔kip〕v. 保留
  replace〔rı'ples〕v. 更換　　reason〔'rizn̩〕n. 原因；理由
  within〔wıð'ın〕prep. 在…之內

29. (**A**) Did you like the comedian?
    A. I thought he was hilarious.
    B. I don't often go to the movies.
    C. No, I'd rather be a singer.
    D. It sounds great.

    * comedian〔kə'midıən〕n. 喜劇演員
      hilarious〔hə'lɛrıəs〕adj. 引人發笑的；滑稽的
      go to the movies 去看電影
      would rather 寧願
      singer〔'sıŋɚ〕n. 歌手　　sound〔saund〕v. 聽起來
      great〔gret〕adj. 很棒的

30. (**C**) You shouldn't scratch that mosquito bite.
    A. I can catch it.
    B. It already bit me.
    C. But it itches.
    D. Where did it go?

    * scratch〔skrætʃ〕v. 抓；搔
      mosquito〔mə'skito〕n. 蚊子
      bite〔baıt〕n. 咬傷；咬痕　v. 咬
      （三態變化爲：bite-bit-bitten）
      catch〔kætʃ〕v. 抓到　　itch〔ıtʃ〕v. 癢

Part C

31. (**C**) M: Are there a lot of tests in this class?

W: Yes. The teacher tests us at two-week intervals.

M: So there should be another test next week, right?

W: Right.

(TONE)

Q : How often do they take a test?

A. They will take a test next week.

B. They will have two tests every week.

C. They are tested every other week.

D. There will be no more tests after next week.

* test〔tɛst〕*n. v.* 測驗　　interval〔'ɪntəvl〕*n.* 間隔
How often…? …多久一次？　　***take a test*** 接受測驗
every other week 每隔一週；每兩週

32. (**C**) W: This pie is delicious.

M: Thank you. I made it myself.

W: You're kidding! You must give me the recipe.

(TONE)

Q : What does the woman want?

A. She wants the man to prove that he made the pie.

B. She wants to take a piece of pie home.

C. She wants to know how to make the pie.

D. She wants the man to make another pie for her.

* pie〔paɪ〕*n.* 派；餡餅　　delicious〔dɪ'lɪʃəs〕*adj.* 美味的
kid〔kɪd〕*v.* 開玩笑　　recipe〔'rɛsəpɪ〕*n.* 食譜
prove〔pruv〕*v.* 證明　　piece〔pis〕*n.* 片；塊

33. (**C**) M: Do you know anyone who'd like a dog?

W: Not that I can think of. Why?

M: My dog just had a big litter and there are too many for me to keep.

(TONE)

Q: Which of the following is true?

A. The man does not like little dogs.

B. The man's dog had one little baby.

C. The man's dog had many puppies.

D. The man wants to give away his dog because it is too big.

   * ***Not that I can think of.*** 我想沒有。（ = *I can't think of anyone.* = *Not that I know of.* = *I don't know.* ）

   litter〔'lɪtɚ〕 *n.* (一胎所生的) 小狗；小豬

   keep〔kip〕 *v.* 飼養　　following〔'faləwɪŋ〕 *n.* 下列的事物

   puppy〔'pʌpɪ〕 *n.* 小狗　　　***give away*** 贈送

34. (**A**) W: Did you listen to the President's speech?

M: Yes. He talked a lot about the economy.

W: And what did he say?

M: We should see some recovery from the recession soon.

(TONE)

Q: What did the President say?

A. He expects the economy to improve soon.

B. The victims of the crisis will recover soon.

C. The economy is booming, but may slow down soon.

D. The economy must be reformed to prevent a recession.

* president〔'prɛzədənt〕 n. 總統　　speech〔spitʃ〕 n. 演講
economy〔ɪ'kɑnəmɪ〕 n. 經濟
recovery〔rɪ'kʌvərɪ〕 n. 恢復；復甦
recession〔rɪ'sɛʃən〕 n. 蕭條；不景氣
soon〔sun〕 adv. 很快地　　expect〔ɪk'spɛkt〕 v. 預期
improve〔ɪm'pruv〕 v. 改善　　victim〔'vɪktɪm〕 n. 受害者
crisis〔'kraɪsɪs〕 n. 危機　　recover〔rɪ'kʌvɚ〕 v. 恢復
booming〔'bumɪŋ〕 adj. 趨於繁榮的　　**slow down** 減慢
reform〔rɪ'fɔrm〕 v. 改革　　prevent〔prɪ'vɛnt〕 v. 預防

35. (**A**)　M: Excuse me.　Can you make an announcement over
　　　　　　 the loudspeaker?

　　　　 W: Did you lose something?

　　　　 M: No, there's a car in the parking lot with its lights on.

　　　　 (TONE)

　　　　 Q : What does the man want the woman to do?

　　　　 A.　Warn the car owner that his lights are still on.

　　　　 B.　Shout at people who leave their lights on.

　　　　 C.　Turn the lights on so that he can find his car.

　　　　 D.　Tell his friends that he is lost.

* announcement〔ə'naʊnsmənt〕 n. 宣佈
over〔'ovɚ〕 prep. 透過；經由
loudspeaker〔'laʊd'spikɚ〕 n. 擴音器　　lose〔luz〕 v. 遺失
parking lot 停車場　　light〔laɪt〕 n. 燈
on〔ɑn〕 adv. 開著　　warn〔wɔrn〕 v. 警告
owner〔'onɚ〕 n. 擁有者　　shout〔ʃaʊt〕 v. 吼叫
leave〔liv〕 v. 使⋯處於某種狀態　　**turn on** 打開
so that 以便於　　lost〔lɔst〕 adj. 迷路的

36. (**C**) M: How about having sushi for lunch?

W: No thanks, I never eat it.

M: Why not?

W: I can't stand raw food.

(TONE)

Q : Why won't the woman eat sushi?

A. She doesn't like Japanese food.

B. She can't stand the smell of fish.

C. She doesn't like uncooked food.

D. She already ate lunch.

* ***How about…?*** …如何？   have〔hæv〕v. 吃
sushi〔'suʃɪ〕n. 壽司   stand〔stænd〕v. 忍受
raw〔rɔ〕adj. 生的   Japanese〔ˌdʒæpə'niz〕adj. 日本的
smell〔smɛl〕n. 氣味；味道
uncooked〔ʌn'kʊkt〕adj. 未烹調的；生的

37. (**B**) W: What did you think of the play?

M: I thought it was lousy.

W: Yeah, I've seen better.

(TONE)

Q : What is their opinion?

A. They like the play very much.

B. They didn't like the show.

C. They could have played better themselves.

D. They cannot agree.

* play〔ple〕n. 戲劇   v. 參加（體育活動、比賽等）；表演
lousy〔'laʊzɪ〕adj. 很糟的   yeah〔jɛ〕adv. 是的（= yes）
opinion〔ə'pɪnjən〕n. 意見   show〔ʃo〕n. 表演；演出
agree〔ə'gri〕v. 同意

38. (**C**)　M: Why did you buy such a small vase?

W: It looked much bigger in the catalog.

M: I think that picture is misleading.

(TONE)

Q: What does the man mean?

A. The vase is bigger than the catalog.

B. The woman looked at the wrong picture when she ordered the vase.

C. The picture makes the vase look bigger than it really is.

D. The woman should have bought the vase in the catalog picture instead.

* vase〔ves〕*n.* 花瓶　　catalog〔ˈkætl͵ɔg〕*n.* 目錄
misleading〔mɪsˈlidɪŋ〕*adj.* 誤導的；給人錯誤印象的
mean〔min〕*v.* 意思是　　wrong〔rɔŋ〕*adj.* 錯誤的
order〔ˈɔrdə〕*v.* 訂購　　instead〔ɪnˈstɛd〕*adv.* 取而代之

39. (**C**)　M: I have a new project that I need some help with.

W: Is that the Baker project?

M: Yes.　Are you interested?

W: Sure.　Let's work on it together.　After all, it's in our mutual best interest.

(TONE)

Q: What does the woman mean?

A. Baker will be happy if they both work on the project.

B. Everyone is interested in the Baker project.

C. Finishing the Baker project will benefit both of them.

D. The Baker project is the most interesting project.

　　* project〔'prɑdʒɛkt〕n. 計畫
　　　interested〔'ɪntrɪstɪd〕adj. 有興趣的
　　　work on 從事於；致力於　　**after all** 畢竟
　　　mutual〔'mjutʃuəl〕adj. 相互的
　　　interest〔'ɪntrɪst〕n. 利益
　　　in one's best interest 爲了某人　　finish〔'fɪnɪʃ〕v. 完成
　　　benefit〔'bɛnəfɪt〕v. 使獲益；有益於
　　　interesting〔'ɪntrɪstɪŋ〕adj. 有趣的

40. (**B**)　M: Isn't Keiko Japanese?

　　　　　W: Yes, she's Japanese, but I'm not sure where she's from.

　　　　　M: Were her parents born in Japan?

　　　　　W: I'm not sure.

　　　　　(TONE)

　　　　　Q : What do they say about Keiko?

　　　　　A. She does not live with her parents.

　　　　　B. They do not know where she was born.

　　　　　C. She does not look Japanese.

　　　　　D. She may not speak Japanese.

　　　　　* Japanese〔͵dʒæpə'niz〕adj. 日本人的　n. 日語；日本人
　　　　　parents〔'pɛrənts〕n. pl. 父母　　**be born** 出生
　　　　　look〔luk〕v. 看起來像

41. (**A**)　W: It looks like the typhoon is headed straight for us.

　　　　　M: That's right. It will hit the island tomorrow.

　　　　　W: At least we'll get a day off.

　　　　　M: Not necessarily.

(TONE)

Q : What does the man mean?

A. They may have to work tomorrow.

B. Tomorrow is not a national holiday.

C. The typhoon may jump over the island.

D. It is never necessary to work during a typhoon.

* typhoon〔taɪˈfun〕*n.* 颱風　　head〔hɛd〕*v.* 使朝…前進
straight〔stret〕*adv.* 直直地；直接地　　hit〔hɪt〕*v.* 襲擊
island〔ˈaɪlənd〕*n.* 島　　***at least*** 至少
get a day off 休假一天　　***not necessarily*** 未必
national〔ˈnæʃənḷ〕*adj.* 國家的
national holiday 國定假日　　***jump over*** 跳過
necessary〔ˈnɛsəˌsɛrɪ〕*adj.* 必要的
during〔ˈdjʊrɪŋ〕*prep.* 在…期間

42.(**D**)　W: Did you have a nice holiday yesterday?

M: Yes, I did.

W: Where did you go?

M: Nowhere.

(TONE)

Q : What does the man mean?

A. He cannot remember where he went.

B. He went to a new place yesterday.

C. He did not have a holiday yesterday.

D. He stayed at home on the holiday.

* nowhere〔ˈnoˌhwɛr〕*adv.* 什麼地方都沒有
remember〔rɪˈmɛmbɚ〕*v.* 記得　　stay〔ste〕*v.* 停留

43. (**B**) W: How do you like working in the Kaohsiung office?

M: I like it a lot.

W: When will you return to Taipei?

M: Oh, this is a permanent move.

(TONE)

Q: What does the man mean?

A. The company has moved its office from Taipei to Kaohsiung.

B. The man will work at the Kaohsiung office from now on.

C. His permanent home is in Taipei.

D. The company has forced him to move to Kaohsiung.

* Kaohsiung〔'gaʊ'ʃjʊŋ〕*n.* 高雄　　office〔'ɔfɪs〕*n.* 辦公室

a lot 非常　　permanent〔'pɜmənənt〕*adj.* 永久的

company〔'kʌmpənɪ〕*n.* 公司　　move〔muv〕*n. v.* 遷移

from now on 從現在起；今後　　force〔fors〕*v.* 強迫

44. (**C**) M: This is an important game.

W: Yeah, the winner will go on to the championship.

M: Do you think we'll win this one?

W: I'm afraid there is no possibility of the Jets winning the game.

(TONE)

Q: What does the woman mean?

A. The Jets might become the champions.

B. She is afraid that the Jets will win the game.

C. Their team will probably lose the game.

D. It's possible that neither team will win.

* important〔ɪm'pɔrtṇt〕*adj.* 重要的
winner〔'wɪnɚ〕*n.* 獲勝者　　***go on*** 前進；繼續
championship〔'tʃæmpɪən,ʃɪp〕*n.* 冠軍賽；錦標賽
possibility〔,pɑsə'bɪlətɪ〕*n.* 可能性
champion〔'tʃæmpɪən〕*n.* 冠軍
afraid〔ə'fred〕*adj.* 害怕的　　team〔tim〕*n.* 團隊
probably〔'prɑbəblɪ〕*adv.* 可能　　lose〔luz〕*v.* 輸掉
possible〔'pɑsəbḷ〕*adj.* 可能的
neither〔'niðɚ〕*adj.* 兩者都不…的

45. (**C**) M: Now be sure to act surprised when you open the door.
W: Why?
M: Everyone went to a lot of trouble to plan this surprise party for you.
W: All right. I'll do my best.

(TONE)

Q : What will happen at the party?

A. The woman will be surprised by her friends.
B. The woman will do her best to surprise her friends.
C. The woman will pretend to be surprised.
D. Everyone will be surprised to see the woman.

* act〔ækt〕*v.* 表現得　　surprised〔sə'praɪzd〕*adj.* 驚訝的
trouble〔'trʌbḷ〕*n.* 麻煩；費事
go to trouble 盡力設法；不怕費事　　plan〔plæn〕*v.* 計畫
surprise〔sə'praɪz〕*adj.* 令人吃驚的　*v.* 使驚訝
All right. 好吧。　　***do one's best*** 盡力
pretend〔prɪ'tɛnd〕*v.* 假裝

English Listening Comprehension Test
Test Book No. 7

This listening comprehension test will test your ability to understand spoken English. In this test, each conversation, statement and question will be spoken JUST ONE TIME. They will not be written out for you. There are three parts to this test. Special instructions will be given to you at the beginning of each part.

Part A

In Part A, you will see several pictures in your test book. For each picture, you will be asked 1 to 3 questions. For each question, you will hear four possible answers. Choose the best answer according to what you see in the picture.

Example:

<u>You will see</u>:

<u>You will hear</u>: What is this?
        A. This is a table.
        B. This is a chair.
        C. This is a watch.
        D. This is a doll.

The best answer to the question "What is this?" is B: "This is a chair." Therefore, you should choose answer B.

A. <u>Questions 1-2</u>

B. <u>Questions 3-4</u>

C. <u>Questions 5-6</u>

D. <u>Questions 7-8</u>

E. <u>Questions 9-10</u>

F. <u>Questions 11-12</u>

G. <u>Questions 13-14</u>

H. <u>Question 15</u>

Part B

In Part B, you will hear 15 questions. After you hear a question, read the four possible answers in your test book and decide which one is the best answer to the question you have heard.

Example:

You will hear: What does your father do?

You will read: A. He's 50 years old.

B. He's a teacher.

C. He's hungry.

D. He's in Los Angeles.

The best answer to the question "What does your father do?" is B: "He's a teacher." Therefore, you should choose answer B.

Please go to the next page. ⟹

16. A. Admission is
　　　 NT$200.
　　 B. One ticket admits
　　　 two people.
　　 C. I bought it new, not
　　　 used.
　　 D. Three drivers have
　　　 been issued tickets.

17. A. I'll have the tuna
　　　 sandwich.
　　 B. Because I'm really
　　　 upset.
　　 C. In the classroom.
　　 D. It's bubble gum.

18. A. I listen to it every
　　　 afternoon.
　　 B. I took it back to the
　　　 store.
　　 C. I turned the volume
　　　 down.
　　 D. It belongs to the
　　　 whole family.

19. A. No. When I got there
　　　 the robbery had
　　　 already happened.
　　 B. Yes. It's over there
　　　 on the street corner.
　　 C. No, I was too busy to
　　　 watch it.
　　 D. Oh, yes. I've been
　　　 looking forward to it
　　　 all week.

20. A. No, I was late.
　　 B. No. I just took a
　　　 leisurely walk.
　　 C. Yes. I run every
　　　 morning.
　　 D. No, I didn't go there.

21. A. No. I prefer pop music
　　　 to classical music.
　　 B. I went to his concert
　　　 last month.
　　 C. I've read several of
　　　 his books.
　　 D. No, I haven't read it.

22. A. The speed limit is 80 kph.
    B. Petrol is too expensive now.
    C. You must have a driver's license.
    D. It's a 3,500 dollar fine.

23. A. We should sell enough to make a profit soon.
    B. It is a story set in the eighteenth century.
    C. I hope to write a book after I retire.
    D. It's coming out in the spring.

24. A. Yes, he can make it at 3:00.
    B. The tennis court costs NT$100 per hour.
    C. He's been playing for five years.
    D. No, he's an amateur.

25. A. You're right. It's too foggy to drive.
    B. I saw the weather forecast at 6:00.
    C. The weather is usually better at the seashore.
    D. It looks like it's cold outside.

26. A. Not until dusk.
    B. No one knows who started the fire.
    C. Yes, they were beautiful.
    D. Over the lake.

27. A. No, I can't come out now.
    B. We need six players.
    C. Yes, it's outside.
    D. We won by six points.

28. A. I'd love a cup, thank you.
    B. They're chocolate biscuits.
    C. I'll take cream and sugar.
    D. I don't care for any, thanks.

29. A. No, it's a hen.
    B. I'll call the waiter.
    C. No, it's a soda.
    D. Yes, I would.

30. A. They had a lot of reports to finish this week.
    B. 50 kilometers is a long way to pedal a bike.
    C. I'm not interested in cycling, either.
    D. They had to pick up a lot of cans, bottles, and paper.

Part C

In Part C, you will hear 15 conversations between a man and a woman. After each conversation, you will hear a question about the conversation. After you hear the question, read the four possible answers in your test book and choose the best answer to the question you have heard.

Example:

You will hear: (Man)   How do you go to school every day?

(Woman) Usually by bus. Sometimes by taxi.

(Tone)

Question: How does the woman go to school?

You will read: A. She always goes to school on foot.
B. She usually rides a bike.
C. She takes either a bus or a taxi.
D. She usually goes to school by bus, never by taxi.

The best answer to the question "How does the woman go to school?" is C: "She takes either a bus or a taxi." Therefore, you should choose answer C.

Please go to the next page. ⇨

31. A. At a clinic, waiting for
    a physician.
    B. On the street, at a
    bus stop.
    C. At their office, in the
    hallway.
    D. At a hospital.

32. A. Hurry and sign up for
    classes.
    B. Remind his professor
    to assist him.
    C. Talk with his advisor.
    D. Make an appointment
    for a scholarship
    application.

33. A. He's depressed because
    she didn't invite him.
    B. He's envious but
    happy for her.
    C. He's doubtful that
    she's telling the truth.
    D. He resents that she is
    so lucky and he isn't.

34. A. To try for the
    scholarship
    opportunity.
    B. To apply for the
    employment
    opportunity.
    C. To pay the application
    fee.
    D. To train diligently
    and be confident.

35. A. She's crazy about
    rock and roll music.
    B. She thinks it's too
    loud and wild.
    C. She likes hard rock
    and dislikes country
    rock.
    D. She likes some kinds
    and dislikes other
    kinds.

36. A. That world religions are too powerful.
    B. That a major earthquake is predicted soon.
    C. Why there are so many weather related tragedies.
    D. Why disasters are depressing everyone so much.

37. A. At a video arcade.
    B. At a coin-operated laundromat.
    C. At a coin-operated car wash.
    D. At a supermarket check-out counter.

38. A. Find a solution to our medical problems.
    B. Change the stressful educational environment.
    C. Eliminate the testing system.
    D. Change the textbook content.

39. A. She can't believe that baseball players would do that.
    B. She thinks it is amusing and humorous.
    C. She thinks that gambling is a horrible vice.
    D. She is extremely upset.

40. A. He's going to a costume party at school.
    B. He's going to the circus after school.
    C. He's going to the school gymnasium.
    D. He's going to drama class in the school theater.

41. A. Mathematics and
       natural science.
    B. History and geography.
    C. Sociology and political
       science.
    D. Chinese and English.

42. A. Her neighbor is a law
       enforcement officer.
    B. She has neighbors who
       aren't considerate.
    C. She has reported her
       neighbor to the police.
    D. Her neighbors are a
       burden.

43. A. The information is not
       given.
    B. She's very supportive
       of Peter's choice.
    C. She strongly opposes
       his choice.
    D. She will try to persuade
       him to change it.

44. A. Hurry up and get
       engaged.
    B. Be more mature and
       give up the playboy
       lifestyle.
    C. Not to wait for her
       because she's
       already married.
    D. Aggressively look
       for a perfect life
       companion.

45. A. Just about two
       months.
    B. A little bit less than
       one month.
    C. Forty weeks.
    D. Seven days a week
       for three weeks.

Listening Test 7 詳解

Part A

For questions number 1 and 2, please look at picture A.

1. (**A**) Question number 1: What is the child on the left doing?

   A. Pretending to be a ghost.
   B. Going to a party.
   C. Crying.
   D. Telling a funny joke.

   * left〔lɛft〕n. 左邊　　pretend〔prɪˋtɛnd〕v. 假裝；裝扮
   ghost〔gost〕n. 鬼　　funny〔ˋfʌnɪ〕adj. 好笑的
   joke〔dʒok〕n. 笑話

2. (**D**) Question number 2: What is the young girl's reaction?

   A. She is scaring him.
   B. She feels frustrated.
   C. She is scary.
   D. She is frightened.

   * reaction〔rɪˋækʃən〕n. 反應
   scare〔skɛr〕v. 驚嚇
   frustrated〔ˋfrʌstretɪd〕adj. 沮喪的
   scary〔ˋskɛrɪ〕adj.（事物）恐怖的；嚇人的
   frightened〔ˋfraɪtn̩d〕adj. 害怕的

For questions number 3 and 4, please look at picture B.

3. (**B**) Question number 3: Why is the girl so happy in this picture?

    A. It was her birthday.

    B. She bought many nice things.

    C. She loves Bill.

    D. She gave the man $250.

4. (**C**) Question number 4: Why do the man's eyes seem so large?

    A. Yes, they do.

    B. That's his normal face.

    C. He is shocked.

    D. So that he can carry the packages.

    * seem〔sim〕v. 看來   normal〔'nɔrml〕adj. 正常的

    shocked〔ʃɑkt〕adj. 震驚的   ***so that*** 以便於

    carry〔'kærɪ〕v. 搬運   package〔'pækɪdʒ〕n. 包裹

For questions number 5 and 6, please look at picture C.

5. (**D**) Question number 5: What is happening to the boy in this picture?

    A. It is flying.

    B. It is happening at night.

    C. A bird is disturbing him.

    D. A mosquito is keeping him awake.

    * disturb〔dɪ'stɝb〕v. 打擾   mosquito〔mə'skito〕n. 蚊子

    keep〔kip〕v. 使保持   awake〔ə'wek〕adj. 醒著的

6. (**C**) Question number 6: According to the clock, what time is it?

    A. It's midday.

    B. It's his bedroom.

    C. It's after twelve.

    D. It's on the wall.

    * midday ('mɪd,de) *n.* 中午   wall (wɔl) *n.* 牆壁

For questions number 7 and 8, please look at picture D.

7. (**D**) Question number 7: How would you describe this scene? What is taking place?

    A. The robbers cannot be seen.

    B. Three thieves are wearing hats.

    C. This is a scenic movie.

    D. This is a bank robbery.

    * describe (dɪ'skraɪb) *v.* 描述

    scene (sin) *n.* 場面；情景   ***take place*** 發生

    robber ('rɑbɚ) *n.* 強盜   thief (θif) *n.* 小偷

    scenic ('sinɪk) *adj.* 風景的；風景優美的

    bank (bæŋk) *n.* 銀行   robbery ('rɑbərɪ) *n.* 搶案

8. (**A**) Question number 8: How many people are on the floor?

    A. Two women are.

    B. There are three behind the counter.

    C. Five altogether in the bank.

    D. Two men are.

＊ floor〔flor〕n. 地板　　behind〔bɪˈhaɪnd〕prep. 在…後面
counter〔ˈkaʊntɚ〕n. 櫃台
altogether〔͵ɔltəˈgɛðɚ〕adv. 總共

For questions number 9 and 10, please look at picture E.

9. (**B**)　Question number 9:　Why is the girl holding up the handbag?

A.　She is feeling jealous.
B.　It is her designer handbag.
C.　It's a handsome puppet.
D.　She is selling it.

＊ ***hold up*** 舉起　　handbag〔ˈhænd͵bæg〕n. 手提包
jealous〔ˈdʒɛləs〕adj. 嫉妒的
designer〔dɪˈzaɪnɚ〕adj. 設計師設計的
handsome〔ˈhænsəm〕adj. 英俊的；精巧的
puppet〔ˈpʌpɪt〕n. 木偶　　sell〔sɛl〕v. 賣

10. (**A**)　Question number 10:　What can we conclude about the two girls on the right?

A.　They both want a designer bag.
B.　They admire the parcel.
C.　They envy the equipment.
D.　They are fond of the packet.

＊ conclude〔kənˈklud〕v. 斷定；下結論
right〔raɪt〕n. 右邊　　admire〔ədˈmaɪr〕v. 讚賞；佩服
parcel〔ˈpɑrsḷ〕n. 包；小包　　envy〔ˈɛnvɪ〕v. 羨慕；嫉妒
equipment〔ɪˈkwɪpmənt〕n. 裝備　　***be fond of*** 喜歡
packet〔ˈpækɪt〕n. 小包；包裹

For questions number 11 and 12, please look at picture F.

11. (**D**) Question number 11: What is going on in this picture?

    A. The house is going to start shaking.

    B. Starvation is everywhere.

    C. She will stay on the floor.

    D. An earthquake is occurring.

    * ***go on*** 發生   start〔stɑrt〕*v.* 開始
      shake〔ʃek〕*v.* 搖動
      starvation〔stɑr'veʃən〕*n.* 飢荒
      stay〔ste〕*v.* 停留
      floor〔flor〕*n.* 地板
      earthquake〔'ɝθ,kwek〕*n.* 地震
      occur〔ə'kɝ〕*v.* 發生

12. (**C**) Question number 12: Look at the picture carefully. How does the girl feel?

    A. The room is flooding.

    B. The fish are swimming.

    C. She feels afraid.

    D. She feels comfortable.

    * flood〔flʌd〕*v.* 淹水   fish〔fiʃ〕*n.* 魚
      swim〔swɪm〕*v.* 游泳
      afraid〔ə'fred〕*adj.* 害怕的
      comfortable〔'kʌmfɚtəbḷ〕*adj.* 舒服的

For questions number 13 and 14, please look at picture G.

13. (**B**) Question number 13: What might this love letter symbolize?

    A. The symbol is on the envelope.

    B. It is a sign of affection.

    C. A symbol is not required.

    D. They are simply embarrassed.

    * letter (ˈlɛtɚ) *n.* 信　　***love letter*** 情書

       symbolize (ˈsɪmbḷˌaɪz) *v.* 象徵

       symbol (ˈsɪmbḷ) *n.* 象徵；記號

       envelope (ˈɛnvəˌlop) *n.* 信封

       sign (saɪn) *n.* 信號；表示

       affection (əˈfɛkʃən) *n.* 情感

       require (rɪˈkwaɪr) *v.* 要求

       simply (ˈsɪmplɪ) *adv.* 只是

       embarrassed (ɪmˈbærəst) *adj.* 尷尬的

14. (**C**) Question number 14: What is the boy doing?

    A. He is pleased.

    B. He is embarrassed.

    C. Accepting the letter.

    D. Sending the letter.

    * pleased (plizd) *adj.* 高興的

       accept (əkˈsɛpt) *v.* 接受

       send (sɛnd) *v.* 寄；送

For question number 15, please look at picture H.

15. (**D**) Question number 15: Where are these two young teenagers?

    A. They are boyfriend and girlfriend.

    B. On a high-rise journey.

    C. They feel very happy.

    D. In a meadow at night.

    * boyfriend ('bɔɪ,frɛnd) *n.* 男朋友

     girlfriend ('gɝl,frɛnd) *n.* 女朋友

     teenager ('tin,edʒɚ) *n.* 十幾歲的青少年

     high-rise ('haɪ,raɪs) *adj.* 高層的 *n.* 高層建築物

     journey ('dʒɝnɪ) *n.* 旅行

     meadow ('mɛdo) *n.* 草地

Part B

16. (**B**) How many people can use that ticket?

    A. Admission is NT$200.

    B. One ticket admits two people.

    C. I bought it new, not used.

    D. Three drivers have been issued tickets.

    * ticket ('tɪkɪt) *n.* 票；入場券；罰單

     admission (əd'mɪʃən) *n.* 入場費

     admit (əd'mɪt) *v.* 准許進入

     used (juzd) *adj.* 舊的；二手的

     driver ('draɪvɚ) *n.* 駕駛人   issue ('ɪʃju) *v.* 發給

17. (**D**)　What are you chewing?

　　　　A.　I'll have the tuna sandwich.

　　　　B.　Because I'm really upset.

　　　　C.　In the classroom.

　　　　D.　It's bubble gum.

　　　　＊ chew〔tʃu〕v. 嚼　　tuna〔'tunə〕n. 鮪魚
　　　　　 sandwich〔'sændwɪtʃ〕n. 三明治　　*bubble gum* 泡泡糖

18. (**B**)　What did you do with that faulty radio?

　　　　A.　I listen to it every afternoon.

　　　　B.　I took it back to the store.

　　　　C.　I turned the volume down.

　　　　D.　It belongs to the whole family.

　　　　＊ *do with* 處置　　faulty〔'fɔltɪ〕adj. 有缺陷的；有毛病的
　　　　　 turn down 關小聲　　volume〔'vɑljəm〕n. 音量
　　　　　 belong to 屬於　　whole〔hol〕adj. 整個的

19. (**A**)　Did you see the incident at the bank?

　　　　A.　No.　When I got there the robbery had already
　　　　　　 happened.

　　　　B.　Yes.　It's over there on the street corner.

　　　　C.　No, I was too busy to watch it.

　　　　D.　Oh, yes.　I've been looking forward to it all week.

　　　　＊ incident〔'ɪnsədənt〕n. 事件　　robbery〔'rɑbərɪ〕n. 搶案
　　　　　 over there 在那邊　　corner〔'kɔrnɚ〕n. 轉角
　　　　　 look forward to 期待

20. (**B**) Did you go running this afternoon?

    A. No, I was late.

    B. No. I just took a leisurely walk.

    C. Yes. I run every morning.

    D. No, I didn't go there.

    * late〔let〕*adj.* 遲到的　　***take a walk*** 散步

    leisurely〔'liʒəlɪ〕*adj.* 悠閒的

21. (**C**) Have you ever heard of this novelist?

    A. No. I prefer pop music to classical music.

    B. I went to his concert last month.

    C. I've read several of his books.

    D. No, I haven't read it.

    * ***hear of*** 聽說過　　novelist〔'nɑvḷɪst〕*n.* 小說家

    prefer A ***to*** B　喜歡 A 甚於 B

    pop〔pɑp〕*adj.* 流行的

    classical〔'klæsɪkḷ〕*adj.* 古典的

    concert〔'kɑnsɝt〕*n.* 音樂會

    several〔'sɛvərəl〕*pron.*　幾個

22. (**D**) What is the penalty for speeding here?

    A. The speed limit is 80 kph.

    B. Petrol is too expensive now.

    C. You must have a driver's license.

    D. It's a 3,500 dollar fine.

    * penalty〔'pɛnḷtɪ〕*n.* 罰金；罰款

    speeding〔'spidɪŋ〕*n.* 超速

speed〔spid〕*n.* 速度　　limit〔'lɪmɪt〕*n.* 限制

speed limit 速限　***kph*** 公里／小時（= *kilometers per hour*）

petrol〔'pɛtrəl〕*n.* 汽油

expensive〔ɪk'spɛnsɪv〕*adj.* 昂貴的

license〔'laɪsn̩s〕*n.* 執照　***driver's license*** 駕照

fine〔faɪn〕*n.* 罰金；罰款

23. (**D**) When will your book be published?

A. We should sell enough to make a profit soon.

B. It is a story set in the eighteenth century.

C. I hope to write a book after I retire.

D. It's coming out in the spring.

* publish〔'pʌblɪʃ〕*v.* 出版　　sell〔sɛl〕*v.* 賣

make〔mek〕*v.* 賺　　profit〔'prɑfɪt〕*n.* 利潤

soon〔sun〕*adv.* 很快地　　set〔sɛt〕*v.* 設定

century〔'sɛntʃərɪ〕*n.* 世紀　　retire〔rɪ'taɪr〕*v.* 退休

come out （書籍等）問世；出版

spring〔sprɪŋ〕*n.* 春天

24. (**D**) Does Greg make much money playing tennis?

A. Yes, he can make it at 3:00.

B. The tennis court costs NT$100 per hour.

C. He's been playing for five years.

D. No, he's an amateur.

* tennis〔'tɛnɪs〕*n.* 網球　***make it*** 趕上；來得及

court〔kort〕*n.* 球場　　per〔pɚ〕*prep.* 每

amateur〔'æməˌtʃur〕*n.* 業餘愛好者

25. (**A**)　How can you see in this weather?

　　A.　You're right.　It's too foggy to drive.

　　B.　I saw the weather forecast at 6:00.

　　C.　The weather is usually better at the seashore.

　　D.　It looks like it's cold outside.

　　＊ weather〔'wɛðɚ〕 n. 天氣　　foggy〔'fɑgɪ〕 adj. 多霧的

　　　forecast〔'for,kæst〕 n. 預報

　　　seashore〔'si,ʃor〕 n. 海岸

　　　outside〔'aʊt'saɪd〕 adv. 在外面

26. (**A**)　When will they set off the fireworks?

　　A.　Not until dusk.

　　B.　No one knows who started the fire.

　　C.　Yes, they were beautiful.

　　D.　Over the lake.

　　＊ *set off* 燃放　　fireworks〔'faɪr,wɝks〕 n. pl. 煙火

　　　not until… 直到…才～　　*start the fire* 引起那場火災

　　　dusk〔dʌsk〕 n. 黃昏　　lake〔lek〕 n. 湖

27. (**D**)　What was the outcome of the game?

　　A.　No, I can't come out now.

　　B.　We need six players.

　　C.　Yes, it's outside.

　　D.　We won by six points.

　　＊ outcome〔'aʊt,kʌm〕 n. 結果　　player〔'pleɚ〕 n. 選手

　　　win〔wɪn〕 v. 贏　　by〔baɪ〕 prep. 相差

　　　point〔pɔɪnt〕 n. 分

28. (**D**)　How about some biscuits with your tea?

　　　　A.　I'd love a cup, thank you.

　　　　B.　They're chocolate biscuits.

　　　　C.　I'll take cream and sugar.

　　　　D.　I don't care for any, thanks.

　　　　* ***How about…?*** ～如何？

　　　　　biscuit〔'bɪskɪt〕 *n.* 餅乾

　　　　　cup〔kʌp〕 *n.* 一杯的量

　　　　　chocolate〔'tʃɔkəlɪt〕 *adj.* 巧克力的

　　　　　take〔tek〕 *v.* 拿；買　　cream〔krim〕 *n.* 奶油

　　　　　sugar〔'ʃugɚ〕 *n.* 糖　　***care for*** 想要；喜歡

29. (**C**)　Is that a cocktail?

　　　　A.　No, it's a hen.

　　　　B.　I'll call the waiter.

　　　　C.　No, it's a soda.

　　　　D.　Yes, I would.

　　　　* cocktail〔'kɑk,tel〕 *n.* 雞尾酒　　hen〔hɛn〕 *n.* 母雞

　　　　　call〔kɔl〕 *v.* 叫　　waiter〔'wetɚ〕 *n.* 服務生

　　　　　soda〔'sodə〕 *n.* 汽水

30. (**B**)　The cyclists look so tired.

　　　　A.　They had a lot of reports to finish this week.

　　　　B.　50 kilometers is a long way to pedal a bike.

　　　　C.　I'm not interested in cycling, either.

　　　　D.　They had to pick up a lot of cans, bottles, and paper.

* cyclist〔'saɪklˌɪst〕n. 騎腳踏車者
tired〔taɪrd〕adj. 疲倦的　　report〔rɪ'port〕n. 報告
finish〔'fɪnɪʃ〕v. 完成　　kilometer〔'kɪləˌmitə〕n. 公里
pedal〔'pɛdl̩〕v. 踩…的踏板　　bike〔baɪk〕n. 腳踏車
interested〔'ɪntrɪstɪd〕adj. 感興趣的
cycling〔'saɪklˌɪŋ〕n. 騎腳踏車兜風
either〔'iðə〕adv. 也（不）　　**pick up** 撿起
can〔kæn〕n. 罐子　　bottle〔'batl̩〕n. 瓶子

Part C

31. (**C**)　M：You look as pale as a ghost.　Are you OK?

W：I'm really under the weather.　I'm fighting a nasty cold.

M：Have you taken any medication for it?

W：My doctor gave me a strong prescription.

M：Is it doing any good?

W：To tell you the truth, it's really wiped me out.　I feel so dizzy and thirsty.

M：You shouldn't be here.　You should have called in sick.

(TONE)

Q：Where are they having this conversation?

A. At a clinic, waiting for a physician.

B. On the street, at a bus stop.

C. At their office, in the hallway.

D. At a hospital.

* pale〔pel〕adj. 蒼白的　　ghost〔gost〕n. 鬼
  under the weather 身體不適的　　fight〔faɪt〕v. 對抗
  nasty〔'næstɪ〕adj. 嚴重的　　cold〔kold〕n. 感冒
  take〔tek〕v. 吃（藥）
  medication〔͵mɛdɪ'keʃən〕n. 藥物
  strong〔strɔŋ〕adj.（藥性）強的
  prescription〔prɪ'skrɪpʃən〕n. 藥方；處方的藥
  do good 有用；有效　　truth〔truθ〕n. 事實
  to tell you the truth 老實說
  wipe sb. out 使某人筋疲力竭　　dizzy〔'dɪzɪ〕adj. 頭暈的
  thirsty〔'θɝstɪ〕adj. 口渴的　　**call in sick** 打電話請病假
  conversation〔͵kɑnvɚ'seʃən〕n. 對話
  clinic〔'klɪnɪk〕n. 診所　　physician〔fə'zɪʃən〕n. 醫師
  stop〔stɑp〕n. 車站　　hallway〔'hɔl͵we〕n. 走廊
  hospital〔'hɑspɪtḷ〕n. 醫院

32.（**A**）W: Have you registered for the spring semester yet?

M: No, I still need to make an appointment with my advisor. I need her permission to take an extra class.

W: You had better hustle, the deadline is this Friday!

M: Thanks for the reminder. Oh, by the way, where do you register?

W: At the administration building, in the main conference room.

(TONE)

Q: What is the woman suggesting the man do?

A. Hurry and sign up for classes.

B. Remind his professor to assist him.

C. Talk with his advisor.

D. Make an appointment for a scholarship
   application.

* register〔'rɛdʒɪstɚ〕n. 註冊
  semester〔sə'mɛstɚ〕n. 學期　　yet〔jɛt〕adv. 已經
  appointment〔ə'pɔɪntmənt〕n. 約定；約會
  advisor〔əd'vaɪzɚ〕n. 指導教授（= adviser）
  permission〔pɚ'mɪʃən〕n. 准許
  take〔tek〕v. 修（課）；上（課）
  extra〔'ɛkstrə〕adj. 額外的
  had better 最好　　hustle〔'hʌsḷ〕v. 趕快
  deadline〔'dɛd,laɪn〕n. 最後期限；截止日期
  reminder〔rɪ'maɪndɚ〕n. 提醒
  by the way 順便一提
  administration〔əd,mɪnə'streʃən〕n. 行政
  building〔'bɪldɪŋ〕n. 建築物；大樓
  main〔men〕adj. 主要的
  conference〔'kɑnfərəns〕n. 會議
  suggest〔səg'dʒɛst〕v. 建議
  hurry〔'hɝɪ〕v. 趕快　　sign up 報名參加
  remind〔rɪ'maɪnd〕v. 提醒
  professor〔prə'fɛsɚ〕n. 教授　　assist〔ə'sɪst〕v. 幫助
  scholarship〔'skɑlɚ,ʃɪp〕n. 獎學金
  application〔,æplə'keʃən〕n. 申請

33. (**B**)　M：Wow, look at you! Where did you get so tanned?

W：I went camping with my family over the long weekend.

M：Oh, I'm so jealous. I've never gone camping before. Where did you sleep? What did you do?

W：I slept in a cabin one night and in a tent the other two nights. We went swimming, fishing and, best of all, we went canoeing down a river canyon.

M：You're the luckiest person I know!

(TONE)

Q：How does her friend feel about her weekend adventure?

A. He's depressed because she didn't invite him.

B. He's envious but happy for her.

C. He's doubtful that she's telling the truth.

D. He resents that she is so lucky and he isn't.

* get〔gɛt〕v. 變得　　tanned〔tænd〕adj. 曬成褐色的
camp〔kæmp〕v. 露營　　over〔'ovɚ〕prep. 在…期間
long weekend 長週末【指週六、週日，再加上星期五或星期一】
jealous〔'dʒɛləs〕adj. 嫉妒的　　cabin〔'kæbɪn〕n. 小木屋
tent〔tɛnt〕n. 帳篷　　canoe〔kə'nu〕v. 划獨木舟
down〔daʊn〕prep. 沿著；順著…下來
canyon〔'kænjən〕n. 峽谷　　lucky〔'lʌkɪ〕adj. 幸運的
adventure〔əd'vɛntʃɚ〕n. 冒險活動
depressed〔dɪ'prɛst〕adj. 沮喪的
invite〔ɪn'vaɪt〕v. 邀請
envious〔'ɛnvɪəs〕adj. 嫉妒的；羨慕的
doubtful〔'daʊtfəl〕adj. 懷疑的　　resent〔rɪ'zɛnt〕v. 怨恨

34. (**A**) W: Should I apply for the scholarship? I sure could use the financial assistance.

M: Of course you should. You must! You're very qualified.

W: But there are hundreds of applicants, I don't stand a chance.

M: Just fill out an application. You have to participate to win. You know the old saying, you have to be in it to win it.

(TONE)

Q : What is the man encouraging the woman to do?

A. To try for the scholarship opportunity.

B. To apply for the employment opportunity.

C. To pay the application fee.

D. To train diligently and be confident.

* apply〔ə'plaɪ〕v. 申請＜for＞

scholarship〔'skɑləˌʃɪp〕n. 獎學金

could use 需要　　financial〔fə'nænʃəl〕adj. 財務的

assistance〔ə'sɪstəns〕n. 幫助；援助

qualified〔'kwɑləˌfaɪd〕adj. 有資格的

applicant〔'æpləkənt〕n. 申請人

stand a chance 有希望　　***fill out*** 填寫

application〔ˌæplə'keʃən〕n. 申請書

participate〔pɑr'tɪsəˌpet〕v. 參與

saying〔'se·ɪŋ〕n. 諺語　　encourage〔ɪn'kɝɪdʒ〕v. 鼓勵

try for 爭取　　opportunity〔ˌɑpɚ'tjunətɪ〕n. 機會

employment〔ɪn'plɔɪmənt〕n. 工作

fee〔fi〕n. 費用　　diligently〔'dɪlədʒəntlɪ〕adv. 勤勉地

35. (**D**)　M : Do you like rock music?

W : It depends on what kind.　I like classic rock and country rock.

M : What do you think of hard rock?

W : It's too loud and wild.　I don't care for it at all.

M : That's too bad because I have free tickets to a hard rock concert tonight.　The Crazy Monsters are playing.

W : Hey, I've changed my mind.　Hard rock is OK, too.

(TONE)

Q : How does the woman feel about rock music?

A. She's crazy about rock and roll music.

B. She thinks it's too loud and wild.

C. She likes hard rock and dislikes country rock.

D. She likes some kinds and dislikes other kinds.

* rock〔rɑk〕adj. 搖滾樂的　n. 搖滾樂

rock music 搖滾樂　　**depend on** 視…而定

classic〔'klæsɪk〕adj. 古典的；傳統的

country〔'kʌntrɪ〕adj. 鄉村音樂的　　**hard rock** 重搖滾

loud〔laʊd〕adj. 吵雜的　　wild〔waɪld〕adj. 瘋狂的

care for 喜歡　　**not…at all** 一點也不…

concert〔'kɑnsɝt〕n. 音樂會

crazy〔'krezɪ〕adj. 瘋狂的　　monster〔'mɑnstɚ〕n. 怪物

change one's **mind** 改變主意

be crazy about 很喜歡；很迷戀

rock and roll〔'rɑkən'rol〕n. 搖滾樂（ = **rock'n'roll** ）

36. (**C**) W：What a terrible year we've had for world weather patterns.

M：You're telling me. The many hurricanes and tornados have been scary.

W：So many disasters and so much destruction make me wonder.

M：Do you think God's unhappy or has the devil taken over heaven?

W：Don't start talking about religion with me.

(TONE)

Q：What is the woman concerned about?

A. That world religions are too powerful.

B. That a major earthquake is predicted soon.

C. Why there are so many weather related tragedies.

D. Why disasters are depressing everyone so much.

* terrible 〔'tɛrəbḷ〕 *adj.* 可怕的；糟糕的

for 〔fɔr〕 *prep.* 由於　　pattern 〔'pætən〕 *n.* 型態

You're telling me. 還用你說；我早就知道了。

hurricane 〔'hɜɪˌken〕 *n.* 颶風

tornado 〔tɔr'nedo〕 *n.* 龍捲風

scary 〔'skɛrɪ〕 *adj.* 嚇人的　　disaster 〔dɪz'æstə〕 *n.* 災害

destruction 〔dɪ'strʌkʃən〕 *n.* 破壞

wonder 〔'wʌndə〕 *v.* 感到懷疑　　devil 〔'dɛvḷ〕 *n.* 魔鬼

take over 接管　　heaven 〔'hɛvən〕 *n.* 天堂

religion 〔rɪ'lɪdʒən〕 *n.* 宗教　　***be concerned about*** 擔心

major 〔'medʒə〕 *adj.* 重大的　　predict 〔prɪ'dɪkt〕 *v.* 預測

related 〔rɪ'letɪd〕 *adj.* 有關的

tragedy 〔'trædʒədɪ〕 *n.* 不幸事件

depress 〔dɪ'prɛs〕 *v.* 使沮喪

37. (**B**)　M：Excuse me, do you have change for three dollars?

　　　　　W：Sorry, I'm all out of quarters. But, there's a coin machine over there on the corner.

　　　　　M：Thanks. It's my first time here. I forgot my detergent.

　　　　　W：I've got some liquid detergent. Want to borrow some?

　　　　　M：That's a kind offer but the powder cleans my blue jeans so much better.

　　　　　(TONE)

　　　　　Q：Where is this conversation being held?

　　　　　A.　At a video arcade.

　　　　　B.　At a coin-operated laundromat.

　　　　　C.　At a coin-operated car wash.

　　　　　D.　At a supermarket check-out counter.

＊ change〔tʃendʒ〕 n. 零錢　***be out of*** 缺乏；沒有

quarter〔'kwɔrtɚ〕 n. 二角五分的硬幣

coin machine 自動販賣機（＝*slot machine*）

over there 在那裡　　corner〔'kɔrnɚ〕 n. 轉角

detergent〔dɪ'tɝdʒənt〕 n. 清潔劑；洗衣粉

liquid〔'lɪkwɪd〕 adj. 液狀的　　borrow〔'baro〕 v. 借（入）

offer〔'ɔfɚ〕 n. 給予；提供　　powder〔'paudɚ〕 n. 粉末

jeans〔dʒinz〕 n. pl. 牛仔褲　　hold〔hold〕 v. 舉行；進行

video arcade 電玩遊樂中心

coin-operated〔'kɔɪn,ɑpɚ,retɪd〕 adj. 投幣式的

laundromat〔'lɔndrə,mæt〕 n. 自助洗衣店

car wash 洗車場；洗車

check-out〔'tʃɛk,aut〕 n. 結帳　　counter〔'kauntɚ〕 n. 櫃台

38. (**B**) W: Did you hear about the young student who committed suicide?

M: Yes, I did. What a terrible tragedy!

W: It makes me furious that school pressure is so intense.

M: That's a huge problem our society has to deal with.

(TONE)

Q: What does the man say we must do?

A. Find a solution to our medical problems.

B. Change the stressful educational environment.

C. Eliminate the testing system.

D. Change the textbook content.

* ***hear about*** 聽說　　***commit suicide*** 自殺
   furious〔'fjʊrɪəs〕*adj.* 狂怒的　　pressure〔'prɛʃɚ〕*n.* 壓力
   intense〔ɪn'tɛns〕*adj.* 強烈的；極度的
   huge〔hjudʒ〕*adj.* 巨大的
   society〔sə'saɪətɪ〕*n.* 社會　　***deal with*** 處理
   solution〔sə'luʃən〕*n.* 解決之道
   medical〔'mɛdɪkl̩〕*adj.* 醫療的　　change〔tʃendʒ〕*v.* 改變
   stressful〔'strɛsfəl〕*adj.* 壓力大的
   educational〔,ɛdʒʊ'keʃənl̩〕*adj.* 教育的
   environment〔ɪn'vaɪrənmənt〕*n.* 環境
   eliminate〔ɪ'lɪmə,net〕*v.* 廢除；除去
   testing〔'tɛstɪŋ〕*adj.* 試驗的；非常困難的
   system〔'sɪstəm〕*n.* 制度
   textbook〔'tɛkst,bʊk〕*n.* 教科書；課本
   content〔'kɑntɛnt〕*n.* 內容

39.（ **D** ）　M：Did you hear of the latest government scandal?

W：What is it this time?　Fill me in.

M：One minister was arrested for illegal gambling.

W：What did he specifically do?

M：He paid some gangsters to influence the outcome of a baseball game.

W：Unbelievable!　What a criminal!

(TONE)

Q：How does the woman feel about the crime?

A.　She can't believe that baseball players would do that.

B.　She thinks it is amusing and humorous.

C.　She thinks that gambling is a horrible vice.

D.　She is extremely upset.

* **hear of** 聽說　　latest〔'letɪst〕*adj.* 最近的；最新的

scandal〔'skændḷ〕*n.* 醜聞　　**fill** *sb.* **in** 對某人詳細說明

minister〔'mɪnɪstɚ〕*n.* 部長

arrest〔ə'rɛst〕*v.* 逮捕　　illegal〔ɪ'ligḷ〕*adj.* 違法的

gambling〔'gæmblɪŋ〕*n.* 賭博

specifically〔spɪ'sɪfɪkḷɪ〕*adv.* 明確地；具體地

gangster〔'gæŋstɚ〕*n.* 歹徒；流氓

outcome〔'aʊt,kʌm〕*n.* 結果

unbelievable〔ˌʌnbə'livəbḷ〕*adj.* 令人難以置信的

criminal〔'krɪmənḷ〕*n.* 犯罪者；罪犯

crime〔kraɪm〕*n.* 罪；犯罪　　player〔'pleɚ〕*n.* 選手

amusing〔ə'mjuzɪŋ〕*adj.* 有趣的

humorous〔'hjumərəs〕*adj.* 滑稽的；好笑的

horrible〔'hɔrəbḷ〕*adj.* 可怕的　　vice〔vaɪs〕*n.* 惡習

extremely〔ɪk'strimlɪ〕*adv.* 非常

40. (**C**) W：You look ridiculous in that costume. Where are you going?

M：I'm on my way to drama club tryouts in the gym.

W：You look like a clown on your way to the circus.

M：I'm a cowboy, not a clown. You need glasses. Are you nearsighted?

W：Since when do cowboys have red cheeks?

M：Our teacher said we should be creative and wear make-up.

W：Good luck, Mr. Hilarious Cowboy.

(TONE)

Q：Where is the student going?

A. He's going to a costume party at school.

B. He's going to the circus after school.

C. He's going to the school gymnasium.

D. He's going to drama class in the school theater.

* ridiculous〔rɪ'dɪkjələs〕*adj.* 可笑的
costume〔'kɑstjum〕*n.* 服裝
on one's way to~ 在某人去~的途中
tryout〔'traɪ,aut〕*n.* 選拔賽；預演
gym〔dʒɪm〕*n.* 體育館　　clown〔klaun〕*n.* 小丑
circus〔'sɝkəs〕*n.* 馬戲團　　cowboy〔'kau,bɔɪ〕*n.* 牛仔
nearsighted〔'nɪr'saɪtɪd〕*adj.* 近視的
cheek〔tʃik〕*n.* 臉頰　　creative〔krɪ'etɪv〕*adj.* 有創意的
wear〔wɛr〕*v.* 上（妝）　　make-up〔'mek,ʌp〕*n.* 化妝
hilarious〔hə'lɛrɪəs〕*adj.* 極可笑的
costume party 化妝舞會
gymnasium〔dʒɪm'nezɪəm〕*n.* 體育館（ = *gym* ）
theater〔'θiətɚ〕*n.* 劇場；階梯式教室

41. (**A**) M : I'm ready to give up! These equations are too
difficult.

W : Hang in there, don't quit. Just apply the formulas.

M : I'm trying but my answers are wrong every time.

W : Try calculating with a calculator. Here, borrow
mine.

M : Thanks. I should hire you to tutor me.

(TONE)

Q : What subjects might they be studying?

A. Mathematics and natural science.

B. History and geography.

C. Sociology and political science.

D. Chinese and English.

* ***give up*** 放棄   equation〔ɪˈkweʃən〕*n.* 方程式
hang in there 堅持下去   quit〔kwɪt〕*v.* 放棄
apply〔əˈplaɪ〕*v.* 應用   formula〔ˈfɔrmjələ〕*n.* 公式
calculate〔ˈkælkjəˌlet〕*v.* 計算
calculator〔ˈkælkjəˌletɚ〕*n.* 計算機
borrow〔ˈbɑro〕*v.* 借（入）   hire〔haɪr〕*v.* 雇用
tutor〔ˈtutɚ〕*v.* 擔任家教來教…
subject〔ˈsʌbdʒɪkt〕*n.* 科目
mathematics〔ˌmæθəˈmætɪks〕*n.* 數學
natural〔ˈnætʃərəl〕*adj.* 自然的
science〔ˈsaɪəns〕*n.* 科學   history〔ˈhɪstrɪ〕*n.* 歷史
geography〔dʒiˈɑgrəfɪ〕*n.* 地理學
sociology〔ˌsoʃɪˈɑlədʒɪ〕*n.* 社會學
political〔pəˈlɪtɪkḷ〕*adj.* 政治的
political science 政治學

42. (**C**) W: My neighbors are so noisy. They're always arguing loudly and singing KTV tunes late into the night.

M: Have you confronted them about it?

W: I'm too embarrassed and afraid.

M: Next time, you should call the police.

W: That's useless. My neighbor is a police officer.

(TONE)

Q: What is not true about the woman's situation?

A. Her neighbor is a law enforcement officer.

B. She has neighbors who aren't considerate.

C. She has reported her neighbor to the police.

D. Her neighbors are a burden.

* neighbor (ˈnebɚ) n. 鄰居　　noisy (ˈnɔɪzɪ) adj. 吵雜的

argue (ˈɑrgju) v. 談論；爭論

loudly (ˈlaʊdlɪ) adv. 大聲地

tune (tjun) n. 歌曲　　*late into the night* 到深夜

confront (kənˈfrʌnt) v. 勇敢地面對

embarrassed (ɪmˈbærəst) adj. 尷尬的

afraid (əˈfred) adj. 害怕的　　*next time* 下一次

police (pəˈlis) n. 警察　　*the police* 警方

useless (ˈjuslɪs) adj. 無效的　　*police officer* 警官

situation (ˌsɪtʃʊˈeʃən) n. 情況　　law (lɔ) n. 法律

enforcement (ɪnˈfɔrsmənt) n. 執行

officer (ˈɔfəsɚ) n. 警官

considerate (kənˈsɪdərɪt) adj. 體貼的

report (rɪˈport) v. 告發；控告

burden (ˈbɝdn̩) n. 負擔；累贅

43. (**A**)　M：What is Peter majoring in at college?

　　　　　W：He's got a dual major.　He's studying both political science and communications.

　　　　　M：Sounds challenging.　What's he planning on doing after graduation?

　　　　　W：He wants to enter politics.　He hopes to be a politician.

　　　　　M：Oh no!　Did you try to talk him out of it?

　　　　　(TONE)

　　　　　Q：How does the woman feel about Peter's major?

　　　　　A. The information is not given.
　　　　　B. She's very supportive of Peter's choice.
　　　　　C. She strongly opposes his choice.
　　　　　D. She will try to persuade him to change it.

* major〔'medʒɚ〕 v. n. 主修　　college〔'kɑlɪdʒ〕 n. 大學
dual〔'duəl〕 adj. 雙重的　　*political science* 政治學
communications〔kə,mjunə'keʃənz〕 n. 傳播學
sound〔saʊnd〕 v. 聽起來
challenging〔'tʃælɪndʒɪŋ〕 adj. 挑戰性的；刺激的
plan〔plæn〕 v. 計畫；打算
graduation〔,grædʒʊ'eʃən〕 n. 畢業
politics〔'pɑlə,tɪks〕 n. 政治　　*enter politics* 進入政界
politician〔,pɑlə'tɪʃən〕 n. 政治家
talk sb. *out of* 說服某人不去做（某事）
information〔,ɪnfɚ'meʃən〕 n. 資訊
supportive〔sə'portɪv〕 adj. 支持的
choice〔tʃɔɪs〕 n. 選擇　　strongly〔'strɔŋlɪ〕 adv. 強烈的
oppose〔ə'poz〕 v. 反對　　persuade〔pɚ'swed〕 v. 說服

44. (**D**)　W: You're so attractive. I can't understand why you are not married yet.

M: I'm not ready to tie the knot. I don't want to settle down.

W: That's a shame because married life is wonderful. You should try it.

M: I'm waiting for someone like you to come along.

W: You can't wait. You must find your true love.

"A faint heart never won a fair lady."

(TONE)

Q : What is the woman encouraging the man to do?

A. Hurry up and get engaged.

B. Be more mature and give up the playboy lifestyle.

C. Not to wait for her because she's already married.

D. Aggressively look for a perfect life companion.

* attractive〔ə'træktɪv〕*adj.* 有吸引力的
married〔'mærɪd〕*adj.* 已婚的；結婚的
yet〔jɛt〕*adv.* 尚（未）　　ready〔'rɛdɪ〕*adj.* 準備好的
tie the knot 結婚　　*settle down* 成家；安定下來
shame〔ʃem〕*n.* 可惜的事　　*come along* 出現
faint〔fent〕*n.* 膽小的　　heart〔hɑrt〕*n.* 心
win〔wɪn〕*v.* 贏得　　fair〔fɛr〕*adj.* 美麗的
A faint heart never won a fair lady. 【諺】懦夫難得美人心。
hurry up 趕快　　engaged〔ɪn'gedʒd〕*adj.* 訂婚的
mature〔mə'tʃʊr〕*adj.* 成熟的　　*give up* 放棄
playboy〔'ple,bɔɪ〕*n.* 花花公子
lifestyle〔'laɪf,staɪl〕*n.* 生活方式
aggressively〔ə'grɛsɪvlɪ〕*adv.* 積極地
companion〔kəm'pænjən〕*n.* 同伴；伴侶

45. (**B**)　M：How was your winter break?

W：Busy, extremely busy.

M：What did you do?

W：I attended an intensive English language course at a cram school. We studied for ten hours a day, six days a week.

M：Wow! That's a lot of studying. What was the cost? Was it worth it?

W：For three weeks, it was nine thousand dollars. That included meals, all the materials and a one-year English magazine subscription. It was definitely a good experience. I learned a lot.

(TONE)

Q：How long was the woman's English course?

A. Just about two months.

B. A little bit less than one month.

C. Forty weeks.

D. Seven days a week for three weeks.

* break〔brek〕*n.* 假期　　attend〔ə'tɛnd〕*v.* 參加
intensive〔ɪn'tɛnsɪv〕*adj.* 密集的
language〔'læŋgwɪdʒ〕*n.* 語言　　course〔kors〕*n.* 課程
cram school 補習班　　cost〔kɔst〕*n.* 費用
worth〔wɝθ〕*adj.* 值得…的　　include〔ɪn'klud〕*v.* 包含
meal〔mil〕*n.* 一餐　　material〔mə'tɪrɪəl〕*n.* 資料
subscription〔səb'skrɪpʃən〕*n.* 訂閱；訂閱費
definitely〔'dɛfənɪtlɪ〕*adv.* 確實地
experience〔ɪk'spɪrɪəns〕*n.* 經歷
bit〔bɪt〕*n.* 一點點　　**less than** 不到

English Listening Comprehension Test
Test Book No. 8

This listening comprehension test will test your ability to understand spoken English. In this test, each conversation, statement and question will be spoken JUST ONE TIME. They will not be written out for you. There are three parts to this test. Special instructions will be given to you at the beginning of each part.

Part A

In Part A, you will see several pictures in your test book. For each picture, you will be asked 1 to 3 questions. For each question, you will hear four possible answers. Choose the best answer according to what you see in the picture.

Example:

<u>You will see</u>:

<u>You will hear</u>: What is this?
  A. This is a table.
  B. This is a chair.
  C. This is a watch.
  D. This is a doll.

The best answer to the question "What is this?" is B: "This is a chair." Therefore, you should choose answer B.

A. <u>Questions 1-2</u>

B. <u>Questions 3-4</u>

C. <u>Questions 5-6</u>

D. <u>Questions 7-8</u>

E. <u>Questions 9-10</u>

F. <u>Questions 11-12</u>

G. <u>Questions 13-14</u>

H. <u>Question 15</u>

Part B

In Part B, you will hear 15 questions. After you hear a question, read the four possible answers in your test book and decide which one is the best answer to the question you have heard.

Example:

You will hear: What does your father do?

You will read: A. He's 50 years old.
B. He's a teacher.
C. He's hungry.
D. He's in Los Angeles.

The best answer to the question "What does your father do?" is B: "He's a teacher." Therefore, you should choose answer B.

Please go to the next page. ⇨

16. A. Sorry, I don't know how.
    B. I'll put a piece aside for you.
    C. It was only NT$100.
    D. Yes, please.

17. A. That's because she studies hard.
    B. I know. She writes for the school newspaper.
    C. I wish she would speak up.
    D. Yes. She plays three sports.

18. A. It's not my company.
    B. I'd love to own a store, too.
    C. OK. Let's go now.
    D. Yesterday afternoon.

19. A. He just passed his driver's test.
    B. He was stopped for speeding last week.
    C. Yes, he forgave him for taking it.
    D. He forgot that he had used it.

20. A. No, it's over there.
    B. Yes, I made it myself.
    C. Yes. It was dirty.
    D. No, I don't need one.

21. A. I'll turn it off.
    B. It's because it's full tonight.
    C. Yeah, a new bulb really made a difference.
    D. I know. You can barely see it.

22. A. It was on sale.
    B. Yes, it's very painful.
    C. Thank you. It's my
       favorite dress.
    D. I have a big test in one
       hour.

23. A. Nearly half of them are
       sick.
    B. They have a form of
       the flu.
    C. A number of them have
       recovered.
    D. One hundred and thirty
       two.

24. A. Congratulations.
    B. No. It's just a rumor.
    C. Yes, she's been
       married for five years.
    D. No, that's right.

25. A. No, but I saw it.
    B. Yes, it's behind that
       rock.
    C. No, we couldn't
       hear each other.
    D. Yes, I heard myself
       again and again.

26. A. She wishes it were
       hers.
    B. She's very happy
       for you.
    C. She has one just
       like it.
    D. Did you thank her
       for it?

27. A. No, it's not ready to be picked yet.
　　B. Yes.　Here's a knife.
　　C. Of course you have to pay for it.
　　D. Yes, the peel is edible.

28. A. I don't think I can climb it.
　　B. I like it very much.
　　C. It's 3,000 meters.
　　D. It's near Springfield.

29. A. He thinks I should study medicine.
　　B. I advise you to go to the doctor.
　　C. I admire him very much.
　　D. It will cost NT$500 to run the ad in the newspaper.

30. A. No.　He has a negative attitude.
　　B. No, we're a lot alike.
　　C. Yes.　He's difficult to get along with.
　　D. Of course he is.

Part C

In Part C, you will hear 15 conversations between a man and a woman. After each conversation, you will hear a question about the conversation. After you hear the question, read the four possible answers in your test book and choose the best answer to the question you have heard.

Example:

<u>You will hear</u>: (Man)   How do you go to school every day?

    (Woman) Usually by bus. Sometimes by taxi.

    (Tone)

    Question: How does the woman go to school?

<u>You will read</u>: A. She always goes to school on foot.
B. She usually rides a bike.
C. She takes either a bus or a taxi.
D. She usually goes to school by bus, never by taxi.

The best answer to the question "How does the woman go to school?" is C: "She takes either a bus or a taxi." Therefore, you should choose answer C.

Please go to the next page. ⇨

31. A. She is about to be
cheated by a con artist.
B. She won a billion
dollars.
C. She won a national
essay competition.
D. She won a million free
frequent flyer miles.

32. A. Grandmother's
birthday.
B. Family Anniversary
Day.
C. The Fourth of July.
D. Thanksgiving.

33. A. Soccer.
B. Track and field.
C. Basketball.
D. Baseball.

34. A. He thinks her creation
is excellent.
B. He's not very
interested or excited
about it.
C. He feels that she has
great talent.
D. He thinks she's too
serious about the
dimensions.

35. A. Lend five thousand
dollars to Maggie.
B. Buy a new cell phone
for his mother.
C. Borrow five thousand
dollars from Maggie.
D. Give the cell phone to
Maggie.

36. A. After they finish the
       safety tests.
    B. In exactly one more
       year.
    C. After environmental
       impact studies are
       completed.
    D. No one is sure yet.

37. A. She misunderstood
       the teacher.
    B. She is often very
       absent-minded.
    C. She was daydreaming
       when the test date
       was announced.
    D. Not enough
       information given.

38. A. Being physically
       challenged forces the
       boy to work harder.
    B. Being physically
       challenged doesn't
       stop the boy from
       doing anything.
    C. The new student is
       a great athlete.
    D. The new student
       likes to play football.

39. A. She is a liar.
    B. She doesn't think
       about others.
    C. She doesn't respect him.
    D. She broke her promise
       to their parents.

40. A. They took away David's dog.
    B. The police closed down the pet shop.
    C. The animals were unhealthy and sick.
    D. David has to wait one month to get his puppy.

41. A. Become a vegetarian and go on a diet.
    B. Eat healthier foods.
    C. See a skin doctor.
    D. Take some medication for his rash.

42. A. To cover her head with mosquito oil.
    B. To buy some mosquito repellent from a pharmacy.
    C. To burn some incense to eliminate the mosquitoes.
    D. To cover her bed with a net.

43. A. At a hotel front desk.
    B. At a check-out counter.
    C. At an information desk.
    D. At a conference registration desk.

44. A. She opens a window and closes a door.
    B. She forgets about a meal in the oven.
    C. She notices smoke pouring from the oven.
    D. She notices a horrible smell.

45. A. A very old motorcycle.
    B. An antique bicycle.
    C. An old automobile.
    D. The man's grandmother.

Listening Test 8 詳解

Part A

For questions number 1 and 2, please look at picture A.

1. (**C**) Question number 1: What does the youngest girl like?

   A. She looks very cute.

   B. She doesn't like to blow bubbles.

   C. Chasing bubbles.

   D. Because there are bubbles.

   * cute〔kjut〕adj. 可愛的　　blow〔blo〕v. 吹
     bubble〔'bʌbḷ〕n. 泡泡
     blow bobbles 吹出肥皂泡泡
     chase〔tʃes〕v. 追趕

2. (**B**) Question number 2: Who is providing the fun?

   A. Yes, it is fun.

   B. The tall girl.

   C. They are all having fun.

   D. Yes, she thinks it's funny.

   * provide〔prə'vaɪd〕v. 提供
     fun〔fʌn〕n. 樂趣　adj. 好玩的；有趣的
     have fun 玩得愉快
     funny〔'fʌnɪ〕adj. 有趣的

For questions number 3 and 4, please look at picture B.

3.(**D**) Question number 3: Why do you think the girl is punching him?

    A. She hit him first.   B. In order to break it.

    C. She is hitting a boy.   D. He broke her vase.

    * punch〔 pʌntʃ 〕v. 用拳頭打；毆打   hit〔 hɪt 〕v. 打

    in order to 為了   break〔 brek 〕v. 打破

    vase〔 ves 〕n. 花瓶

4.(**A**) Question number 4: What will probably happen next?

    A. She might scold him.

    B. It is his fault.

    C. He said he was sorry.

    D. He will escape with her.

    * probably〔 ˋprɑbəblɪ 〕adv. 可能

    happen〔 ˋhæpən 〕v. 發生   next〔 nɛkst 〕adv. 接下來

    scold〔 skold 〕v. 責罵   fault〔 fɔlt 〕n. 過錯

    escape〔 əˋskep 〕v. 逃走

For questions number 5 and 6, please look at picture C.

5.(**C**) Question number 5: How do they feel?

    A. It is windy.   B. A tornado is coming.

    C. Terrified.   D. It feels cold.

    * windy〔 ˋwɪndɪ 〕adj. 多風的

    tornado〔 tɔrˋnedo 〕n. 龍捲風

    terrified〔 ˋtɛrəˏfaɪd 〕adj. 害怕的

6. (**B**) Question number 6: Where is the danger?

    A. It's a tornado.   B. Near the house.

    C. Yes, it is.   D. What should we do?

    * danger〔'dendʒə〕*n.* 危險

For questions number 7 and 8, please look at picture D.

7. (**C**) Question number 7: Where do you think the kids were playing baseball?

    A. Out of the door.

    B. They will play outside now.

    C. Indoors.

    D. The ball broke the vase.

    * kid〔kɪd〕*n.* 小孩   ***out of ~*** 在~外面
    indoors〔'ɪn'dorz〕*adv.* 在室內

8. (**B**) Question number 8: What is the mother's reaction to this incident?

    A. This is a disaster.

    B. She is furious.

    C. It could be fatal.

    D. The kids are fleeing.

    * reaction〔rɪ'ækʃən〕*n.* 反應
    incident〔'ɪnsədənt〕*n.* 事件
    disaster〔dɪz'æstə〕*n.* 災難
    furious〔'fjʊrɪəs〕*adj.* 狂怒的
    fatal〔'fetl̩〕*adj.* 致命的   flee〔fli〕*v.* 逃走

For questions number 9 and 10, please look at picture E.

9. (**C**) Question number 9: What might the boy be thinking to himself?

    A. She must be drowning.

    B. It's a real emergency.

    C. The water is shallow.　　D. He cannot swim.

    * drown〔draʊn〕v. 淹死　　real〔'riəl〕adj. 眞正的
      emergency〔ɪ'mɝdʒənsɪ〕n. 緊急情況
      shallow〔'ʃælo〕adj. 淺的　　swim〔swɪm〕v. 游泳

10. (**D**) Question number 10: What is a possible reason for the girl's actions?

    A. This is the Pacific Ocean.

    B. She is attacking a shark.

    C. She is having a nightmare.

    D. She wants him to jump in.

    * *Pacific Ocean* 太平洋　　attack〔ə'tæk〕v. 攻擊
      shark〔ʃɑrk〕n. 鯊魚　　nightmare〔'naɪt,mɛr〕n. 惡夢

For questions number 11 and 12, please look at picture F.

11. (**A**) Question number 11: What are these three kids doing?

    A. They are imagining things.

    B. It's a Halloween party.

    C. They are sightseeing.　　D. They are wishful.

    * imagine〔ɪ'mædʒɪn〕v. 想像
      Halloween〔,hælo'in〕n. 萬聖節前夕
      sightsee〔'saɪt,si〕v. 遊覽；觀光
      wishful〔'wɪʃfəl〕adj. 渴望的

12. (**D**) Question number 12: Which child thinks the shooting star is an angel?

    A. All three are holy.   B. The girl on the left.

    C. Aliens are from outer space.

    D. The boy in the middle.

    * ***shooting star*** 流星   angel〔'endʒəl〕*n.* 天使

    holy〔'holɪ〕*adj.* 神聖的   left〔lɛft〕*n.* 左邊

    alien〔'eljən〕*n.* 外星人   ***outer space*** 外太空

    middle〔'mɪdḷ〕*n.* 中間

For questions number 13 and 14, please look at picture G.

13. (**B**) Question number 13: What is this a picture of?

    A. Three students are taking an examination.

    B. The different reactions of three students.

    C. A scholarship application.

    D. Three drawings from Math class.

    * take〔tek〕*v.* 參加

    examination〔ɪg,zæmə'neʃən〕*n.* 考試

    different〔'dɪfərənt〕*adj.* 不同的

    scholarship〔'skɑlɚˏʃɪp〕*n.* 獎學金

    application〔ˏæplə'keʃən〕*n.* 申請

    drawing〔'drɔ·ɪŋ〕*n.* 圖畫   math〔mæθ〕*n.* 數學

14. (**A**) Question number 14: How does the boy seem to feel?

    A. Fortunate and relieved.

    B. Depressed and disappointed.

    C. Excited and jealous.

    D. Satisfied and nervous.

* seem〔sim〕v. 似乎　　fortunate〔'fɔrtʃənɪt〕adj. 幸運的
relieved〔rɪ'livd〕adj. 放心的；鬆了一口氣的
depressed〔dɪ'prɛst〕adj. 沮喪的
disappointed〔,dɪsə'pɔɪntɪd〕adj. 失望的
excited〔ɪk'saɪtɪd〕adj. 興奮的
jealous〔'dʒɛləs〕adj. 嫉妒的
satisfied〔'sætɪs,faɪd〕adj. 滿意的
nervous〔'nɝvəs〕adj. 緊張的

For question number 15, please look at picture H.

15. (**C**) Question number 15: How many adults are in this picture?

A. Three are present.

B. There are five altogether.

C. There are two grown-ups.

D. Only two kids are there.

* adult〔ə'dʌlt,'ædʌlt〕n. 大人
present〔'prɛzn̩t〕adj. 在場的；出席的
altogether〔,ɔltə'gɛðɚ〕adv. 總共
grown-up〔'gron,ʌp〕n. 大人

Part B

16. (**B**) Would you save me some cake?

A. Sorry, I don't know how.

B. I'll put a piece aside for you.

C. It was only NT$100.　　D. Yes, please.

* save〔sev〕v. 留給　　piece〔pis〕n. 片；塊
put aside 保留

17. (**D**) Joan is quite an athlete.

    A. That's because she studies hard.

    B. I know. She writes for the school newspaper.

    C. I wish she would speak up.

    D. Yes. She plays three sports.

    * ***quite a*** 了不起的   athlete〔'æθlɪt〕*n.* 運動員；運動選手

    speak up 大聲說   play〔ple〕*v.* 參加（競賽）；打（球）

    sport〔sport〕*n.* 運動；競賽

18. (**C**) I'd like to accompany you when you go to the store.

    A. It's not my company.

    B. I'd love to own a store, too.

    C. OK. Let's go now.   D. Yesterday afternoon.

    * accompany〔ə'kʌmpənɪ〕*v.* 陪伴   own〔on〕*v.* 擁有

19. (**B**) Why did Rick's father forbid him to use the car?

    A. He just passed his driver's test.

    B. He was stopped for speeding last week.

    C. Yes, he forgave him for taking it.

    D. He forgot that he had used it.

    * forbid〔fɚ'bɪd〕*v.* 禁止   pass〔pæs〕*v.* 通過

    speeding〔'spidɪŋ〕*n.* 超速   forgive〔fɚ'gɪv〕*v.* 原諒

20. (**B**) Did you knit this scarf?

    A. No, it's over there.   B. Yes, I made it myself.

    C. Yes. It was dirty.   D. No, I don't need one.

    * knit〔nɪt〕*v.* 編織   scarf〔skɑrf〕*n.* 圍巾

    over there 在那裡   dirty〔'dɝtɪ〕*adj.* 髒的

21. (**B**)　I can't believe how bright the moonlight is!

    A.　I'll turn it off.

    B.　It's because it's full tonight.

    C.　Yeah, a new bulb really made a difference.

    D.　I know. You can barely see it.

> * bright〔braɪt〕*adj.* 明亮的
> moonlight〔'mun͵laɪt〕*n.* 月光　　***turn off*** 關掉
> full〔fʊl〕*adj.* 充滿的；滿月的
> yeah〔jɛ〕*adv.* 是的 (= *yes*)　　bulb〔bʌlb〕*n.* 電燈泡
> difference〔'dɪfərəns〕*n.* 不同；差別
> ***make a difference*** 有差別　　barely〔'bɛrlɪ〕*adv.* 幾乎不

22. (**D**)　Why are you in such a panic?

    A.　It was on sale.　　B.　Yes, it's very painful.

    C.　Thank you. It's my favorite dress.

    D.　I have a big test in one hour.

> * panic〔'pænɪk〕*n.* 恐慌　　***on sale*** 特價中；拍賣中
> painful〔'penfəl〕*adj.* 痛的　　dress〔drɛs〕*n.* 服裝
> big〔bɪg〕*adj.* 重要的

23. (**D**)　What is the precise number of students with the illness?

    A.　Nearly half of them are sick.

    B.　They have a form of the flu.

    C.　A number of them have recovered.

    D.　One hundred and thirty two.

> * precise〔prɪ'saɪs〕*adj.* 精確的
> number〔'nʌmbɚ〕*n.* 人數　　illness〔'ɪlnɪs〕*n.* 疾病
> nearly〔'nɪrlɪ〕*adv.* 將近　　flu〔flu〕*n.* 流行性感冒
> ***a number of*** 許多　　recover〔rɪ'kʌvɚ〕*v.* 康復

24. (**B**) Is it true that Josie is getting married?

    A. Congratulations.

    B. No. It's just a rumor.

    C. Yes, she's been married for five years.

    D. No, that's right.

    * ***get married*** 結婚
      congratulations (kən͵grætʃə'leʃənz) *n. pl.* 恭喜
      rumor ('rumɚ) *n.* 謠言　　***That's right.*** 沒錯。

25. (**D**) Did you hear your echo in the cave?

    A. No, but I saw it.

    B. Yes, it's behind that rock.

    C. No, we couldn't hear each other.

    D. Yes, I heard myself again and again.

    * echo ('ɛko) *n.* 回音　　cave (kev) *n.* 洞穴
      behind (bɪ'haɪnd) *prep.* 在…後面
      rock (rɑk) *n.* 岩石　　***again and again*** 一再地

26. (**A**) Gail could hardly control her jealousy when she saw my new watch.

    A. She wishes it were hers.

    B. She's very happy for you.

    C. She has one just like it.

    D. Did you thank her for it?

    * hardly ('hɑrdlɪ) *adv.* 幾乎不
      control (kən'trol) *v.* 控制
      jealousy ('dʒɛləsɪ) *n.* 嫉妒　　wish (wɪʃ) *v.* 希望
      like (laɪk) *prep.* 像　　thank (θæŋk) *v.* 感謝

27. (**B**) Do I need to peel this fruit before eating it?

A. No, it's not ready to be picked yet.

B. Yes. Here's a knife.

C. Of course you have to pay for it.

D. Yes, the peel is edible.

* peel〔pil〕v. 剝皮；削皮　n. 果皮

　　ready〔'rɛdɪ〕adj. 準備好的　　pick〔pɪk〕v. 摘；採

　　yet〔jɛt〕adv. 還（沒）　　knife〔naɪf〕n. 刀子

　　of course 當然　　***pay for*** 付…的錢

　　edible〔'ɛdəbḷ〕adj. 可食用的

28. (**C**) What's the altitude of the mountain?

A. I don't think I can climb it.

B. I like it very much.

C. It's 3,000 meters.

D. It's near Springfield.

* altitude〔'æltə‚tjud〕n. 高度

　　mountain〔'maʊntṇ〕n. 山

　　climb〔klaɪm〕v. 登上；攀登

　　meter〔'mitɚ〕n. 公尺

　　Springfield〔'sprɪŋ‚fild〕n. 春田（美國伊利諾州的首府）

29. (**A**) What did your adviser say?

A. He thinks I should study medicine.

B. I advise you to go to the doctor.

C. I admire him very much.

D. It will cost NT$500 to run the ad in the newspaper.

* adviser〔əd'vaɪzə〕*n.* 指導教授（= *advisor*）

medicine〔'mɛdəsn̩〕*n.* 醫學

advise〔əd'vaɪz〕*v.* 勸告；建議

go to the doctor 去看醫生　　admire〔əd'maɪr〕*v.* 欽佩

run〔rʌn〕*v.*（連續）刊登　　ad〔æd〕*n.* 廣告

30. (**A**)　Don't you like Simon?

A. No.　He has a negative attitude.

B. No, we're a lot alike.

C. Yes.　He's difficult to get along with.

D. Of course he is.

* negative〔'nɛgətɪv〕*adj.* 消極的；否定的；負面的

attitude〔'ætə,tjud〕*n.* 態度　　***a lot*** 非常

alike〔ə'laɪk〕*adj.* 相像的

difficult〔'dɪfə,kʌlt〕*adj.* 困難的　　***get along with*** 相處

Part C

31. (**A**)　M：Hello, may I speak to Mary Jones, please?

W：Speaking.　Who is this?

M：My name is Thomas Smith.　I'm calling to notify you that you have won one million dollars in our lottery sweepstakes!　Congratulations!　You're the lucky winner.

W：Are you kidding me?　Is this a joke?　I can't believe it!

M：It's the truth ma'am; you're the lucky winner.　Your name was drawn by our computer.　Now we want to transfer the money into your bank account today. May I have your account number, please?

(TONE)

Q：What is happening to Miss Mary Jones?

A. She is about to be cheated by a con artist.

B. She won a billion dollars.

C. She won a national essay competition.

D. She won a million free frequent flyer miles.

* **_Speaking_**. 【電話用語】我就是。　　call〔kɔl〕v. 打電話
notify〔'notə,faɪ〕v. 通知　　win〔wɪn〕v. 贏得
million〔'mɪljən〕adj. 百萬的　　lottery〔'lɑtərɪ〕n. 抽獎
sweepstakes〔'swip,steks〕n. 彩票；獎券；獨得獎金
congratulations〔kən,grætʃə'leʃənz〕n. pl. 恭喜
winner〔'wɪnɚ〕n. 優勝者；得獎者
kid〔kɪd〕v. 開~玩笑；欺騙　　joke〔dʒok〕n. 玩笑
truth〔truθ〕n. 事實　　ma'am〔mæm〕n. 小姐
draw〔drɔ〕v. 抽中　　computer〔kəm'pjutɚ〕n. 電腦
transfer〔træns'fɝ〕v. 轉（帳）；劃撥
account〔ə'kaʊnt〕n. 帳戶　　happen〔'hæpən〕v. 發生
be about to V. 即將~；正要~　　cheat〔tʃit〕v. 欺騙
con artist 騙子　　billion〔'bɪljən〕adj. 十億的
national〔'næʃn̩〕adj. 全國性的
essay〔'ɛse〕n. 論說文；散文
competition〔,kɑmpə'tɪʃən〕n. 比賽
free〔fri〕adj. 免費的　　frequent〔'frikwənt〕adj. 頻繁的
flyer〔'flaɪɚ〕n. 飛行者　　mile〔maɪl〕n. 哩
frequent flyer miles 飛行哩程數【一種航空公司為經常搭乘飛
　機的乘客，累積飛行距離的方式，當乘客累積到一定的飛行距離
　之後，可以兌換免費的機票，或是選擇機位升等】

32. (**D**) W: Are you excited about going to grandma's for the holiday?

M: Not really. It's a long way to drive and I don't even like to eat turkey.

W: What about the family reunion? All your cousins and relatives will be there. That will be fun.

M: I just saw everybody last month for grandpa's 75th birthday.

(TONE)

Q: What holiday are the speakers talking about?

A. Grandmother's birthday.

B. Family Anniversary Day.

C. The Fourth of July.

D. Thanksgiving.

* excited〔ɪk'saɪtɪd〕*adj.* 興奮的

grandma's *n.*（外）祖母家

not really 事實上沒有

even〔'ivən〕*adv.* 甚至　　turkey〔'tɝkɪ〕*n.* 火雞

What about~? ~如何；~怎樣？

reunion〔ri'junjən〕*n.* 團圓

cousin〔'kʌzn̩〕*n.* 堂（表）兄弟姊妹

relative〔'rɛlətɪv〕*n.* 親戚　　fun〔fʌn〕*adj.* 好玩的

anniversary〔͵ænə'vɝsərɪ〕*adj.* 周年紀念的

the Fourth of July 七月四日；美國獨立紀念日

Thanksgiving〔͵θæŋks'gɪvɪŋ〕*n.* 感恩節

33. (**C**)　M：Who won the game?

W：We did! We won by five points, but it was very close until the last minute. The other team played tough.

M：Did you score any points? Any rebounds, steals or assists?

W：I scored fifteen points; I'm not sure about the other stats.

M：That's so terrific. I'm proud of you. You're quite a player.

(TONE)

Q：What sport or competition did the girl take part in?

A. Soccer.

B. Track and field.

C. Basketball.

D. Baseball.

* win〔wɪn〕*v.* 贏　　game〔gem〕*n.* 比賽
by〔baɪ〕*prep.* 相差　　point〔pɔɪnt〕*n.* 分
close〔klos〕*adj.* 接近的　　team〔tim〕*n.* 隊
tough〔tʌf〕*adv.* 強硬地；粗暴地　　score〔skor〕*v.* 得（分）
rebound〔rɪ'baʊnd〕*n.* 籃板球　　steal〔stil〕*n.* 抄截
assist〔ə'sɪst〕*n.* 助攻
stats〔stæts〕*n. pl.* 統計數字（= *statistics*）
terrific〔tə'rɪfɪk〕*adj.* 很棒的；厲害的
be proud of 以～爲榮　　proud〔praʊd〕*adj.* 光榮的
quite a 了不起的　　competition〔ˌkɑmpə'tɪʃən〕*n.* 比賽
take part in 參加　　soccer〔'sɑkɚ〕*n.* 足球
track and field 田徑

34. (**B**) W: See what I made in art class. Guess what it is.

M: I don't have a clue. Is it a tree stump? A pig in the mud?

W: Don't be ridiculous. It's a cute penguin! See the little nose and its cute flippers.

M: Since when are penguins brown?

(TONE)

Q: How does the man feel about her artwork?

A. He thinks her creation is excellent.

B. He's not very interested or excited about it.

C. He feels that she has great talent.

D. He thinks she's too serious about the dimensions.

＊ art〔ɑrt〕*adj.* 美術的　　guess〔gɛs〕*v.* 猜

clue〔klu〕*n.* 線索

I don't have a clue. 我完全不知道。

stump〔stʌmp〕*n.* 樹椿　　mud〔mʌd〕*n.* 泥巴

ridiculous〔rɪ'dɪkjələs〕*adj.* 可笑的；荒謬的

cute〔kjut〕*adj.* 可愛的　　penguin〔'pɛngwɪn〕*n.* 企鵝

nose〔noz〕*n.* 鼻子　　flippers〔'flɪpəz〕*n. pl.* 鰭狀肢

since〔sɪns〕*prep.* 自從　　brown〔braʊn〕*adj.* 棕色的

creation〔krɪ'eʃən〕*n.* 作品

excellent〔'ɛkslənt〕*adj.* 極好的

interested〔'ɪntrɪstɪd〕*adj.* 感興趣的

great〔gret〕*adj.* 很棒的　　talent〔'tælənt〕*n.* 天賦；才能

serious〔'sɪrɪəs〕*adj.* 認真的

dimensions〔də'mɛnʃənz〕*n. pl.* 大小；重要性

35. (**C**) M : Maggie, can you do me a big favor?

W : It depends on what it is.

M : Can you lend me five thousand dollars for one week?

W : Sorry, I'm broke at the moment. Why do you need it?

M : I lost my brother's cell phone. He's going to kill me.

(TONE)

Q : What does the man want to do?

A. Lend five thousand dollars to Maggie.

B. Buy a new cell phone for his mother.

C. Borrow five thousand dollars from Maggie.

D. Give the cell phone to Maggie.

* ***do sb. a favor*** 幫某人的忙　　***depend on*** 視…而定
  lend〔lɛnd〕*v.* 借（出）
  broke〔brok〕*adj.* 破產的；沒錢的　　***at the moment*** 現在
  lose〔luz〕*v.* 遺失　　***cell phone*** 手機
  kill〔kɪl〕*v.* 殺死　　borrow〔'baro〕*v.* 借（入）

36. (**D**) W : When will the high speed railway be completed?

M : Nobody knows. The completion date keeps being extended. They are already one year behind schedule.

W : Is it true that the train will travel at 300 kilometers per hour? How long will it take to go from Taipei to Kaohsiung?

M : The speed is correct. It can go even faster. The trip from north to south will be less than ninety minutes.

W : That's really amazing, but what happens if there is an earthquake when it's going that fast?

(TONE)

Q：When will the high speed train start running?

A. After they finish the safety tests.

B. In exactly one more year.

C. After environmental impact studies are completed.

D. No one is sure yet.

* speed〔spid〕n. 速度　　railway〔'rel͵we〕n. 鐵路

complete〔kəm'plit〕v. 完成

completion〔kəm'pliʃən〕n. 完成

date〔det〕n. 日期　　keep〔kip〕v. 持續

extend〔ɪk'stɛnd〕v. 把（期限）延長

behind schedule 比預定的進度慢

travel〔'trævḷ〕v. 行進　　kilometer〔'kɪlə͵mitɚ〕n. 公里

per〔pɚ〕prep. 每　　take〔tek〕v. 花費

Kaohsiung〔'gau'ʃjuŋ〕n. 高雄

correct〔kə'rɛkt〕adj. 正確的　　even〔'ivən〕adv. 更加

trip〔trɪp〕n. 路程　　north〔nɔrθ〕n. 北方

south〔sauθ〕n. 南方

amazing〔ə'mezɪŋ〕adj. 令人驚訝的

happen〔'hæpən〕v. 發生

earthquake〔'ɝθ͵kwek〕n. 地震

run〔rʌn〕v. 運作　　safety〔'seftɪ〕adj. 安全的

exactly〔ɪg'zæktlɪ〕adv. 正好

environmental〔ɪn͵vaɪrən'mɛntḷ〕adj. 環境的

impact〔'ɪmpækt〕n. 影響　　studies〔'stʌdɪz〕n. pl. 研究

yet〔jɛt〕adv. 尚（未）

37. (**D**) M : Are you ready for the big test tomorrow? I'm pretty nervous.

W : Tomorrow? Are you kidding? Isn't it next week?

M : I wish. That would be nice. No, tomorrow is the big day.

W : What a nightmare! I totally forgot. I'm going to be burning the midnight oil tonight.

M : Don't stay up all night. Make sure you get some sleep. Being too exhausted won't help you on the exam.

(TONE)

Q : Why did the woman forget about the examination?

A. She misunderstood the teacher.

B. She is often very absent-minded.

C. She was daydreaming when the test date was announced.

D. Not enough information given.

* ready〔'rɛdɪ〕 *adj.* 準備好的   big〔bɪg〕 *adj.* 重要的
pretty〔'prɪtɪ〕 *adv.* 非常   nervous〔'nɝvəs〕 *adj.* 緊張的
kid〔kɪd〕 *v.* 開玩笑   wish〔wɪʃ〕 *v.* 希望；但願
nightmare〔'naɪt,mɛr〕 *n.* 惡夢   totally〔'totḷɪ〕 *adv.* 完全
burn the midnight oil 讀書到深夜   ***stay up*** 熬夜
make sure 一定   ***get some sleep*** 睡一會兒覺
exhausted〔ɪg'zɔstɪd〕 *adj.* 筋疲力盡的
exam〔ɪg'zæm〕 *n.* 考試（= *examination* ）
misunderstand〔,mɪsʌndɚ'stænd〕 *v.* 誤會
absent-minded〔'æbsṇt'maɪndɪd〕 *adj.* 心不在焉的
daydream〔'de,drim〕 *v.* 做白日夢
announce〔ə'naʊns〕 *v.* 宣佈
information〔,ɪnfɚ'meʃən〕 *n.* 資料   give〔gɪv〕 *v.* 提供

38. (**B**) W: We have a new student in our class. He's physically challenged. He's quite an amazing boy.

M: Why do you say that?

W: Well, he lost both legs in a car accident when he was six, but he can still do almost anything. He rides a special bicycle to school, he loves to swim, he also plays baseball and basketball.

M: I'm very impressed. He sounds extraordinary. I'd like to meet him sometime.

(TONE)

Q: Which statement best captures the main idea of this conversation?

A. Being physically challenged forces the boy to work harder.

B. Being physically challenged doesn't stop the boy from doing anything.

C. The new student is a great athlete.

D. The new student likes to play football.

* physically ('fɪzɪklɪ) adv. 身體上
challenged ('tʃælɪndʒd) adj. 殘障的
quite (kwaɪt) adv. 相當
amazing (ə'mezɪŋ) adj. 令人驚訝的　　lose (luz) v. 失去
leg (lɛg) n. 腿　　*car accident* 車禍
ride (raɪd) v. 騎　　special ('spɛʃəl) adj. 特別的
impress (ɪm'prɛs) v. 使印象深刻；使感動
sound (saʊnd) v. 聽起來像；似乎
extraordinary (ɪk'strɔrdṇ,ɛrɪ) adj. 特別的；非凡的
would like 想要　　meet (mit) v. 認識

sometime〔ˈsʌmˌtaɪm〕adv. 哪一天;(今後的)有一天
statement〔ˈstetmənt〕n. 敘述
capture〔ˈkæptʃə〕v. 抓到;掌握
main〔men〕adj. 主要的   idea〔aɪˈdiə〕n. 思想
main idea 主旨   force〔fors〕v. 強迫;迫使
stop sb. ***from V-ing*** 使某人無法~
athlete〔ˈæθlit〕n. 運動員;運動選手
football〔ˈfʊtˌbɔl〕n. 美式足球;橄欖球

39. (**B**) M：It's 8 pm, my turn. Please hand over the remote control.
W：Back off. The program is not over. You have to wait till it's finished.
M：No way. You promised me I could watch what I wanted at eight.
W：No, I didn't. Don't put words in my mouth. You're lying.
M：I'm telling Mom and Dad. You're so selfish. I hate you. I hope you catch a disease and die!

(TONE)
Q：What does the boy say about his sister?
A. She is a liar.
B. She doesn't think about others.
C. She doesn't respect him.
D. She broke her promise to their parents.

* ***pm*** 下午   turn〔tɜn〕n. 輪流   ***my turn*** 輪到我了
hand over 交出   ***remote control*** 遙控器
back off 退後   program〔ˈprogræm〕n. 節目
till〔tɪl〕conj. 直到   finished〔ˈfɪnɪʃt〕adj. 結束的

no way 絕對不行;不要　　promise〔'prɑmɪs〕*v.* 答應
put words in one's *mouth* 無中生有;硬說某人說過某話
lie〔laɪ〕*v.* 說謊(現在分詞為 lying)
selfish〔'sɛlfɪʃ〕*adj.* 自私的　　hate〔het〕*v.* 討厭
catch〔kætʃ〕*v.* 感染(疾病)　　disease〔dɪ'ziz〕*n.* 疾病
die〔daɪ〕*v.* 死掉　　liar〔'laɪɚ〕*n.* 說謊者
respect〔rɪ'spɛkt〕*v.* 尊重
break one's *promise to sb.* 違反和某人的約定
parents〔'pɛrənts〕*n. pl.* 父母

40. (**C**)　W: Did you hear about David's new dog?

M: No, what about it?

W: It was smuggled here from mainland China.

M: How do you know that?

W: The pet shop that sold him the puppy was closed down by the police. All the animals were illegally purchased and taken here.

M: What happens now?

W: David's dog has to go through a thirty-day quarantine for infectious diseases. Then, he can take the dog home.

(TONE)

Q: Which information below is not true?

A. They took away David's dog.

B. The police closed down the pet shop.

C. The animals were unhealthy and sick.

D. David has to wait one month to get his puppy.

* *hear about* 聽說…的事　　smuggle〔'smʌgl̩〕v. 走私運入
  mainland China 中國大陸　　pet〔pɛt〕adj. 寵物的
  puppy〔'pʌpɪ〕n. 小狗　　*close down* 使歇業
  the police 警方　　illegally〔ɪ'ligl̩ɪ〕adv. 非法地
  purchase〔'pɝtʃəs〕v. 購買　　*go through* 通過；經歷
  quarantine〔'kwɔrənˌtin〕n. 檢疫
  infectious〔ɪn'fɛkʃəs〕adj. 傳染性的
  below〔bə'lo〕adv. 在下面　　*take away* 帶走
  unhealthy〔ʌn'hɛlθɪ〕adj. 不健康的
  sick〔sɪk〕adj. 生病的

41. (**B**) M : What's the matter with Kevin's face? It's as red as
　　　　　　a tomato.

　　　　　W : He told me he has allergies. But I just think it's
　　　　　　acne.

　　　　　M : He must have very oily skin. He shouldn't eat greasy
　　　　　　foods.

　　　　　W : A poor diet doesn't have anything to do with skin
　　　　　　problems.

　　　　　M : I strongly disagree with you. What you eat certainly
　　　　　　does affect your complexion.

　　　　　(TONE)

　　　　　Q : According to the man, what should Kevin do?

　　　　　A. Become a vegetarian and go on a diet.

　　　　　B. Eat healthier foods.

　　　　　C. See a skin doctor.

　　　　　D. Take some medication for his rash.

* ***What's the matter with ~?*** ～怎麼了？

tomato〔təˋmeto〕*n.* 番茄　　allergy〔ˋælədʒɪ〕*n.* 過敏症

acne〔ˋæknɪ〕*n.* 面皰；青春痘　　oily〔ˋɔɪlɪ〕*adj.* 油性的

skin〔skɪn〕*n.* 皮膚　　greasy〔ˋgrizɪ〕*adj.* 油膩的

poor〔pur〕*adj.* 清淡的；不好的　　diet〔ˋdaɪət〕*n.* 飲食

doesn't have anything to do with … 和…毫無關係（＝*has*

　　nothing to do with…）　　strongly〔ˋstrɔŋlɪ〕*adv.* 強烈地

disagree〔͵dɪsəˋgri〕*v.* 不同意

certainly〔ˋsɝtn̩lɪ〕*adv.* 一定

does〔dʌz〕*aux.*【強調肯定句】真的；確實

affect〔əˋfɛkt〕*v.* 影響

complexion〔kəmˋplɛkʃən〕*n.* 氣色；臉色

according to 根據

vegetarian〔͵vɛdʒəˋtɛrɪən〕*n.* 素食主義者

go on a diet 節食　　healthy〔ˋhɛlθɪ〕*adj.* 健康的

take〔tek〕*v.* 吃（藥）

medication〔͵mɛdɪˋkeʃən〕*n.* 藥物　　rash〔ræʃ〕*n.* 疹子

42. (**D**)　W : What an awful night.　I was eaten alive!

　　　　M : Oh, so you have mosquitoes in your room, too?

　　　　W : I sure do.　There's a whole army of them living in my
　　　　　　 bedroom.

　　　　M : You should buy a mosquito net.　It's the only way to
　　　　　　 get a good night's sleep.　I guarantee you.　You won't
　　　　　　 regret the purchase.

　　　　W : I'll do it today.　Where can I pick one up?　Would a
　　　　　　 local pharmacy have one?

　　　　(TONE)

　　　　Q : What is the man's suggestion?

A. To cover her head with mosquito oil.

B. To buy some mosquito repellent from a pharmacy.

C. To burn some incense to eliminate the mosquitoes.

D. To cover her bed with a net.

* awful〔'ɔfʊl〕adj. 可怕的　　alive〔ə'laɪv〕adj. 活的
  mosquito〔mə'skito〕n. 蚊子　　whole〔hol〕adj. 整個的
  army〔'ɑrmɪ〕n. 軍隊　　bedroom〔'bɛd,rum〕n. 房間
  net〔nɛt〕n. 網子　　**mosquito net** 蚊帳
  only〔'onlɪ〕adj. 唯一的　　way〔we〕n. 方式
  get a good night's sleep 晚上睡個好覺
  guarantee〔,gærən'ti〕v. 向～保證
  regret〔rɪ'grɛt〕v. 後悔　　purchase〔'pɝtʃəs〕n. 購買
  pick up 購買　　local〔'lokl̩〕adj. 當地的
  pharmacy〔'fɑrməsɪ〕n. 藥房
  suggestion〔sə'dʒɛstʃən〕n. 建議　　cover〔'kʌvɚ〕v. 覆蓋
  mosquito oil 防蚊液 (= *anti-mosquito oil*)
  repellent〔rɪ'pɛlənt〕n. 驅蟲劑　　burn〔bɝn〕v. 燃燒
  incense〔'ɪnsɛns〕n. 香；香料
  eliminate〔ɪ'lɪmə,net〕v. 消除；消滅

43. (**A**)　M: I have a reservation. I'm here to check in. Should I
　　　　　　　fill out a form?

　　　　　W: Just a moment, please. I'll be right with you.

　　　　　M: I've already been standing here for five minutes.

　　　　　W: I apologize for the wait. We're understaffed today.
　　　　　　　We have a convention going on next door. May I ask
　　　　　　　your name and how you spell it?

　　　　　M: Sure, I'm Robert Smith. That's S-M-I-T-H.

　　　　　W: OK, Mr. Smith. We have a suite reserved for you on
　　　　　　　the fourth floor. May I see your ID and a credit card?

(TONE)

Q : Where is Mr. Smith standing?

A. At a hotel front desk.

B. At a check-out counter.

C. At an information desk.

D. At a conference registration desk.

* reservation〔,rɛzə'veʃən〕n. 預定
  check in 登記住宿　　**fill out** 填寫
  form〔fɔrm〕n. 表格　　**Just a moment.** 稍等一下。
  I'll be right with you. 我馬上就來。
  apologize〔ə'pɑlə,dʒaɪz〕v. 道歉　　wait〔wet〕n. 等待
  understaffed〔,ʌndə'stæft〕adj. 人員不足的
  convention〔kən'vɛnʃən〕n. 會議　　**go on** 舉行；進行
  spell〔spɛl〕v. 拼字　　suite〔swit〕n. 套房
  reserve〔rɪ'zɝv〕v. 保留　　floor〔flor〕n. 樓層
  ID 身分證（= identification）　　**credit card** 信用卡
  front desk （旅館的）櫃台　　desk〔dɛsk〕n. 櫃檯
  check-out counter 結帳櫃台　　**information desk** 服務台
  conference〔'kɑnfərəns〕n. 會議
  registration〔,rɛdʒɪ'streʃən〕n. 登記

44. (**D**) W: What's that smell? What an awful odor! Is something burning?

　　　　　M: Oh my God, I left my steak in the oven!

　　　　　W: Quick, close the kitchen door and open the window. Next time grill it outside, OK? Is it still edible?

　　　　　M: Nope. It's burnt to a crisp. Sorry for stinking up the house.

(TONE)

Q：What does the woman do?

A. She opens a window and closes a door.

B. She forgets about a meal in the oven.

C. She notices smoke pouring from the oven.

D. She notices a horrible smell.

* smell〔smɛl〕*n.* 氣味　　awful〔'ɔful〕*adj.* 可怕的
  odor〔'odɚ〕*n.* 氣味　　burn〔bɝn〕*v.* 燒焦
  Oh my God! 噢，天哪！
  leave〔liv〕*v.* 遺留；使維持（某種狀態）
  steak〔stek〕*n.* 牛排　　oven〔'ʌvən〕*n.* 爐子
  quick〔kwɪk〕*adv.* 趕快　　grill〔grɪl〕*v.* 用烤架烤
  edible〔'ɛdəbḷ〕*adj.* 可以吃的　　nope〔nop〕*adv.* 不（= *no*）
  crisp〔krɪsp〕*n.* 酥脆的東西　　***be burned to a crisp*** 烤焦
  stink〔stɪŋk〕*v.* 使充滿惡臭　　***stink up*** 使…臭氣燻天
  meal〔mil〕*n.* 一餐；一頓飯　　notice〔'notɪs〕*v.* 注意到
  smoke〔smok〕*n.* 煙　　pour〔por〕*v.* 湧出
  horrible〔'hɔrəbḷ〕*adj.* 可怕的

45. (**C**)　W：It looks like a piece of junk. You couldn't pay me to
ride in it!

M：Hold your tongue. You'll hurt her feelings. This
baby is my pride and joy.

W：Does she still run?

M：Of course. Her engine is very reliable. She runs like
a tank in a battle.

W：How old is your baby and what's her name?

M：Her name is Fanny Ford and she'll be four decades
old next year.

(TONE)

Q : What is the topic of this conversation?

A. A very old motorcycle.

B. An antique bicycle.

C. An old automobile.

D. The man's grandmother.

* piece〔pis〕*n.* 片；個
  junk〔dʒʌŋk〕*n.* 垃圾　　pay〔pe〕*v.* 付錢給～
  ride〔raɪd〕*v.* 乘坐　　tongue〔tʌŋ〕*n.* 舌頭
  Hold your tongue. 住口。　　hurt〔hɝt〕*v.* 傷害
  her 在此指「那部車的」。凡是車、船、國家等，代名詞用
  　she，受格則用 her。
  feelings〔'filɪŋz〕*n. pl.* 感情　　pride〔praɪd〕*n.* 驕傲
  joy〔dʒɔɪ〕*n.* 喜悅；令人高興的事物
  run〔rʌn〕*v.* 行駛　　engine〔'ɛndʒən〕*n.* 引擎
  reliable〔rɪ'laɪəbl̩〕*adj.* 可靠的
  tank〔tæŋk〕*n.* 坦克車　　battle〔'bætl̩〕*n.* 戰爭
  Ford〔fɔrd〕*n.* 福特公司製造的汽車
  decade〔'dɛked〕*n.* 十年　　topic〔'tɑpɪk〕*n.* 主題
  conversation〔ˌkɑnvɚ'seʃən〕*n.* 對話
  motorcycle〔'motɚˌsaɪkl̩〕*n.* 摩托車
  antique〔æn'tik〕*adj.* 古董的
  automobile〔ˌɔtə'mobil〕*n.* 汽車
  grandmother〔'grænˌmʌðɚ〕*n.* 祖母

全民英語能力分級檢定測驗簡介

「全民英語能力分級檢定測驗」（General English Proficiency Test），簡稱「全民英檢」（GEPT）旨在提供我國各階段英語學習者一公平、可靠、具效度之英語能力評量工具，測驗對象包括在校學生及一般社會人士，可做為學習成果檢定、教學改進及公民營機構甄選人才等之參考。

本測驗為標準參照測驗（criterion-referenced test），參考當前我國英語教育體制，制定分級標準，整套系統共分五級——初級（Elementary）、中級（Intermediate）、中高級（High-Intermediate）、高級（Advanced）、優級（Superior）。每級訂有明確能力標準（詳見表一綜合能力說明與表二分項能力說明），報考者可依英語能力選擇適當級數報考，每級均包含聽、說、讀、寫四項完整的測驗，通過所報考級數的能力標準即可取得該級的合格證書。各級命題設計均參考目前各階段英語教育之課程大綱及相關教材之內容分析，期能符合國內各階段英語教育的需求、反應本土的生活經驗與特色。

「全民英語能力檢定分級測驗」各級綜合能力說明 　　《表一》

級數	綜　合　能　力	備　　註	
初 級	通過初級測驗者具有基礎英語能力，能理解和使用淺易日常用語，英語能力相當於國中畢業者。	建議下列人員宜具有該級英語能力	一般行政助理、維修技術人員、百貨業、餐飲業、旅館業或觀光景點服務人員、計程車駕駛等。
中 級	通過中級測驗者具有使用簡單英語進行日常生活溝通的能力，英語能力相當於高中職畢業者。		一般行政、業務、技術、銷售人員、護理人員、旅館、飯店接待人員、總機人員、警政人員、旅遊從業人員等。
中 高 級	通過中高級測驗者英語能力逐漸成熟，應用的領域擴大，雖有錯誤，但無礙溝通，英語能力相當於大學非英語主修系所畢業者。		商務、企劃人員、祕書、工程師、研究助理、空服人員、航空機師、航管人員、海關人員、導遊、外事警政人員、新聞從業人員、資訊管理人員等。

級數	綜　合　能　力	備		註
高級	通過高級測驗者英語流利順暢，僅有少許錯誤，應用能力擴及學術或專業領域，英語能力相當於國內大學英語主修系所或曾赴英語系國家大學或研究所進修並取得學位者。	建議下列人員宜具有該級英語能力	高級商務人員、協商談判人員、英語教學人員、研究人員、翻譯人員、外交人員、國際新聞從業人員等。	
優級	通過優級測驗者的英語能力接近受過高等教育之母語人士，各種場合均能使用適當策略作最有效的溝通。		專業翻譯人員、國際新聞特派人員、外交官員、協商談判主談人員等。	

「全民英語能力檢定分級測驗」各級分項能力說明　　《表二》

能力\級數	聽	讀	說	寫
初級	能聽懂與日常生活相關的淺易談話，包括價格、時間及地點等。	可看懂與日常生活相關的淺易英文，並能閱讀路標、交通標誌、招牌、簡單菜單、時刻表及賀卡等。	能朗讀簡易文章、簡單地自我介紹，對熟悉的話題能以簡易英語對答，如問候、購物、問路等。	能寫簡單的句子及段落，如寫明信片、便條、賀卡及填表格等。對一般日常生活相關的事物，能以簡短的文字敘述或說明。
中級	在日常生活情境中，能聽懂一般的會話；能大致聽懂公共場所廣播、氣象報告及廣告等。在工作情境中，能聽懂簡易的產品介紹與操作說明。能大致聽懂外籍人士的談話及詢問。	在日常生活情境中，能閱讀短文、故事、私人信件、廣告、傳單、簡介及使用說明等。在工作情境中，能閱讀工作須知、公告、操作手冊、例行的文件、傳真、電報等。	在日常生活情境中，能以簡易英語交談或描述一般事物，能介紹自己的生活作息、工作、家庭、經歷等，並可對一般話題陳述看法。在工作情境中，能進行簡單的詢答，並與外籍人士交談溝通。	能寫簡單的書信、故事及心得等。對於熟悉且與個人經歷相關的主題，能以簡易的文字表達。

能力級數	聽	讀	說	寫
中高級	在日常生活情境中，能聽懂社交談話，並能大致聽懂一般的演講、報導及節目等。在工作情境中，能聽懂簡報、討論、產品介紹及操作說明等。	在日常生活情境中，能閱讀書信、說明書及報章雜誌等。在工作情境中，能閱讀一般文件、摘要、會議紀錄及報告等。	在日常生活情境中，對與個人興趣相關的話題，能流暢地表達意見及看法。在工作情境中，能接待外籍人士、介紹工作內容、洽談業務、在會議中發言，並能做簡報。	能寫一般的工作報告及書信等。除日常生活相關主題外，與工作相關的事物、時事及較複雜或抽象的概念皆能適當表達。
高級	在日常生活情境中，能聽懂各類主題的談話、辯論、演講、報導及節目等。在工作情境中，參與業務會議或談判時，能聽懂報告及討論的內容。	能閱讀各類不同主題、體裁的文章，包括報章雜誌、文學作品、專業期刊、學術著作及文獻等。	對於各類主題皆能流暢地表達看法、參與討論，能在一般會議或專業研討會中報告或發表意見等。	能寫一般及專業性摘要、報告、論文、新聞報導等，可翻譯一般書籍及新聞等。對各類主題均能表達自法，並作深入探討。
優級	能聽懂各類主題及體裁的內容，理解程度與受過高等教育之母語人士相當。	能閱讀各類不同主題、體裁文章。閱讀速度及理解程度與受過高等教育之母語人士相當。	能在各種不同場合以正確流利之英語表達看法；能適切引用文化知識及慣用語詞。	能撰寫不同性質的文章，如企劃報告、專業/學術性摘要、論文、新聞報導及時事評論等。對於各類主題均能有效完整地闡述並作深入探討。

「全民英語能力檢定分級測驗」中級題型、題數及測驗時間　　《表三》

測 驗 項 目		題　　　　型		題　　　數		測驗時間
初試	聽力測驗	第一部份	看圖辨義	15 題	45 題	約 30 分鐘
		第二部份	問答	15 題		
		第三部份	簡短對話	15 題		
	閱讀能力測驗	第一部份	詞彙和結構	15 題	40 題	45 分鐘
		第二部份	段落填空	10 題		
		第三部份	閱讀理解	15 題		
複試	寫作能力測驗	第一部份	中譯英	1 段		40 分鐘
		第二部份	英文作文	1 篇		
	口說能力測驗	第一部份	朗讀短文	2~3 篇		約 15 分鐘
		第二部份	回答問題	10 題		
		第三部份	看圖敘述	1 圖		

※ **考情資訊**：中級英語檢定考試，初試訂於每年 2 月中旬及 8 月
　　　　初舉行，複試於每年 4 月底及 10 月中舉行，詳情
　　　　請參閱網站 http://www.gept.org.tw

||||||||||||| ●學習出版公司門市部 ●|||||||||||||||

台北地區：台北市許昌街 10 號 2 樓 TEL：(02)2331-4060・2331-9209
台中地區：台中市綠川東街 32 號 8 樓 23 室
　　　　　TEL：(04)223-2838

|||||||||||||||||||||||||||||||||||||||||||||

中級英語聽力檢定⑤

主　　　編／劉　毅
發 行 所／學習出版有限公司　　　　☎ (02) 2704-5525
郵 撥 帳 號／0512727-2 學習出版社帳戶
登 記 證／局版台業 2179 號
印 刷 所／裕強彩色印刷有限公司
台 北 門 市／台北市許昌街 10 號 2 F　　☎ (02) 2331-4060・2331-9209
台 中 門 市／台中市綠川東街 32 號 8 F 23 室　☎ (04) 223-2838
台灣總經銷／紅螞蟻圖書有限公司　　☎ (02) 2799-9490・2657-0132
美國總經銷／Evergreen Book Store　☎ (818) 2813622

售價：新台幣二百二十元正
2006 年 1 月 1 日初版